KV-141-426

SUNRISING

Also by David Cook

ALBERT'S MEMORIAL
HAPPY ENDINGS
WALTER
WINTER DOVES

LINCOLNSHIRE RECREATIONAL SERVICES — LIBRARIES
This book should be returned on or before
the last date shown below.

C15

0436106744

7/86 DAY CENTRE

BURLAND COURT

2.W.

m.2

F.MS

R.5.

HOME LIBRARY SERVICE

FH   COOK/1

Sunrising

AD 02995165

L 5/9

SUNRISING

A novel by

David Cook

An Alison Press Book
Secker & Warburg
London

First published in England 1984 by
The Alison Press/Martin Secker & Warburg Limited
54 Poland Street, London W1V 3DF

Copyright © 1984 by David Cook

ISBN 0-436-10674-4

British Library Cataloguing in Publication Data

Cook, David, 1940–
    Sunrising
    I. Title
    823'.914[F]   PR6053 0/

LINCOLNSHIRE
COUNTY LIBRARY

Photoset in Great Britain by
Rowland Phototypesetting Limited, Bury St Edmunds, Suffolk
and printed by St Edmundsbury Press
Bury St Edmunds, Suffolk

For
Ian McKellen

This book was written with the assistance of a Bursary from the Arts Council of Great Britain and a Writing Fellowship at St Martin's College, Lancaster.

'Mr John Bovrill steward at Compton aged 64 years,
Daniel Wells aged 26 years, Richard Turner aged
53 years laid this floor August 1834. William
Ainge aged 56 years, Richard Ainge aged 52 years
both resided on the farm and gave them plenty of
cider. Finish carrying wheat 8th day of August
1834 and the best crop that as been in a number
of years. William Bustin aged 42 years was hanged
for setting fire to Edward Sheldon Esq's ricks
13 in number and William Baker's August 15th 1834.
He was native somewhere near Stow.'

That inscription was found on a floorboard in Tysoe
Manor. The writing is in a sloping hand, typical of the early
19th century, and the names all fit people of the area alive at
that time. Bustin was hanged publicly outside the prison at
Warwick.

This book begins in 1830, before the date of the inscription.
Very few of its characters are 'real' people, but some of the
events described in it did happen, and all of them could have
happened.

PART ONE

The Incendiarists

The Byre

A stillborn calf had been tied into the membrane of its sac with plaited straw, and hung up by a nail over the stall above the head of its mother. Brown liquid dripped from the parcel, and the mother cow blinked her eyelids to prevent the blood and fluid of her dead offspring from running into her eyes. Through the torn membrane, already becoming crisp and brown and stinking as it dried, Cath could see the outline of the baby calf, less than eighteen inches long. It had been hung where it was as a discouragement to the mother cow against aborting again.

Cath placed a hand over her nose and mouth, and moved away. She had come to the byre, hoping to steal milk. She had eaten nothing of substance for four days, only what she could get from the woods and hedges. She had found oregon grapes and bullace, had puckered her lips over sloe and crab-apple and horse chestnut, which had griped her guts. She had eaten dandelion leaves and wild borage, which had calmed and exhilarated her, but left her still hungry. She had supped on watercress and jack-in-the-hedge, had longed for bread and potatoes, and forced herself not to think of meat. For a whole day, she had lain in the ditch close to this farm, watching the farmer and his movements, before daring to enter the byre.

The udders of the mother cow were large and swollen with milk intended for the calf. Cath watched some of it leak from the tits onto the ground. Wasted. She had taken such a risk to find it, and now a decomposing parcel had made her throat too tight to swallow. Meanwhile the cow would be in pain, and the farmer would leave her so for a few hours as an added punishment before he came to collect the special milk. The calf's milk.

Cath moved slowly to the door, and peered through a crack in the wood. She could see the farmer in the yard, some distance away, moving about his business without haste. She could not leave now, even if she had the strength. Her legs and arms were shaking; if she tried to run, she would surely fall, nor had she anywhere to run.

Her eyes were playing tricks, clouding over suddenly or trying to close themselves when she needed them to stay open, alert and watchful. Just for a moment, safe behind the door of the byre, perhaps she might allow them to close. She leaned her forehead against the door, folded her arms across her chest, and hugged herself to stop the shaking. Her eyes closed.

It couldn't last much longer. Berries, leaves and wild fruit might sustain her through the rest of August and into September, but October and November would be colder. She was sure she would not see Christmas, and had no wish to. She was dying slowly because she lacked the bravery to die quickly. As John had done.

Now, here in this cow-shed, she was waiting without anything to wait for, since he had been dead seven days. She had no reason to hide or to run, yet she continued hiding and running. And waiting.

What she had been doing was not reasonable. Only thieves were forced to hide and run, and she was not a thief. She had gone without food, or begged, or eaten from the hedgerows, and only now had she made the intention to creep into the byre and steal milk, and even now the putrefying body of the dead calf kept her from it. So she had run and hidden for a week without reason. And as to the waiting, the remaining on Childs Hill, close to the village of Tysoe and that other hill they called Sunrising, there was no reason in that either. He would not come back from the dead. Crows and magpies had picked out his eyes. She had asked herself why she waited but the best of answers she had been able to find was simply that there was nothing else for her to do, nothing else she wished to do.

She had been wrong, had made mistakes, and it was too late to correct them, a whole week too late. From that moment

4

when she had turned away from him, and listened to the crowd sigh, from that moment on, any other mistakes she might make would be of little consequence.

The dead calf dropped from its decaying parcel, and landed at its mother's feet. The cow backed, and shook its head, then cautiously moved forward to sniff at the corpse. Cath also moved forward, dragging her feet through the straw and muck, and swaying slightly until she reached the cow, and could hold onto it for support. Then, turning her head away from the dead calf, she sank to her knees, and knelt beside the cow, closed her eyes and felt with her fingers at the swollen udder. She found one of the leaking tits, lifted it to her lips, forced it into her mouth, and began to suck. The mother cow surrendered up her dead calf's milk slowly, but without protest, bending her neck to lick the salt from Cath's cheeks, and Cath drank hungrily until she was full.

At the back of the shed, she sat down on a pile of hay. She must wait until all was dark outside, but not too long, or the farmer would return and find her. She must wait, but she must not sleep. So far, even when she had allowed her tired eyes to close, she had not slept. Without real food or warmth at night, sleep had been impossible to find. But now, with the warm milk inside her, she feared that her mind might give in to her body. Lifting a handful of hay, she rubbed it over her hands and arms, then pressed it to her face, and held it there.

The Hay

The yellowhammers were in the stubble, and the sunflowers had gone to seed in the village gardens, and behind their front doors the village folk sat, thinking of themselves as Godfearing people. For days now she had watched them from a safe distance. From the safety of Childs Hill, she had observed them going about their work. She had seen them burning the autumn leaves, had heard the voices of women and children laughing as they gathered the last of the gleanings or burned small patches of wheat-stubble. She who had burned the hay.

It was difficult for her to think of them now as ordinary people, hard to remember them as they had been when she and John had watched them together. Then they had looked like ants, being more than half a mile away, yet their voices, carried up the hill on a light breeze which made the heat so pleasant, had sounded as clear as the bells which struck the hour on the church tower. She and John had laughed, and felt safe, and made plans to go down and call on the ants at the foot of the hill that evening, and beg for food. They had laughed at the noises their own stomachs made in noisy protest (hunger then had been laughable), had laughed because the sun was hot, and because everything they looked at together made a picture, had laughed at each other and with each other, had become drunk on laughter, staggering and rolling and laughing, hugging and kissing and laughing, aching with it and never wanting it to stop, laughing at their laughter, their closeness, their daring, their good fortune, their happiness.

Lying side by side in the heat of the afternoon, they had

talked of the future – *their* future, the future of two young people who not only shared their food, but shared their thoughts as fairly as they shared their bodies. The excitement and pleasure of this sharing seemed to fill the air about them, just as the silences between their words were filled with smiles and looks and touching.

Then, as if testing their happiness, as if daring and challenging it, they had remarked on their various faults. She had admired John's hands, and he had described them as they once had been, smooth and pink and not unlike, he said, her own. Cath had laughed at this, knowing her hands to be coarse and hard. Imagine his astonishment, said John, when one morning he had waked to discover, not smooth pink hands, but sun-burned lumps of skin and bone hanging from the ends of his arms, with veins and muscles all drawn out, and tufts of dark hair protruding from the back of every finger. He had curled his fingers, and formed one hand in the shape of a claw, while Cath had kissed each talon, and complained that her own fingers were too fat and her thighs too thin, and John had replied that there was much pleasure to be found inside thin thighs, and anyway when all four of their thighs were, in their most natural state, pressed together, they amounted to much the same as two pairs of a middling size.

He had kissed her neck, and commented on its perfection. His own neck, he had told her, was indeed most miserably thin, and she had moved the backs of her fingers over it to judge for herself whether his dissatisfaction was justified or mere praise-seeking. She had stroked every inch of skin from his shoulder to his chin, kissing it as she did so, had made the most exact scrutiny of his Adam's apple, and had agreed; his neck was much too thin; painfully thin; she could not imagine how she had hitherto overlooked this thinness; she wondered how he would ever manage to eat when eventually they saw food again. Not even an ant had a neck so narrow. It would be a pity to have come so far, only to perish of starvation caused by the slenderness of one's neck.

This had set them to laughter again, laughing more and more with each fantastical suggestion as to how they could set about fattening up John's neck, while leaving the rest of him as it was. First he must wear a very tight collar, and only swallow every alternate mouthful so that less nourishment escaped into his stomach. Then he must somehow contrive to swallow a large dinner plate, so that it would rest on his collar bone, and collect the food as it came down, giving his neck first refusal of all the choicest bits. He had laughed until he coughed, and she had slapped his back, but the laughter had only grown stronger with her attempts to discourage it. Still laughing he had taken out his clay pipe, and, laughing also, she had grabbed the roll of brown paper which contained the precious matches, in order to light it for him. She had cried out, then laughed again, as she burned her finger, and threw the match away from her, and laughing he had taken her hand, and gently kissed the burned finger.

Only the sound of yellowhammers rising suddenly from the stubble in the next enclosure and taking to the sky in a flock had stopped their laughter.

Then there were voices, men's voices behind them, and getting closer, breathless voices of men running. And they had stood and stared as the hay flared up in front of them, sending a tower of crackling flames into the air which still echoed with their laughter. They had stood, unable to believe what was happening, and so allowed the men's voices to get closer. Then John pushed at her, and told her to run, but she had reached for his hand, and he had pushed it away, and shouted angrily, and she had run, thinking that he would follow. But when she turned, she had seen him trying to put out the fire, with the men running across the field towards him.

She had not returned. She had run to the nearest barn, and hidden there. She had told herself that the men would let him go when he had explained how it had happened, that it was she who had burnt the hay. Then they would come to her. There would be a charge, a fine, and she would pay it. She would work to pay it, she and John together; they would both work to pay off the fine, as was right, until their child was due.

So she had waited. But no one had come.

The Peacock

John did not return, nor did any men come to charge her with firing the hay. Cath waited until the dawn, and then began walking down the hill to find him.

She could smell the burned hay, and as the light grew and she came lower down the hill, she could see the blackened stubble. A crow waddled in and out between the larger tufts of burned grass, as if searching for something he had lost. The crow's back shone with health. This was his ground. He knew the lie of it well, patrolled it every day, found food there – grubs and insects and the corpses of birds and animals, some prey to Nature herself, some the leavings of larger predators. No fire would keep the crow from his work of laying out and cleaning up the corpses which had fallen to his share. There were good days and bad in any calling, but a habit of thoroughness and a conscientious disposition allowed him to sleep well at night. Cath wished that she could find food for herself as easily. As for sleep, she did not expect it until she had talked with John.

The village of Tysoe was a parish of three parts, Temple, Church and Upper Tysoe, each separated from the other. Cath began to walk more slowly. Some villages were accustomed to the passage of strangers; others were not. But as she entered Church Tysoe, a small girl ran from a doorway to tug at her skirt and ask her if she had seen the fire. Cath smiled, nodded, and walked on, but not before the little girl had told her that it was safe now, because her uncle had caught the man who'd done it, and locked him up in the Peacock.

The people of Church Tysoe did not in any way resemble

9

ants when seen close to, nor was the exterior of the Peacock in any way remarkable. Men entered and left it, and most of them looked at her with interest, but so they would look at any stranger. No one stopped to question her. No one accused her of any misdemeanour. She studied all the windows at the front of the inn, hoping to see John, but he did not appear. There were windows at the rear also, and a yard. She leaned against the gate of the yard, and pretended to watch a boy grooming a horse, but her eyes searched the upper windows. She asked the boy if he had seen the man who caused the fire, but he did not answer. She asked for water, and he lifted the bucket and threw the dirty contents at her.

She walked up and down, trying to think what next to do. She had no money to enter the inn, nowhere to stay and nothing for food. Yet she could not leave its vicinity until she had seen John. She must speak to someone to get information, but must phrase her question cautiously. She must not refer to 'the man who caused the fire' since that had earned her only a bucket of dirty water. Nor, of course, must she use John's name.

A man was leaving the inn, a gentleman by his appearance, and more likely therefore to treat her politely. Cath asked, 'Is the young man being kept here?', hoping that the gentleman would know which young man she meant, and he nodded curtly and replied, 'Yes, he'll be locked in until the hearing. Then you'll be able to see what he looks like', and walked on.

Locked in! A hearing – what was to be heard, and whom? The gentleman's answer had set up a train of further and urgent questions. He seemed to be in a hurry, but she ran after him and asked when the hearing was to be. Whereupon the gentleman stopped in his tracks, swung round, taking her by surprise, and demanded, 'Not a friend of yours, is he?' And she, without thinking, answered 'No', like Peter who had denied his Lord, and had then stuttered, and tried to change her answer, but the gentleman was already speaking again, saying, 'Good! We know how to deal with them, if and when they come', and while she was still trying to understand this, added one other statement she did understand, which was that the hearing was to be at ten o'clock on Thursday morning, and walked on again.

Two days later she saw the gentleman again. During those two days she had not dared to linger outside the Peacock, but had walked past it often, looking up at the windows, but pretending that she had business elsewhere. She had lived on water, and what she could find in the hedgerows. But this day, Thursday, she had waited openly outside the inn from seven in the morning, and at half past eight had watched others arrive, except that they did not join her in waiting, but went on past into the inn to take their places. When the church clock showed only a quarter of an hour to go before the time set for the hearing, then Cath decided that she might safely walk up to the door of the inn, and find a place inside, and at that moment the gentleman approached, carrying documents under his arm, stopped, touched his hat and said, 'Punctuality is a virtue not often to be found in young women', studied her face closely, then stood politely back and allowed her to precede him.

The few seats available were soon occupied, only to be given up as the occupant recognised the later arrival of a more worthy personage who could not be expected to stand. Cath saw the women among the audience look at her, and whisper amongst themselves. But their gossip was only concerned with the state of her clothing. They did not know that she had burned the hay.

The gentleman sat himself in a chair behind a table on which he placed his documents. Twelve other chairs had been set aside for the feoffees of the village. As each feoffee presented himself, the gentleman gave him a sheet of paper and a pencil. Five of the chairs remained empty, there being five feofees of such great age that leaving their houses would have been considered hazardous. Of the seven who attended, three were brothers of one family, two of another. Six of the seven were farmers; the seventh was the landlord of the Peacock.

By nine thirty the taproom was crowded, as the people of the three parts of Tysoe and surrounding parishes continued to push their way in. From outside a man's loud voice could be heard calling that a public hearing was not public if honest people were kept out. His voice was joined by those of others in the street who were in agreement. The gentleman at the table asked the feoffees whether they recognised any of the angry voices outside, and when they shook their heads, he signalled to a man near the door who, with the assistance of others standing close to him, managed to close it and to secure it with a lock and chain. Whereat the loud-voiced man outside shouted even more loudly, but was not further heeded.

Cath, pressed hard against one of the walls, and faint from the heat and from lack of nourishment, watched John being led from another room. His hands were bound, and he wore a leg-iron. His face was pale and his sparse beard untidy, and he kept his head lowered, as if searching for something among the clean sawdust which had been scattered on the floor.

She stood on her toes as high as she could, in order to see him and be seen, but John had looked at no one, not even at the gentleman who asked him questions. He was asked to give his name, and did so, but his voice was frail and he was asked to speak louder. His answers were written down by the gentleman, and one of the feoffees also made marks upon his piece of paper, which may have been writing. John was asked where he had come from, and had answered truthfully that he had come from Finstall in Worcestershire, but the gentleman did not seem to believe him, remarking that it was a considerable distance, and asking the reason for such a journey. And John had answered truthfully again that he was on his way south in search of employment as a farmhand. At this the gentleman had interrupted John by raising one hand, after which he had declaimed, almost shouted, a single word, and that word was 'Machinery!'

Even after the word had been pronounced, had fallen into silence, reached out to the furthest walls of the room and dissipated in the hot and sticky air, the gentleman remained with his arm held aloft, and turned slowly so as to be seen by all the crowd. Then the people, knowing that it was their turn, had begun softly to throw words of their own into the sticky air, whispering excitedly among themselves like angry bees. The whispering grew, and persisted, until Cath's head was full of it, and was then cut off by the gentleman's lowering his hand and turning again to John.

'So you know about machinery?'

John had not said so. It was the gentleman who appeared to know about machinery, he and the buzzing crowd. But there was no one to make that point.

'Who sent you here?'

'Nobody.'

'Speak up.'

'I came on my own.' The first lie.

'I didn't ask you that. Who told you to come here?'

It had been she, Cath, who had said, 'Let's go this way. Let's rest here awhile.'

'Have you been to Banbury?'

'No, sir.'

'To Netherthrop?'

'I don't think so, sir.'

'Think more carefully. You may have been there.'

'I never was there, sir.'

'Then who is the man outside? Who is the man whose voice we heard shouting?'

'I cannot tell, sir.'

'Cannot or will not?'

'I don't know him, sir.'

'Were you ever at Otmoor?'

John considered the question, but the gentleman was impatient. 'I dare venture that Otmoor is a place you may have heard of, and having been there would not easily forget.'

They had been through so many villages on their way, had not known the names of many and had forgotten those they had been told. 'I may have passed close to it, sir.'

'Hah!'

Cath willed him to tell them that he had a friend who could vouch for him. She prayed that he would not lie, not tell a direct lie as she had done. If he would only name her as a friend, she could undo the lie, stand up and tell them all that John was honest and true and it was she who had burned the hay. If only she were not caught up in the press, she could get closer to him, and then (if he would but look up) he would see her. Surely he must know she would be there, would never have run away. Why did his eyes not search for her in the crowd? They only lived for each other. They shared everything. They had sworn so.

More questions. An infinity of questions. Had John spoken with anyone concerning the fire on Sunrising Hill? Had anyone offered him money or reward of any kind? Had he met with anyone on the road? Had he been threatened with violence unless he did what he was asked? Come now! If he had been threatened with violence, let him tell; it would be better for him to speak out now. Was he a member of any organisation calling itself a Trades Union or some such? Or any organisation, any organisation at all?

To all these questions John had answered, 'No, sir', and at last, when the gentleman appeared to have come to a temporary stop, lifted his head and asked, 'Please, sir! If I may speak?'

The gentleman nodded his head gravely, and the crowd grew very silent. Cath closed her eyes, and silently mouthed the words, 'Please tell them the truth', but John had already begun to speak. What he said was, 'I am very sorry for what happened, but it was by no purpose. No one else was concerned in it with me. I was lighting my pipe, sir, and I dropped the match. I was alone at this time, and the fire moved so fiercely, I could not put it out. I have no money to pay for the damage, but I will work without wages until the whole sum be repaid, if that is acceptable. I'm sorry. It is of little help, I know, but it is all I can say.' Then the gentleman made a sign with his hand, and John was taken from the room.

The gentleman consulted with the feoffees, and collected their pencils. Most of them had written nothing on their pieces of paper (which did not in any case seem to interest him): the landlord of the Peacock folded his carefully and put it in his pocket. Around Cath the crowd buzzed, the crowd bubbled. She heard nothing, her mind being too full of the words she had not spoken, mixed up with the words which John had found the voice to say. He had lied for love, and she had lied for fear, her lie being the first.

'The Accused will be taken to Warwick Assizes. I shall not disclose when that journey will be undertaken.' The gentleman collected up his documents, placed the feoffees' pencils neatly in an inside pocket, and left by the door through which John had been taken. The door to the street was unbolted, and the crowd moved out into the fresh air. There they met and mingled with those who had been excluded, who asked for news of what had passed, received it, discussed it, gave it in turn to others, so that the whole street became a collection of shifting and re-forming groups of talking and gesticulating villagers, among which could be heard the loud voice of the loud-voiced man informing all who would listen that the Peacock was the worst inn between Bicester and Coventry, as he moved away up the road towards Brailes.

Cath had remained in the room. The chairs used for the hearing were being moved to the sides by the boy who had thrown the bucket of water at her. The door through which John had been taken was no more than seven or eight strides away, but to Cath, who was still leaning against the wall where she had been pressed by the crowd, it seemed to be in another country.

When the chairs had been repositioned to the boy's liking, he began raking the sawdust on the floor. Cath moved, edging her way towards that door, taking small steps. The boy stopped work, and leaned on his rake to watch her. She reached the door. It was locked, had been locked from the other side. And when she turned away from it, the boy was smiling.

Stepping out into the main street of Tysoe, she was blinded for a moment by the brilliant sunlight. Out of the light, in a cloud of noise and dust, there came a coach and pair into the street from behind the Peacock. Just for a moment, Cath caught sight of the gentleman and John, sitting side by side in the coach, before the sunlight and dust began to sting her eyes and cause them to shed water.

Warwick Assizes

At Kineton she had knocked at the door of a cottage, and been given a little bread and some elderflower tea. She had crossed over Windmill Hill, and passed Pillerton Lazer, reaching Pillerton Hersey as night fell. There she rested in a dry ditch.

As she had walked, and now as she rested, she attempted to prepare what she was going to say. She must choose her words carefully, and practise saying them out loud. In her head they remained confused, as they had at the hearing. Only when she had given voice to them would she be able to tell whether they expressed what she meant to say.

She must tell them that it was she who had burned the hay, and that John had lied to protect her. No, she must not use the word 'lie'. She would have so little time to explain, and they would be impatient, as the gentleman had been. She must be careful, she must make them listen. She would use the word 'blame'. John had taken the blame, because he loved her. They loved each other, and she was carrying his child. She would tell them that, and they would listen.

She slept little, and at dawn began to walk again. She and John had walked mile after mile together, seldom noticing the hardness of the rutted roads, or the dust, the steepness of the hills or their own tiredness. When they had lain down for the night, they had held each other close and fallen asleep, drifting together into the depths of sleep, until either the daylight or birdsong had woken them.

She washed her face and hands in a stream outside Combrook, then broke off a small branch of willow and used it to brush some of the dried dirt from her clothes before standing upright, clearing her throat, and addressing herself to the trees.

'Sir! If I may speak for one moment . . .' (John had asked for the right to speak, and had been allowed by the gentleman.) 'It was I, sir, threw down the match. John was there with me, but it was I did it.'

If John were with her now, he might be laughing at the sight of her, shouting at a willow tree. It was six days since they had laughed together, five weeks since she had left Finstall to travel south with him. She had tried to discourage John from talking about the baby, had warned him that it was most unlikely that she could carry it for the whole nine months, and that they were not to plan for it, not to build up hopes, not to consider its welfare at the expense of their own. They were young, too young to share their joint life with someone else. She had said all that, and he had laughed. And now not even a light wind moved the withies of the willow tree.

Close to the Fosse, by Compton Verney, she stopped to rest, and was offered a mouthful of cider and a cold potato by some women picking stones in a field. They said they could find her a few days' work if she were willing, but she explained that she had urgent business in Warwick, and thanked them.

Along the Fosse she continued to practise what she would say. She must ask for permission to speak as John had done, and then she must be brief and clear. At Moreton Morrell she followed a sign for Newbold Pacey, and judged that she would arrive before dark, but by walking more quickly and not stopping for rest she got as far as Wiggerland, and spent the night in Wiggerland Wood.

Next morning, between ten and eleven, she walked into the town of Warwick. The journey had taken nearly two days. She enquired for the County Gaol. It was in the centre of the town, close by St Mary's Church, and was bounded by Northgate Street on one side, Bridewell on another. The prison and the County Hall, in which the Assize Court was held, were side by side.

Cath approached a man in uniform who seemed to be in charge of the gate of the court, and asked him when the Assizes would be held, and what happened there, since she had a friend who was to appear.

'In what capacity, miss?'

'As a prisoner, sir.'

'Ah!' The man seemed to have a considerable store of knowledge about the workings of the legal system, and since there were very few people going either into or out of the building, showed a happy disposition to impart it.

'Is it a capital offence?'

Cath did not know what a capital offence was, but replied that she did not think so. The man told her that if the offence was not capital, and did not concern a debt of more than forty pound, then the Mayor might sit on her friend, or perhaps the Recorder, or even his Deputy, and in that case they would sit on a Wednesday, unless the Wednesday were in the middle of Whit week, or Easter week, or at Christmastide. Any of these three might sit, and there were also three Senior Aldermen, men of considerable substance, who might sit, except that they hardly ever sat these days, which was a great pity, in the man's view, since two of them at least were not above being fair.

Cath wondered whether the value of the burned hay could possibly amount to more than forty pounds. It did not seem likely, but when she asked the man for his view of the affair, and told him of the circumstances, he drew his breath in noisily through his mouth, and closed his eyes.

'Well, that's incendiarism, miss. That's a very different matter, a grave matter, miss, a matter of grave concern that is, incendiarism.'

'It was an accident, sir.'

'That is for the court to decide. An accident is what they may or may not decide to call it, but until they do, you may take my word it is a grave matter, miss, and if you have any money you had better get your friend a talker.' The man explained that a 'talker' was a legal gentleman, a barrister-at-law, trained and paid to show off whosoever was paying him in a good light. The prosecution always had them, and they didn't come cheap. Some travelled from Coventry, or Birmingham, or even from London itself if the case were interesting and paid well.

Luckily Cath would have time to find a talker for her friend. The law would not be rushed. If the friend had only been brought to Warwick two days ago, his case would not be heard for at least two, and more probably three, weeks. When his case was to be heard, his name would be posted on the gate.

She thanked the man, left him, and made her way to the Post Office in Market Square. Cath could read printed letters, and she found a sign there informing the public that letters from London arrived every morning at eight minutes past seven, and letters to London were despatched every evening at fourteen minutes before eight. Letters from Birmingham, Manchester or Liverpool reached Warwick at twenty minutes past nine am, and letters to those cities would be carried by the coach *Mercury* promptly at three every afternoon. The charge for sending letters to all these places was clearly printed on the notice, but nothing about it indicated how long it would take a letter to reach Finstall in Worcestershire or what charge would be made for sending it.

No one would talk for John. Even if a letter could be sent, there would not be enough money in the box hidden behind the kindling wood in the cupboard by the fireplace, nor had she the right to ask for it. There would be very little money in that box. They had always had just enough to live on, and that was what there would be in the box, just enough for those left at home to live on.

She herself would have to talk, unpaid, for John. In two weeks, she would be well rehearsed. She would find work, and get new clothes, and practise until every word was just right.

The Hotel and Commercial Inn was close by the Post Office. She enquired there at the back door for work, and was refused. She tried the Warwick Arms in the High Street and the Swan Hotel in Jury Street without success.

Standing by the water pump in the back yard of the Woolpack Hotel on Market Place, she watched an old man empty chamberpots into buckets. The old man placed the filled buckets in a corner of the yard to await collection by the Nightsoil Men. Cath wondered how she could make her appearance more respectable. She had washed those parts of herself that did not require undressing, but her clothes were badly stained and torn. If all the hotels of Warwick refused her work, she might be forced back into the country, and her plans would come to nothing.

The door of the Woolpack's kitchen was open, and into the

yard drifted the smell of roasting mutton and a great deal of noise. Cath took water from the pump, and tried once more to rub away the stains of mud and grass from her skirt, before approaching the open door slowly.

'More fire!' A short stout woman shouted the words to a small boy, as she ran from the large table in the centre of the kitchen to one of the three ovens next the fire and back again. The small boy heaped on more fuel, and shielded his eyes from the sparks as he poked at the ashes of an enormous fire. Sweat poured from his and the cook's faces, and their clothes were soaked with it. The two women at work at the other end of the room were also sweating and working hurriedly. Cath stood at the doorway, and was noticed by the cook on one of her many runs to and from the ovens.

'Give her some of that stale pudding, Dotty, and send her on her way. She's keeping the air out. We shall all melt into pools on this floor in a minute.'

The larger and more muscular of the two women tore off a piece of dry pease pudding, and threw it to Cath, who caught it, and stood back from the doorway for a moment, so as to allow the air in as she had been told. Then, shouting so as to be heard above the noise and clatter, she asked, 'I would very much like to work here. May I come back when you are not so busy, with the mutton being cooked and everything?'

On hearing the word 'mutton', the cook ran from the table at twice her normal speed, flung wide the door of the largest oven, and was immediately enveloped in thick black smoke and lost to sight.

'Damp the fire, Arnold! Damp it!' The small boy pulled and pushed at several flues, and then tipped a large jug of water onto the flames, so that the black smoke, which had been spreading itself evenly around the kitchen, was changed into white steam.

'You're about as much use to me as the parson's dangler is to Mrs Parson.' Cath backed away from the door as the entire staff of the kitchen, all coughing, moved forwards towards the fresh air of the yard. It seemed to her that it would be better to return at a time of less turmoil.

At twelve minutes to four, the door was still open, but there was no sound coming from the kitchen. The fire had been damped down, and the staff sat on stools or flopped over the central table, with the scraps of their own meal still left on their plates, and half-consumed mugs of tea in their exhausted hands.

The cook was asleep, her head resting on the table. Cath waited at the door. Dotty, the larger of the other two women, spoke to Edith, the smaller. 'Think she'd have seen enough, wouldn't you?' The cook opened one eye, and focused it on the shape in the doorway. 'I'm going to die right here and now at this table, unless folks can learn to stop blocking that door-hole and keeping the air from me.' She made a limp gesture with one hand, indicating that Cath should step forward into the room, and Cath did so.

'No lice or fleas, have you?' Cath shook her head. 'Say so now, if you have. We should find out soon enough, and I should be so very angry at the deception, your name would be mentioned everywhere you might look for a position.' Cath swore that she had no lice or fleas, and endured the scrutiny of the cook's one open eye as it searched her soul for falsehood. Then the cook grunted, opened her other eye, and heaved the upper half of her body into a more vertical position.

'And how many hedges have you struggled through, to get here looking like that?' The question did not require an answer. 'It has been known for guests to ask to come into this kitchen. They usually have very poor stomachs for it when they get here, and one sight of you looking like that would take away their appetites for ever, and then where's the profit?' Cath explained that she had nothing else to wear, but that she could wash and mend what she had on.

'And what shall you be wearing, miss, when you're a-bending over and a-washing? A garland of roses?' The cook found this question most humorous, roaring with laughter and looking about for appreciation from the others. 'We could make a fortune, charging sixpence at that door for the people to watch you a-bending and a-scrubbing in a garland of roses.' Her exhaustion quite gone, the cook stood and tiptoed with exaggerated grace to the wash-bowl, swaying her shoulders from side to side, and singing 'A-bending and a-scrubbing, a-bending and a-scrubbing' over and over. At the bowl, she looked coyly over her shoulder, then lifted up the back of her skirts and wriggled her posterior.

Edith went pink in the cheeks, and covered her mouth to laugh at the cook's good humour, while Dotty, who was less amused, got up to clear the table and glare more closely at Cath. Meanwhile the boy, Arnold, decided to join the game, by feigning lechery for the cook, and running at her with arms outstretched. As he approached her, the cook swung round, lifted up the front of her skirts, and swiftly buried Arnold inside them, continuing thereafter her posing and wriggling while the muffled voice of Arnold could be heard from within her skirts, asking to be let out.

'He's only a shrimp, but he does do his best.' As suddenly as she had first engulfed him, the cook plucked Arnold from under her skirts, and put him on the table among the remaining dishes, which Dotty now forebore to clear. There she plucked him like poultry, stripping off his trousers and revealing to the four women present the most intimate third of his skinny white body.

'He's no good at fire-keeping, and his dangler's not worth turning over in bed for. Just look at that sad little piglet! The poor thing won't ever grow, Arnold, if you keep tormenting it.' The small boy scrambled to his feet on the table-top, pulling his clothes round him, his face the colour of boiled beetroot, his nose running, tears in his eyes, and the cook, who had begun to sweat again, wiped her face with a dirty rag, realising that somehow the fun had gone out of the game, and looking elsewhere for a mark. 'Edith's the one whose skirts you should be a-sniffing up. She hasn't been near a wash-tub the best part of a month.'

This remark drew noises of protest from Edith, and irritated Dotty, who said angrily, 'A lady guest gave Margaret some of her old clothes last week. Margaret was going to ask a price for them at John Powers's Pawnshop.'

For a moment the cook was nonplussed. 'What do I want old clothes for?'

'Her. If you want her. She's still here.' Dotty pointed to Cath, who remained just inside the doorway.

The cook looked at Cath almost as if she was seeing her for the first time. 'Who said I wanted her to start?' Dotty shrugged her shoulders. 'You're getting a bit too forward, madam. You may be trying for a position at the George before long, away from your precious Edith.'

For a full minute, no one spoke, and the kitchen staff went about their work of clearing up, while Cath waited, standing at the door. Then, as she turned to go, the cook said, 'What size was this so-called lady?'

Dotty indicated a size with her hands.

'Tell Margaret to bring the wearables to me. They count as remuneration. We're due our share.' Dotty began to leave. 'Clothes or money, tell her, it's all the same. I won't have all these private dealings.'

Dotty left the kitchen, and the cook turned her attention to Cath. 'They have to keep in sweet with me, or they get very poor portions, and poor portions cut two ways. A hungry guest doesn't feel so generous when it comes to feeling in his pockets.' The cook considered this statement for a while, as if there were a joke in it somewhere which she had not quite discovered. Then she said, 'You knew that mutton was burning, didn't you?'

'It smelled as though it might be done.'

'I can't smell anything with this nose so stuffed up all the time, and those two couldn't smell a sewer if they were swimming in it.'

Cath started work there and then. The clothes were brought, and Arnold was locked inside the pantry while the women watched Cath change. She was to have her food, and be paid threepence halfpenny a day for every day Cook wished her to work. At first she would be 'on test' to see if she suited. She was to help Arnold tend the fire and clear the ashes, to fetch water and scrub the pans and dishes, to remove slops and waste and wash the kitchen floor and walls once a week, and to perform any other tasks which the cook might put on her. If she suited, she would become part of the regular establishment, work for six and a half days a week, and be given Sunday afternoon as a half-day of rest; her full days would be from six thirty in the morning until nine thirty at night. Under no circumstances was she to enter or leave by any other than the back door, and should she ever be spied in any other part of the hotel but the kitchen, she would at once be 'taken in' as a suspicious person. Almost at once she was given the nickname of 'Nose', since the cook, whenever calling for her, would shout, 'Where's my nose?' or sometimes, 'Run, Nose! Run, run, run!'

Nobody asked her where she came from or where she was going, but on the evening of her third day at work, Dotty and Edith asked where she was staying. When Cath replied that she was suited, and thanked them for the offer of assistance they had not made, they stared at her suspiciously, and shortly afterwards the cook asked to see her arms, giving bed-bugs as a reason. Cath bared the underside of her upper arms for inspection.

'I don't claim to see into the future, Nose, but I shall be able to tell your lodging by counting the bites.' There were no bites. Oddly enough, this did not please Cook. 'There's an ill flavour to your blood, miss, or else you've made your lodging in an ice-house, if the bugs take no interest.' Cath smiled, and covered her arms, hoping that she would not be pushed into the admission that she slept sitting upright in a doorway, but Dotty had already guessed (or perhaps she knew, and had been asking in order to shame Cath into admission), for she whispered to the cook, who said with the satisfaction of one who has been proved correct, 'Well, there you are: I said it must be cold. You'll get your threepence halfpenny tonight, miss, and then you can have the grace to be bitten like everyone else. Arnold knows all the lodging houses near here. Him and his mother, they've been flung out of all of them at one time or another for pissing the beds.'

Instructed to give Cath the benefit of his experience, Arnold led Cath that evening to a room above a shop in Paradise Street, where she was shown a small bed in one corner, and told she might have the use of it for three halfpence a night, payable in advance, for which she would get the use of the kitchen as well. Arnold, wishing to demonstrate his worldliness, attempted to barter with the landlord.

'She won't need to use the kitchen, Mr Buller. She's working for me at the Woolpack, and has the use of ours all day long.'

The landlord sighed, put his hands in his pocket, and gazed dolefully at the small boy in front of him. 'It's no good, Mr Bennett. If I was to start making adjustments to my rates, where would it end? Every lodger would require a different consideration. I'd never be able to keep the details straight.'

Arnold pointed out that it was inhuman to expect a working woman to part with half her wages for the mere privilege of a bed. He paced the room, mumbling that he wished he had never brought Cath to such a rogue.

'A rogue, Mr Bennett?'

'A rogue, Mr Buller. I don't know what Cook will say.'

'How is the dear lady? She never comes to see me these days.'

'Three halfpence a night for a flea-ridden mattress!'

'At least, Mr Bennett, it's sweeter than when you and your dear mother was here to honour us with your patronage.'

Cath sat down on the bed, and this was taken as a sign that the deal had been struck. There were five other beds in the room. She wondered how many of them would be occupied.

Next day, Cook asked Arnold, 'Where have you put my Nose?' When told, she giggled and said, 'Buller! Well, at least he won't try to hop into bed with you. He's been badly ruptured these last five years, and walks like a duck on hot coals.' Demonstrating Mr Buller's walk, she paraded the full length of the kitchen, clutching the front of her clothes. 'Do you know how he chose his wife?' No one knew. 'He timed her.' Everyone waited. No more was said. Cath realised that she was expected to ask. 'Timed her doing what?'

The cook swung round in triumph. 'Boning seventy sparrows for a pie.' Laughter in the kitchen. 'She was the quickest, and didn't waste a wing.'

It wasn't long before the cook had told Cath the life histories of all those who worked with her, never allowing any to speak for themselves, because she so much enjoyed the telling and the elaboration of other people's lives. If they dared to offer a forgotten detail or attempt to amend an inaccuracy, she would snap, 'I'm coming to that. Leave it to you, you'd get it told from coffin to crib, and wonder why the congregation had left before the collection.'

Dotty was thirty-five and unmarried, the eldest of a family of seven, and had been keeping home for her father for the last twelve years since the death of her mother. All the rest of her family had married, and left home; the father was now fifty-one, and over-fond of drink. Edith was twenty-seven, and now lived with Dotty; they had met while Edith was in service at Stratford, under circumstances which they did not communicate. Arnold and his mother had run away from the rest of a very large family in Birmingham. Why his mother had chosen Arnold as a partner in escape, when she had eight other children to choose from, was quite beyond Cook's comprehension, but this had been done, and there was no accounting for taste.

Cath did not talk much about herself or her situation, and this, together with her polite manners and willingness to work, intrigued the other women. She feared that her reticence might cause them to dislike her.

'You've not been on the road long; that's my guess.' Cath shook her head. Cook was in one of her mellow moods which always followed a temper tantrum, brought on in this case by Edith's slicing into her own finger. Other people's pain invariably threw the cook into a rage. Edith's finger had been wrapped in a hem torn from one of Cook's own petticoats, and she had been despatched to the Free Dispensary in Chapel Street, accompanied by Arnold in case of fainting.

'I hope you're going to last, Nose. We turn dozens of boys and girls away from that door, particularly in winter when the streets are cold. Young people travel about too much; that's my view. Once they've filled their stomachs and got warm, off they go, London way most of them. I've known some tear their clothes off in the street, to be taken up and put in prison, all for the shilling piece that's handed to them when they come out. They could work all that time, and get the same money, but they'd have to pay for their beds.'

'Is it bad in prison, ma'am?'

'If it was a bower of roses, my girl, that would defeat the object.' Cath had been every evening to look for John's name, posted on the gate of the Assize Court, even though she had been told that it was much too soon, and had lingered outside the walls of the gaol itself, looking up at the few barred windows and wondering if he might see her.

'Yes, I hope you stay, for I can see that you were a well-brought-up Nose. I've no pretensions, never have had and never shall, but I wasn't all that badly brought up myself. It's these kitchens fetch you down. You come all down to earth with a clatter when you have to sweat to make the meat stretch further than ever it did round the poor old animal. I'm sure if I'd gone in for more pastry and less general, I could have stayed a lady.' Cook rose from her chair to continue work. 'Where's that scab they christened Edith? All she ever uses that finger for is picking her nose. Run and fetch her back from the Dispensary. I'll stitch it up myself.'

For the second time within the same hour, Cath stood before the notices posted on the gate of the Assize Court. She had read the list of names five times, but the name she longed to see there was not among those to be tried within the coming week.

It was Sunday, her half-day of rest. So far it had been spent either here, or walking around the town, listening to her own footfalls, and convinced that the people of Warwick were staring at her clothes, which had been cast aside by a hastily departing hotel guest, and now hung loosely about Cath, moving not as she moved, but in a manner which suggested the movements of their previous occupier.

Her shoes were tight. The hotel guest's feet must have been pointed. Cath's own feet had lived for so long without shoes that they had spread sideways, and now resisted being squeezed for fashion. Furthermore, the regular pattern of sound made by each shoe as it hit the rough cobblestones and tortured its lodger had been accompanied, during her walk, by other less tentative footsteps. As these had continued, street after street, Cath had become convinced that she was being followed. The small hairs on the back of her neck had begun to tingle, and she had returned to the gate of the Assize Court by a roundabout route.

Now, as she pretended to read the list of names for the sixth time, the shadow of a head larger and higher than her own moved over the print of the poster, and came to rest.

'I study humankind myself. That is one of my main interests.' Cath turned, and found herself confronting a face which was a particularly fierce shade of red, and had a gloss which reflected light. Even more remarkable was the woman's nose, which almost exactly resembled a large bluebottle, having the same colour and proportion, and seeming to be covered with a translucent skin of gossamer. Had it also

27

possessed legs, Cath felt sure that it would have walked across the woman's face, and flown away. It was a bluebottle anchored for ever by greed to a piece of overripe fruit.

'We are all students of the world, are we not? I have seen a great deal in my short life.' Cath estimated the woman's age as being close to fifty. 'We attend here regularly to advance our education.'

The woman must be a widow, since a frill of dull purple and black surrounded the fierce red glow of her face, the upper two thirds of the frill being a bonnet, the lower third a collar encircling a rather wide and unfeminine neck.

'Please don't presume that we spend our whole life here. We attend only those cases where much is at stake.' The 'we', Cath realised, was not royal, but included a fat young man with a large head, who stood at some distance, touching the iron railings with a gloved hand. Cath was sure that, when she had first turned to look at the woman, there had been two men leaning against the railings. Now the remaining man moved a little nearer, and she noticed that his face was smooth, pink and white, and gave no sign of having aged.

Nodding politely, Cath turned, and began to move away, but the woman continued talking, falling in beside her, and matching her step for step, while the baby-faced man followed four paces behind.

'This town is so very quiet on Sundays. Well, it is the Lord's day, of course, so quietness is suitable, but this town is so very very quiet; it is quite *dis*quieting. Nothing moves, my dear, without its movement being noted. Each week we plan to do something different, something which might change our lives, but then we wander about the town as usual, and I always get the same feelings of . . .' The woman raised a gloved hand to her forehead, and sighed. The purple glove against the shiny red face was like the pistil of some monstrous flower. 'I'm lost for a word. My husband swore I was a gypsy, or a great actress hiding from my public here in Warwick, but they find words so easily.' Cath had never seen an actress, on or off the stage, but she could easily imagine that this was how one might behave. 'It is grey. That is how best I can explain it. This whole town is grey on Sundays, is that not so, Angel?' The 'Angel' did not refer to Cath, but to the overweight young man who followed them, who nodded agreement, and smiled an almost lipless smile.

'The whole world might be grey on Sundays, for all we should know of it, but nowhere could be greyer than this town.' Cath stopped walking, and was about to express her desire to be excused, when both purple-gloved hands came forward, clasped her own ungloved right hand, first shook it, and then held it. 'Rebecca. That is my Godgiven name. What is yours, my dear?'

'Cath, ma'am.' Cath felt uncomfortable in calling the bluebottle woman 'ma'am', for although her clothes were of good quality, and her language seemed elegant, there was something about the woman's voice which did not fit the clothes or language, and had a hint of coarseness.

'Cath! That has an honest sound about it.' By this time, Cath had realised that, wherever she walked, the woman and her guardian Angel would walk with her, he following four paces behind, and studying the cobblestones. 'But you cannot have been given that name in church. Therefore it must be short for . . . ?' The woman waited for Cath to finish the sentence.

'Catherine.'

'Why, of course!' The woman seemed to be waiting again, this time for an explanation, but Cath did not wish to give one.

'*Cath! Cath! Want Cath!*' It was Luke, her brother, who had shortened her name, being unable to master the whole of it, and his short version had stuck. To remember her brothers and sisters now was painful to her. She had deserted them for John, had left them angry and weeping. They had predicted that God would punish her, had told her never to return. Luke had clung to her, repeating 'Cath! Cath!' over and over as she tore herself free from him. She would not go back. But she would always be Cath.

'Names are of paramount importance. If I were to tell you Angel's real name, you would certainly burst out laughing. For the life of me, I can't think what his father and I were doing when we gave him that name; it is an unsuitable name for a young man. We laugh at it ourselves, Angel and I, his father being dead of course. Quite out of the blue, one of us will say the name, and then we burst out laughing.' Already the woman was chuckling. 'It really will amuse you, I'm sure, for what we

29

always say about it is, *It's not a name you'd want to go to bed with*.' The chuckling had grown, so that walking had become impossible, and now the woman threw back her head and laughed aloud, holding on to Cath for support.

'Reginald!'

The laughter stopped abruptly. It was not the woman who had spoken the name, but the owner of that name himself, and its effect was quite other than to move them both to laughter. Mother and son stared at each other in silence for perhaps five seconds, then the woman turned away, still holding Cath's arm, and continued walking.

'There are people in this town, my dear, complete strangers who, without introduction, will engage you in conversation here in the street, and this, I find, happens more often of a Sunday than any other day. These are people who either live alone or in a situation which is oppressive to them. They wander into the streets of Warwick every Sunday, and seek me out. Angel takes no part. He listens, but seldom relieves me of the burden of conversation. Angel is quiet, but he thinks a great deal. There are times when he quite shatters my composure with one of his ideas. Suddenly out it will come. After he has been silently thinking for hours, he'll open his mouth, and out will come . . . well, goodness knows what. Isn't that so, Angel?' Behind her, Angel nodded. 'Except when there's a third party present. Then all his ideas seem to fail him.'

The woman was right about the town, which was indeed grey, and the afternoon sky matched it perfectly. The clothes of the townspeople who passed were sombre – smart, but sombre Sunday-best – but beside Cath, splendid in purple and black, strode the woman, nodding and smiling to the passers-by, her bluebottle of a nose preceded only by her ample bosoms, sailing out in front like two great ships with the wind behind them.

'And the confidences these people make to me!' The woman raised her hand to acknowledge a greeting which had not been made. 'Innermost secrets, my dear. If I were not a student of humankind, I should be overwhelmed by some of their private thoughts.' Cath's own private thoughts were of John, of the Assize Court, and of her speech, which still had to be re-hearsed. 'It is my profession makes them talkative with me.

When all your customers confide in you, then you must either practise the art of good conversation, or seek out a quieter calling in life. And what *is* my profession? I expect you are curious to know.'

Cath nodded. It seemed the polite thing to do.

'If I was to call my establishment an Inn, and you were to visit me there, then I should be found out in a lie, for an inn it is not. Yet it is more, much more, my dear, than a mere Beer-House, for it fits nicely in between the two, and has the best qualities of both. You won't find a more cheerfully comfortable ingle-nook in the whole of Warwickshire, and certainly not in this grey town. We call our little establishment the Good Intent, and you may find us on the corner of George Street and Ironhouse Lane. But wait!' The woman stopped suddenly, and held her free hand in the air as if summoning some vehicle. 'Why do I direct you? Why should you seek us out, when we can take you there? We'll stand on no ceremony, and accept no excuses. Angel and I shall conduct you there as our guest. The high point of a grey Sunday in Warwick must be afternoon tea with Angel and Mrs Fleckwindsor.'

Without waiting for a word of acceptance or refusal, the woman set Cath and herself in motion again, this time with a clear objective and destination. Cath's only way of escape would have been to push the large woman aside and run, a course of action in which she felt little confidence, being by now quite crippled in both feet and legs. Meanwhile Angel, as if the announcement of tea had cured him of his shyness, took four short shuffling steps to draw level, and spoke to Cath.

'If you take "rid" away from "Reginald", you're left with the correct letters to make an Angel.'

Mrs Fleckwindsor beamed at her son. 'What did I tell you? He stores them all up inside.'

'Oh, I do like my tea served properly. Thank you, my Angel.'

They were sitting in a tiny front parlour. The furniture was covered with velvet, and large tassels hung even from places, such as the legs of armchairs, where one would not usually expect tassels to be. The parlour smelled of beeswax and brewer's yeast.

'Do try one of these little pink ones. What have you put inside them, Angel?'

Cath obeyed, and tried a pink one, while Angel stood, wiping the palms of his hands down the sides of his tightly fitting jacket, as he listed the ingredients in all the many kinds of dainty cakes and pastries piled on the heavy metal cakestand before them.

'He's holding his breath to know what you think, my dear. Since he puts all his artistic endeavour into food, it's only fair to give him a little critique.'

'They're very nice.'

'There you are, Angel! And honesty shining from her very eyes as she said it! I should not be at all surprised if you haven't found yourself a disciple.' Angel exuded satisfaction, and Mrs Fleckwindsor turned her attention again to Cath. 'Do try the Almond Fingers. I cannot induce him to stop making them. Almost all my tiny profit goes into Angel's artistic endeavours, and if I were to allow it, he would stand out there in the street, giving dainties away to every passer-by, just for a glint of appreciation.'

'A true artist shouldn't charge.' Angel nibbled at a Cinnamon Slice.

'That may be so, dearest one, but marzipan, cane sugar and nutmeg do not grow on trees.'

'Nutmeg does.'

Cath ate as much as she could politely manage, and Angel's thin smile became wider with each mouthful. Crumbs fell from Mrs Fleckwindsor's mouth onto her projecting bosom, and had to be flicked across the room with a handkerchief trimmed with lace. The teapot was drained dry and twice refilled. Outside the tasselled window-curtains, the grey town faded into dark.

'Oh, it is such a pleasure to have honest to goodness company! Isn't it, Angel?' Angel agreed. 'I intend from now on only to spend Sundays in the company of honest people; it is much the best way. Have you come far, my dear?'

The question was totally unexpected. Cath choked on marzipan, and looked desperately around the room, which now seemed even smaller than when she had entered it. The heavy dark furniture pressed in on her; the tassels weighed her down.

Mrs Fleckwindsor and her son waited, she seated, he standing behind her holding a delicate tea-cup between moist fingers and smiling his thin-lipped smile. The smell of hops and yeast from the next room grew stronger and more sickly.

'Please don't distress yourself, my dear.' Though Mrs Fleckwindsor had expressed her pleasure at the unpretentious honesty of Cath's name, she had not yet brought herself to use it. 'I don't intend to pry, I assure you. Let us speak of something else. Angel, where is one of your shattering ideas when we so badly need it?'

'I've come from Otmoor.' It was a place she had heard of, and would not easily forget. 'I came to be with a friend.'

'How wise to come *from* Otmoor! We hear such stories of the dreadful rioting. And do the men really dress as women, and blacken their faces?'

Cath stared at her. '*I dare venture that Otmoor is a place you have heard of, and having been there would not easily forget.*' She had chosen badly. Perhaps those who really came from Otmoor did not own to it.

The silence stretched out between them. Then Mrs Fleckwindsor brushed cake-crumbs from her dress. 'But how thoughtless I am,' she said. 'You have been sent here to avoid the violence, and doubtless left loved ones behind you. It is distressing for you to hear us chatter on. Not another word, Angel, about Miss Cathy's past. We must make that a rule if she is to continue to visit us.'

Angel smiled and nodded.

On the following Tuesday, Cath took supper with the Fleckwindsors. She had been unable to think of a polite excuse not to go, nor was Mrs Fleckwindsor, now covered from neck to ankle in bright red satin, in the habit of accepting excuses.

In the room next to the tiny parlour the smell of yeast and hops had been overpowered by that of tobacco smoke and human sweat, for the room had filled with men, their pipes alight and beer at their elbows, and from them there arose a gentle chatter of good-humoured gossip. Mrs Fleckwindsor bounced in and out, from parlour to beer-room, carrying pots of beer and hunks of bread and cheese, like a small girl at her very own party.

'I do so enjoy it when we are busy, my dear; my purpose in life is to give pleasure. Thirty-six similar establishments in the town alone! It's such a gratification when one is preferred above all others.'

There was something she had to say to Cath which might very well change all their lives, but clearly it could not be said on the move. However, it was clear that Angel (though he might very well know what it was) was not to be present at its saying, for he was banished to the kitchen. Cath, by herself and seeing the door to the beer-room left ajar, moved to peer through, so that she might see the faces of these men who preferred the Good Intent to the other thirty-five beer-houses.

The room was dark, and made the murkier by the tobacco smoke which drifted from the mouths of the men or twirled upwards from the bowls of clay pipes to hang heavily in the air. The voices of the men were low, almost whispering. It seemed to Cath as if two of the men noticed her at the door, and turned their heads away. The back of one man's head reminded her of someone, and there was a voice (was it from the other?) which she thought she had heard somewhere before.

Someone in the murk of the room struck a match. It flared up, illuminating the room for a second, and burning the hand of whoever had struck it, who laughed, and dropped the match.

The match flared up . . . 'Run. Please run. Quickly.' And the yellowhammers rising suddenly from the stubble.

She was shaking. She moved away quickly from the door, and found herself sitting in the velvet chair, found that Mrs Fleckwindsor was sitting with her, and talking, and holding a tankard of beer in her hand, and talking, a river of unregarded sound mingling with the low-voiced chatter from next door, while Cath sat and went over and over in her mind where she and John might have been and what they might now be doing had she not burned the hay.

'Has my son been forward with you? You look to be in some distress. If so, it must be laid to my fault, not his, for I am always reproaching him for his backwardness in regard to the fair sex. You have quite ensnared him, my dear. He has even begun to neglect his artistic endeavours, and hasn't been seen at the pastry board since Sunday.'

She had written John a letter, telling him that she was in

Warwick, and would be at his trial. She had told him that there would be no one hired to speak for him, because she had been unable to find enough money, but that she would tell them what had happened, and that it had been an accident. She would also tell them about the baby, and everything would come out right, because she loved him.

'Angel is like a daughter in many ways, but not even a mother as devoted as I could pronounce him pretty. But he is very gentle, my dear. He would never harm you.'

She had told John that he must say nothing but what was true, because the truth was their only hope now, and she would be there to admit her part.

'I shall not try to be devious with you.' Mrs Fleckwindsor paused, gathering breath and resolution. 'Angel will not find it easy to come by a wife. His good points lie hidden. I know that he is relying upon me to present him in a favourable light, but you have an honest nature, my dear, I know; you are as honest as your name, and look for honesty in others.'

They would be together again soon, because that was only right, since they had meant no harm to anyone, and besides she loved him so very much.

'You would be more comfortable than you are now. You are of good stock, I know. You would lack for nothing. I have longed for pretty grandchildren.'

She had closed the letter by hoping he was in good health as she was. She had sent him many kisses. She had written, 'Your neck is not thin. It is beautiful.' Though she could read and write too, the spelling of so long a word had given her trouble. 'Love' was not a difficult word to spell. The man who stood by the gate had taken the letter from her, and promised that he would do his best to see that it was delivered.

'I fear for his sanity if you should refuse him.' Mrs Fleckwindsor had been talking, and now she had stopped. She seemed to be expecting some reply. Cath smiled and nodded, hoping that this would be enough to set Mrs Fleckwindsor on again. It was not enough. There was silence. Mrs Fleckwindsor appeared to be at a loss for words. Motionless and with narrowed eyes, she waited for a response. Something had gone wrong.

Finally, when the silence had become embarrassing, Cath

stood, and said, 'I'm very tired. Will you excuse me?'

Mrs Fleckwindsor also stood, and spoke. 'But am I to give him hope?'

'Who?'

'Angel.' There was another long pause. 'My dear, you have not been listening. My son wants to marry you.'

Cath thought for a moment, and then said, 'That's very kind of him, but will you explain that I am in love with someone else, and that we're going to be married?'

'My dear, it will become so hot in here. Shall we survive?' The public gallery of the Assize Court was crowded, but not enough to have prevented Mrs Fleckwindsor from noticing Cath in the front row and pushing her way through the spectators to sit beside her. The jury was being sworn. Mrs Fleckwindsor made herself comfortable on a cushion which she had brought with her.

'Is this case something to do with farming, or with agriculture?' Cath nodded. 'I thought as much. One can always tell by the number of farmers they take on the jury. I suppose they are to be considered expert in such matters.' She stood up again, in order to lift the cushion and beat it with clenched fists. Cath tried to remove Mrs Fleckwindsor's presence from her mind, so as to concentrate on what was to happen and what she must say. In order to gain her place at the front, she had arrived early. She must be able to see John when they brought him in, and must be seen by the judge when it was time for her to speak.

'Angel is so heartbroken, he won't leave the house. His only distraction is food.' The woman's chatter buzzed in Cath's ear. The more she was ignored, the more talkative she became. 'I really do intend to take steps to change my life.'

A door opened, and slowly an officer appeared, followed by John with another officer walking behind him. He looked weak and very frightened. When he had mounted the steps and stood in the dock, he raised his head and looked towards the public gallery. But not at Cath.

'My dear, he's only a child. He can hardly be much older than yourself.'

Mrs Fleckwindsor turned, and Cath could feel the intensity

of the woman's gaze on her face like a burning. 'He really has the most interesting appearance.' A silence. The woman watching Cath, who watched only John. 'It won't go in his favour, I fear. The old judges are just as envious as we women when it comes to physical attraction.' Silence. Watching. 'This gallery will be impossible to get near when the news of that beautiful and tortured face becomes general. He looks far too poor to have instructed anyone to speak for him. I do hope he can be heard.' All were commanded to stand as the judge entered. 'Oh dear! What a sour countenance. I knew his brother once. The whole family is riddled with disease.'

The charge was read, and John required to plead. 'Not guilty, sir.'

'Good. We're in for a fight, at least. It is so disappointing to go through all the preliminaries, and be baulked of a trial.'

It was explained to John that, since no one had been appointed to speak for him, he himself must conduct his case, with the judge acting as legal adviser. Therefore, if he wished to bring witnesses into court to testify to his innocence, he must consult the judge. Cath moved forward, trying to stand and to say that she was present and would give evidence, but she felt Mrs Fleckwindsor's restraining hand on her arm, and before she could speak, John had already replied that he did not wish to call witnesses, and that he would give evidence for himself.

'That is not permitted.'

'Sir?'

A court official instructed John that he must not call the judge 'sir', but 'my lord'.

'My lord?'

'You are not permitted to testify on oath on your own behalf. You may make a statement after evidence has been given against you. I am sure the jury will give proper consideration to it.'

'I will tell the truth, my lord.'

'Whether you tell the truth or not, that is of no consequence; it is not sworn evidence. You may tell the truth if you wish; I am sure that I hope you will. And you will not be questioned; that will be a protection to you.'

37

'I have no objection, my lord, to questions. I would answer all questions truthfully.'

'You are not to be asked questions. You may ask questions of your own to those witnesses who give evidence against you. You will not ask questions until you are told you may do so. You may ask questions then, under direction, and in the proper form. Is that clear to you?'

'Yes, my lord.'

Again Cath stirred in her seat, and again she was restrained.

'You may proceed, Mr Moyle.'

A fat gentleman in a dirty wig stood up and informed the judge that the case was a simple one. At a preliminary examination, the accused had not denied incendiarism, but had made the excuse that there was no intent. (Did that mean it had been an accident? Yes, it must mean that. Was the gentleman saying that there had been an accident? If so, Cath might not have to stand up and speak. But she would do so. She would put it all beyond doubt. Still she felt Mrs Fleckwindsor's hand on her arm.) The accused might appear to be a simple man, but he could not be as simple as he appeared, since he knew enough about the law to make – without any help, with no legal advice, or so he appeared to be saying – such a sophisticated defence, based on the legal maxim, the sophisticated legal maxim – here the gentleman in the dirty wig turned towards the jury, looked solemnly at them, and spoke in a foreign language which Cath assumed to be Latin, and which he immediately translated as meaning that there could be no crime without intent. However, the gentleman continued, this subtle defence would not hold. The crown would bring witnesses to show, not only that the accused had burned a field of hay, the property of Matthew Walton, farmer of the parish of Tysoe, but that he had been accompanied and assisted in his act of incendiarism by at least one co-conspirator, and that conspirator had been *disguised as a woman*.

John said 'No', and was told sharply to be silent. Cath felt herself go cold, and her hands trembled. Mrs Fleckwindsor took the hand nearest to her between her own, and patted it.

Everyone present in the court before his lordship would know, said the dirty-wigged gentleman, the significance of that female disguise. It had been a cover for acts of arson, destruction, for revolutionary activities reminiscent of the worst days of the French Revolution, all over the country in recent years, as far as Wales, as near – the solemn gaze at the jury again – as very near, so near he did not need to remind those present in the Court, he did not believe he needed to utter the name of . . . Otmoor!

There was a buzz in the public gallery, and loud calls for silence in court. Members of the jury looked sideways at each other. '*And do the men really dress as women and blacken their faces?*' Cath shrank away from Mrs Fleckwindsor, and felt the woman cuddle protectively against her, while the woman on her other side dug sharply at Cath's intruding flank with an elbow. The first witness was called.

It was established that the hay had been cut by Farmer Walton, and its value was established in pounds and pence, and Farmer Walton was established as holding a farm building and five fields in the parish of Tysoe, and it was established that the Farmer himself had not seen the accused setting fire to his hay, but that certain men in his employ as day labourers had seen this, and had apprehended a man, and brought him to the Farmer, who had kept him bound until relieved of his presence by an officer of the law (the parish beadle) and that this man was the man standing in the dock.

John had no questions for Farmer Matthew Walton.

Peter Stokes, a day labourer, was one of the men who had apprehended the accused, whom he now recognised. It was at once clear that words of the order of 'apprehend' and even 'accused' were likely to give trouble to Peter Stokes. The judge accordingly cautioned him to be particularly careful in his answers. Peter Stokes twisted his hands, burst out into a sweat, lowered his gaze to the top of the witness-box, from which it was not thereafter lifted, and answered almost every question with either a 'Yes' or a 'No'.

'You saw with your own eyes the accused standing by the blazing hay?'

'Yes, sir.'

'He has stated in his examination at the Peacock Inn that he was alone. Was he alone?'

'No, sir.'

'There was another party with him?'

39

'Yes, sir.'

'What did this other party do as you approached?'

'Sir?'

The dirty-wigged gentleman said, 'It may be necessary to lead this witness, my lord.'

'Oh, lead . . . lead.'

'Did the other party run away from the fire as you approached?'

'Yes, sir.' Mrs Fleckwindsor turned her face to look at Cath.

'And was this bashful other party known to you?'

'No, sir.'

'Or to any of the men who were with you? Did any of you recognise the other party?'

'No, sir.' At any moment now, she would stand and speak. She would tell everyone that she herself was the other party, and they must listen. Cath swallowed, and discovered that her throat was dry.

'And am I correct in suggesting that this other party was dressed in woman's clothing?' Mrs Fleckwindsor was still watching Cath, and now placed a hand on her arm. There was silence from the witness-box. The question had been phrased in too complicated a way. 'Was this other party disguised as a woman?'

'Yes, sir.' But the question had altered its sense. Cath had been present – she would testify to that – but she had not been disguised. She stirred, and the fingers of Mrs Fleckwindsor's hand curled and tightened, so that what had been a hand on an arm had become a grip. Cath looked down at the hand, noticing for the first time that it was without a glove. It was a large hand, muscular, a hand which had known hard work.

'Can you think of any reason, within your experience as a native of these parts, why a man wishing to go out into the fields for recreation, or any other innocent purpose, should first disguise himself in woman's attire?'

A gulp. 'No, sir.' Cath attempted to move her arm. If this man had seen her, as he said, then he had seen a woman – herself. She placed her own hand over Mrs Fleckwindsor's hand, and tried to loosen the grip. She could not. She looked towards Mrs Fleckwindsor, and uttered the word 'Please', but Mrs Fleckwindsor only smiled, and whispered, 'It's more

40

interesting by far than one had expected, don't you agree?'

'But what if such a man had so disguised himself in order to commit wanton and vicious damage?' The gentleman in the dirty wig was going much further than he should in examining the witness, but the accused could not know that, and the learned judge seemed to have no objection. 'Have you ever heard of desperate men disguising themselves in this way in order to go out and commit offences against property – to subvert law and order – to do damage?'

The witness recognised 'do damage'. 'Yes, sir.'

'Tell his lordship where you have heard of such a thing done, and for what reason it was done.'

'At Otmoor, sir. For rioting.'

Cath wrenched her arm free, and stood up at the front of the public gallery, moving forward to the rail. She was sweating, shaking, and breathless; her throat was dry; but she was angry – angry and weeping. With the anger she found energy, the energy to shout.

'Please, may I beg permission to speak?' She did not wait for a reply. 'The person that man saw with John was me. I was there, and I –' A large, muscular hand was placed over her mouth, and she was being pulled backwards, away from the rail.

'Free the working man from slavery! We starve while you grow fat. We sweat while you count your money. One shilling and sixpence an hour!' It was the voice of the man who had shouted outside the Peacock Inn, and at his provocation, others began to shout, so that no one could be heard clearly. The clerk of the court cried, 'Silence!' and no one heeded him. Those in the body of the court looked up into the gallery. The learned judge grew rigid with anger. Officers of the court moved about the public gallery, trying to restore order. The spectators shouted in a confused way, many accusing each other of disruption, and, insofar as there was room to do so, moved agitatedly on the benches. Cath struggled and bit at the hand, kicking and scratching and crying out, trying to make the speech she had rehearsed, trying to make the people understand that it was she who had burned the hay. Nobody heeded her. Nobody heard her.

Only John raised his head, and looked up towards her. She

41

shouted, 'John!' and then, 'Please tell them!', but the shouted words were mere noise in a room which was filled with noise.

The judge stood up.

At first no one noticed. Then those in the well of the court stood also – the members of the jury, the officers, the fat gentleman in the dirty wig. Those ushers who had been attempting to quell the disturbance in the public gallery stood still, and their example was noticed, and after many minutes, all was still. It would have been possible now for Cath, her clothes torn, her face streaked with tears, to speak and be heard, but the silence was overwhelming, and she could not speak, or not immediately.

The judge turned, and left the court by a private door behind his throne. The trial stood adjourned. Nothing more was to be said, and nothing heard, until those in the public gallery had been removed. Nothing.

'I was with John on that hill.'

'Yes, my dear, I know.' Cath and Mrs Fleckwindsor were in the tiny front parlour. Angel had made them tea. 'Your behaviour was not that of a mere spectator. Also Mr Bradshaw, the gentleman who conducted the hearing at Tysoe, recognised you as you left here on Tuesday evening, and enquired after you. He had guessed that you were in some way connected with the fire when he saw you here in Warwick.'

'Then why didn't he tell the court? Why wasn't I arrested?'

Mrs Fleckwindsor placed her tea-cup on the table, and studied the backs of her fingers for a moment. One of her knuckles was bruised. 'It is all politics to these people. They cannot allow it to have been an accident. The landowners will not accept that there are such things, and the agitators want only acts of protest and heroics. Accidents don't further any causes; they are merely accidental. For both sides, it had to be a conspiracy.' She signalled to Angel to refill her cup. 'Once the hay was on fire, there was no saving that young man. His only chance would have been to run. If I had not stopped you speaking, they would have arrested you also.'

'But I burned the hay.'

'That's as may be, my dear, but you are a woman. He was

42

with you, he was older, and I have no doubt that they were his matches.'

'Our matches. We shared everything.'

Mrs Fleckwindsor smiled. 'The short time of our youth is very precious, even in adversity. Mr Bradshaw asked me if it was my opinion that you could ever have been mistaken for a man dressed in woman's clothing. We laughed together at such a preposterous idea. I don't believe for one moment that anyone saw you. It was all a notion of Mr Bradshaw's, don't you agree? He has such an inventive mind. So many ideas!'

Cath stood. 'I must go back to the court. I must know what is happening.'

'They will not let you in.'

'I will stand outside, and wait.' She was moving towards the door.

'But you must know what will happen. I have told you what has to happen.' Cath stopped, and turned. 'As a student of humankind, my dear, I beg you not to expect kindness or, indeed, humanity.'

Mrs Fleckwindsor also stood, and came towards Cath, who was surprised to see that the eyes above the bluebottle nose had tears in them. She took both Cath's hands in hers, leaned forward, and kissed her on the cheek. 'Angel and I are determined to leave this town, and change our lives.'

Cath left the beer-house, went to the Assize Court, and waited there. Eventually Mr Bradshaw left the court, and approached her. For what seemed a very long time, he stood before her in silence. Cath found that she was unable to look at him. This man had guessed that she had burned the hay. Finally he said, 'I believe that you are deeply concerned for that young man, and therefore it grieves me to tell you that he is to be hanged in three days time on the hill where the fire was started.'

It grieves me to tell you . . . it grieves me . . . grieves . . . me . . . There were no tears, no screaming, no shouting, no recriminations, no anger. There was nothing. Nothing but walking. Moving forwards. Walking out of the grey town of Warwick and into the warm colours of the countryside. Moving back, back along the way she had come three weeks earlier, when there had been hope. No hope now. Nothing. She moved back towards the place where they would bring him to be hanged, to the hill called Sunrising where she and John had last been together, lain together, laughed together, where together they had laughed his life away.

Sunrising

Two men had stood with him on the cart, one on either side, holding his arms, his hands being tied behind his back. The hill they called Sunrising was very steep, and mounting it all three men had found standing upright difficult. They had staggered about the cart as it bumped along, almost falling over each other. Since the cart had been surrounded by villagers, men and women carrying pitchforks, the two men guarding John had held on to him as much for their own safety as his confinement.

Someone had suggested that they should walk the hill, mounting the cart again when they reached the top, but that did not accord with tradition. 'He has to be seen. Seen to be an example. That's what we were told.' They had all agreed on that, and enjoyed their common agreement. They had left their work to make sure it was done right. A half-day's holiday to witness the law, their law, being administered to the full in every detail.

It was not possible to stand continuously upright on a cart travelling up such a hill, and everyone there (except for some of the smallest children) was conscious that the three men were marring what should have been a solemn and dignified procession by appearing to be drunk. But there was no help for it, since the gallows had been placed on the very spot where the crime had been committed.

Her crime. Placed where her crime had been committed. Placed thus, it could be seen for miles around, if one's eyesight were not obscured by tears.

'He has to be seen. Hold him upright.'

The two men on the cart, chosen for their size, had found their stature of more hindrance than help, and the fattest of them had become extremely red about the face with embarrassment, and panted like a badger after the chase, bent double and holding the side of the cart. His embarrassment had turned to anger. 'He'll be seen alright when his own eyes have been taken.'

Cath had not waited for that. She had seen the crows circling overhead, and had remembered crows in the blackened field on the morning after she had burned the hay, had remembered their squabbles over territory and their feathers shining with nourishment which they had found and she could not. She had not wished to see John's only beneficiaries claim their inheritance. And the man whose eyes had been so spoken of had lowered those eyes, and concentrated on the earth which could be seen through the cracks in the floor of the cart, and on the life within it which would continue after the shadow of the cart had passed. Cath had seen that expression before. She remembered recoiling from a piece of rotting bark which had seemed to be alive. 'It's only woodlice, Cath. They have to live somewhere.' And he had studied the lice for several minutes, then carefully placed the bark close to the tree from which it had fallen, saying, 'Everything's put here for a purpose.' Cath had argued, challenging him to tell her what possible good purpose woodlice could serve, and saying that she wondered what thoughts the tree might have on the subject, and he had frowned, and shrugged his shoulders, then looked at her with so much affection, and smiled his helpless smile, so that she had hugged him.

John had not looked at her from the cart, had not in any way acknowledged her presence, for she had burned the hay. Only at the end he had looked, had looked at her and into her, and had held that look for a very long time, while they had asked him whether he had anything to say to God. Then, with his eyes fixed on hers, full of puzzlement and wonder and fear, he had said that he prayed God would forgive his sins and accept his soul, and that those left behind who knew him, and knew him to be innocent of this crime, would they also please pray for him, as he prayed for them and for the baby he would never see.

A fat pink farmer had stood beside Cath, sweating, smiling and nodding, his tiny pale-blue eyes never ceasing to stare up at John's, while inside his trouser pocket his right hand moved up and down, continually turning over and over a single coin against a bunch of keys, the blunt tips of his fingers rubbing and rubbing at each side in turn – heads *chink*! tails *chink*!, over and over, rubbing and turning.

Then they had placed a rope around John's neck, and even the small children in the crowd had fallen silent. There had been total silence except for the insects and the birds and the rhythmical chink of coin against keys. She had turned her head away, closing her eyes and covering her ears, as the horse standing between the shafts of the cart was slapped and tugged and commanded to walk forward, pulling the cart from under John's feet.

The noise made by the crowd then was like a sigh. He had lived for eighteen years, and his life had ended in a sigh and the sound of a coin against keys.

PART TWO

Otmoor For Ever

Horses

It was cold and dark, the day only three hours old, and the previous day had seen heavy rain.

'Move on, boy. Go where it's deeper.' The older of the two boys prodded the younger in the back, forcing him further along the only ditch they had found which did not contain water.

'I can't see.' The younger boy moved forward cautiously, his arms outstretched, his feet feeling, one step at a time, for the ground beneath them.

'God didn't mean for you to see in the dark, nor yet did he mean for you to be frit of it.' The younger boy's left foot touched something which was not ditch. He stopped, groping forwards with his hands to feel what was blocking the way.

'Why you stopped now? This ain't deep enough.'

The younger boy's right hand rested on Cath's shoulder, and as his fingers felt the human hair, the boy let out a scream, which was cut short as the older boy placed his right hand over the source of the noise. 'Sssh! That hayward's got good ears, boy.'

The younger boy struggled to move back towards the way they had come. 'There's something there. Quick! I touched hair and an arm. Quick! Tis a body, I swear. Come you away from it.' He was trembling and whimpering, and the older boy allowed him to struggle past.

'You ain't to come grazing with me again, boy, and that's a promise.' He turned in the darkness, and thought for a moment. 'God made everything on this earth, boy, and there ain't nothing He intended we should be frit of.' Slowly he moved forwards. 'You like a rabbit watching a stoat, just letting all the faith drain from you.' His hands had found Cath's head, and his fingers moved gently over her face.

She was sitting upright, her knees pressed against one side of the ditch, her back supported by the other. Her eyes were closed, and her arms folded tightly across her chest. She was unconscious.

'It's a woman.' The older boy's fingers tested the length of matted hair.

The younger boy edged a little further away. 'Is she a witch, James?'

'No, she ain't old enough for that. She has a young skin.' His fingers stroked her neck and shoulders, feeling for a pulse, while he leaned forward, placing an ear close to her mouth to listen for any sign of breathing, and waited.

The sound of a small, almost weightless, silver-grey moth, exploring the latticed window of a dairy. Below the moth lie dead flies, dark-blue and shiny, their bent legs stuck up into the air ridiculously, their stomachs extended with gorging. And outside another moth, waiting on a leaf, at the beginning of a summer storm.

The moth's breath, so very faint and weak.

'Why don't she say something?'

'Shush, boy!'

'Is she gone, then?' No reply. 'She ain't, is she?'

'No, she ain't gone yet.' He raised his head.

'How can you tell?'

'Cos Jesus tells me, and I'm telling you. It was him gave me the sense to know when a body's breathing and when they ain't. Come here, and help me get her warm.' The older boy stepped carefully over Cath's body to get to her other side.

'How can I warm her? I'm freezing to death myself.'

'Same way as you and me was to get each other warm, boy, by getting up close and sharing what little we got. Three people's got more left inside than two.'

Reluctantly the young boy moved towards the body, and reaching out a hand, began, slowly at first, to rub Cath's upper arm. 'She's very stiff and cold, James. Can't be right to interfere with her if she's dead.'

The two boys pressed themselves against Cath's body, one each side, rubbing at her vigorously, trying to make the blood flow more quickly. The older boy placed his mouth against her ear, and spoke quietly. 'We don't aim to harm you, miss, only you won't last much longer less we get some warmth into you. Can you hear what I'm saying?' There was no response. 'We got horses grazing up on Atmot field, miss. When it comes nearly light, we can get you to some fire. Fire enough to make you think it's midsummer.' He listened for her breathing.

A blade of dry grass floated down from the top of the hay-wagon. That had been a time when summers were white-hot, and the earth was for rolling over and on, rolling for-ever downhill until you rolled against the body of another child.

And laughed into a face that gave you pleasure, and gave pleasure to that laughing face.

'I thought it was you and me was going to keep each other warm, James. I'm colder now than I was afore.'

Whose smile you longed for, and whose hand you ached to touch. Whose fingers plucked up primroses, and hurled them into the air, to watch them fall. A primrose falling, half-dead, out of the sky, to land at the feet of a healthy child. A child of love.

And the newly scythed grass smelling sweet, before it dried and burned in the heat, or sweated in the barn, smelling now like a boiling sheep's-head. Like broth for a healthy child. When the summers were too hot.

For almost an hour, the two boys rubbed at Cath's arms, and the older boy talked to her, and listened to her breathing. Then he stood.

'We ain't doing enough, boy. We got to move her. I'll lay underneath. Stop the damp getting up. She'll be in the middle, and you be on top. Perhaps then we can straighten her out. Take her feet your way.' The smaller boy took hold of Cath's ankles. 'Go on. Pull at her. She won't break, at least that's my opinion.' The smaller boy managed to get Cath's feet away from the side of the ditch, and tried to straighten her legs. 'And don't you go touching her clothes, or putting your hands where they ain't ought to be. I knows the way your mind works, Boy Shiltern.'

'We should be able to say you and I laid with a woman, James, both at one and the same time.'

'You go telling that, and I'll remember things about you I'd best forget. Here! Let me get under her, before you go jumping atop.'

They lay along the ditch, one on top of the other, with an old piece of sacking taken from inside the older boy's jacket covering the younger, their arms wrapped around each other, and their breath warming each other's faces until sleep overtook them.

The light grew as they slept. On the other side of the field, the hayward discovered the seven horses unlawfully grazing, which the boys were supposed to be tending, and plaited grass into the mane of each horse. For each horse so 'ticketed', there would be a fine of two pence.

Cath's eyelids opened, and blinked in the strong morning light. A mass of straw-coloured hair lay close to her face, and a small right hand rested gently against her chin. From below her left shoulder came the sound of deep and even snores. Two young but strong arms circled her waist from behind, and the top of a head covered with curly dark-brown hair and speckled with mud was just visible.

Lifting her arm slowly, she stroked the straw-coloured hair, and the head beneath the hair moved, making itself more comfortable. The face was that of an eleven-year-old boy. Cath's fingers moved, playing with the straight fringe which covered the boy's forehead, until the boy's eyes opened slowly, and two circles of deepest amber stared at her.

For a long moment Cath studied the depth of colour and the flecks of pigmentation in the boy's eyes. Then the small hand still touching her chin moved to the dark curls of the head below her, and, grasping them, shook the head. The snoring ceased.

Slowly, and without speaking, the younger boy got to his feet, and backed away along the ditch, brushing down his clothing, and folding the piece of old sacking which had been covering him, and on which he had now trodden. Cath used the sides of the ditch to pull herself upright. Her legs were very weak. The boy who had been lying below her sat up, and rubbed his eyes. Both boys watched Cath as she leaned against

54

the side of the ditch. After a while the older boy spoke. Cath estimated his age as about thirteen years.

'We meant you no harm, miss.' He waited, clearly expecting her to respond. Cath closed her eyes, trying to remember where she was. The boy stood. 'You've no reason to be shamed. He's too young, and I'm a Christian. We did nothing wrong, miss, I swear.'

Cath moved a little way along the ditch towards the older boy. All her life she had made mistakes. Her way of perceiving the world was not that of other people. Too much kindness overwhelmed her. The boy backed away until he saw the tears in her eyes. 'Please don't cry. You were cold. We tried to warm you.' Cath placed her arms over his shoulders, put her head against the side of his, and, hugging him close to her, wept.

Finally two words, repeated over and over, replaced the sobs. 'It's alright . . . it's alright . . .' The younger boy stood watching. The older boy laughed, to conceal his own emotion and embarrassment. 'Jesus ain't ready for you yet, miss. Otherwise he'd not have let me and Boy find you. Have you still got your vittles, Boy? I ate mine.'

Without waiting for a reply he began to search the pockets of the younger boy, and brought forth a crust of dry bread and a withered turnip, which he held out for Cath to eat. She shook her head. 'He wants you to have them, don't you, Boy?' The younger boy nodded, a little uncertainly. 'I'm trying to teach him godliness, but he ain't a very good scholar.' Cath accepted the bread. 'He'll get something to eat when he gets home. This'll learn him for thinking as you were a witch.'

Cath smiled at the boy with straw-coloured hair and amber eyes. 'Do you have a real name?' The boy lowered his head, and picked a stone out of the side of the ditch.

'William, miss.'

Cath came close to him, and touched his hair. 'Thank you for your company last night, William. What do they call this place?'

The boy pointed. 'Bletchingdon's over there, and Hampton Poyle that way. Back there's Frogsnest Farm.'

She took a scrap of paper from her pocket. It had been given to her by a boy of about William's age as she had moved away from the hill they called Sunrising. She had never seen the boy

55

before, and he, having thrust the paper at her, had run away. Now she held it out to William who, not being able to read, passed it to James. The note was printed in capitals. James studied it carefully, and read it aloud. 'The death of your friend must not be wasted. If you need help or shelter, ask for Bevil at the sign of the Crown, Charlton on Otmoor.'

'Do you know where that is?'

'Ten miles. I can take you there. We must find the horses first.'

When the boys returned from rounding up the horses, each with grass plaited into its mane, both seemed doleful and disinclined for conversation. The amber eyes of the younger boy were frightened, and searched the older boy's face for reassurance.

'Shall we be punished much, James?'

James placed an arm over the boy's shoulder, and led him a little way from Cath, intending not to be heard. 'It was my doing, boy. Don't you spoil things now by getting too frit. No one shall harm your skin, not for forty pennies nor forty pounds. You did middling well last night. We saved a soul for Jesus. That's worth more than two weeks' wages.' He ruffled William's hair, and turned to Cath. 'Do you visit a house of God, miss?' Cath nodded. 'Then you might pray for Boy and me, if you will, and we will pray that you find Mr Bevil, and that he's kind to you.'

Cath was too weak to ride by herself, and so shared the largest of the horses with James, while William rode a small piebald, and made sure that none of the horses strayed or lagged behind. Their first stop was at a small weatherbeaten collection of buildings called Rowle's Farm. A woman came out to meet them. James dismounted, sorted two horses out from the group, and ran forward with them. She grasped the tethers, and a conversation ensued which Cath could not hear, but which ended in the woman's striking James about the head with her fists, and striding off towards the house, waving her arms in the air. When she returned, she threw a few coins in the dirt, and kicked James as he scrabbled for them.

'She's paid us off, Boy. We're not to go there again. Wouldn't give me more than a penny towards the fine.'

At Barridon Farm, the large leader-horse had to be left, and the farmer came out to get a closer look at Cath, for James had shown him the note, and read it to him, since the farmer could not read.

'Are you sure that says Bevil's name there?' James assured him that it did.

The farmer looked even more closely at Cath. 'Where'd you see him?' Cath said that she had seen Bevil at Warwick at the Assize Court.

The farmer smiled. 'They do say he was over that way for a hanging. He goes all over, does that Bevil. A right Gyppo!' He patted James on the shoulder. 'You done well, helping this young woman, if she's from Bevil. Pretty she is and all, under all that muck.'

James was given bread and cheese as well as his part of the fine, and told that it was only for Bevil's sake, and not to expect it every time he had a lie with a woman in a ditch. His cheeks were still flushed as he shared the food out with Cath and William.

At Brook Furlong Farm, where the last of the horses was left, Bevil's name and an examination of the note produced smiles and laughter. Money for the fine was given, and more food offered. The whole family came out to look at Cath, and a young woman, whom Cath took to be the eldest daughter, came right up to her, and touched her on the arm, saying, 'Were you with that boy over near Banbury way? The one they hanged for firing hay? I heard tell about that.'

James and William turned to look at Cath, and Cath nodded.

'And did you watch them do it? The hanging?'

They waited. Again she nodded.

'Then would you change some of your clothes with mine? I've got some as are warmer than yours, and it would truly please me to have that dress.'

Cath looked down at the dress which had once belonged to a lady guest at the Woolpack Inn, and was now torn and spattered with mud. The daughter clutched her by the hand, and squeezed it excitedly. 'Please do. It won't take but a minute. I'll put a coin in the pocket for good luck.'

Within the house, as Cath washed, the daughter said, 'And I wouldn't wager against you carrying that poor boy's child, would you?' She waited for an answer, and was given none.

The clothes she had given were, as promised, warmer. Cath said, 'Why do you want mine?'

'It's a good gown. It'll mend.' Cath did not lower her gaze. There was a silence. Then the girl said, 'Do you know what happens here?' Cath shook her head. 'Nothing. That's what happens here – nothing. Ever. But one day soon, something is going to happen, somewhere not far from where you're bound. When it's happened, there'll be celebrating. Dancing and such. I shall wear this dress, and tell everyone how I got it, to prove I met you. What you wear doesn't matter, because you were there.' The daughter held up the dress, and swung it round like a partner. 'What do they call you?'

'Cath.'

'And the boy?'

'He was a man, not a boy. His name was John.'

A horse was lent to James so that he might take Cath the rest of the way, and since William refused to wait at the farm until James's return, all three of them shared it. For most of the journey they travelled in silence, except when James sang them a hymn.

They passed through the village of Oddington, following the line of the River Ray. Cath rode between the two boys, with the younger behind her, holding her round the waist.

'What colour are your father's eyes, William?'

'Like mine, I think, miss.'

'Does he have your hair?'

The boy laughed. 'No, miss, he has his own. But it's much the same colour.' And all three laughed together at this piece of wit, and Cath was reminded that it was a long time since she had done such a thing.

'And James? Do your father and mother have the same colour eyes as you?'

There was a long silence before James answered. 'I live with my aunt, miss. The only father I have is Jesus.' An even longer silence followed before James spoke again. 'Your young man will be in Heaven. He will have seen Our Father there.'

58

Bevil

'I'm Bevil. You asked for me.'

This was the man who had prevented her from telling the court at Warwick what had really happened, who had set on Mrs Fleckwindsor to restrain her, and had started the shouting in the public gallery, as earlier he had shouted in the street outside the Peacock. Would he now explain to her why it was so important that John should be hanged for what she herself had done?

He watched her. He was waiting for her to speak, impatiently as it seemed, his small hazel eyes flickering, searching out hers, then darting away from what they had found.

'You have something to say?' He waited, but she could wait longer. She had waited for days, held him in her mind, and waited for the explanation which was her due. It was the idea of Bevil she had held, the name and a voice; she had not seen the man himself until now. Now she stood on a bridge over the River Ray, in company with a large man with hands as large as those which had covered her mouth and pulled her back from the rail at Warwick, and a large square mouth below darting hazel eyes. It was for him to convince her that the speech he had prevented would not have saved John's life, that there was a necessity in John's death.

'They have given you food? I told them to give you food.' She watched him. Yes, they had given her food. 'Somewhere to sleep?' Yes, she had slept in a warm room on sacks filled with straw. They had told her that Bevil was away on business, and

59

would return, and, having already waited so long, she was content to sleep away this further time.

He had fallen silent again, standing in front of her, uncomfortable and ill at ease. She broke the silence. 'Why?' Her voice was so low that she could not be sure that the word had actually emerged. 'Why?'

'I thought you might need help. You did. They tell me you were almost dead.'

'I burned the hay at Tysoe.'

'So?' It was almost as if he had forgotten about it, and was thinking of something else.

'You stopped me telling the court.' He looked at his hands, which were cut and scratched. She was trembling, almost bursting inside with the effort of speaking without crying. 'I want you to tell me why, and by what right you did such a thing.' The cuts and scratches seemed to have been freshly made. He raised his left hand to his mouth, and sucked at a trickle of escaping blood. 'Why?'

'It would have done no good. They won't hear reason; they shut their ears against it. They'll only heed what we show them, not what we say, and even that only when there are more of us than of them. Some of us have to sacrifice, or we all starve.' She did not understand. 'Your John could have died for nothing.' But he had died for nothing, for nothing that he had done. 'Did he not agree with our cause?'

It is all politics to these people. They cannot allow it to have been an accident. 'What cause? We were not part of it. He hardly knew of it.'

'Did John have money? Own land? Put up fences? Collect rents?' She shook her head. 'Then he was part of it. Everyone is part of it. New-born babies can hardly know of it either, but they soon starve when a man has nothing to give them and the mother's too sick for her milk to be right.' The eyes did not flicker now, but stared angrily at her. He waited for the anger to subside, and then said, 'I've set it about that the girl who helped burn the hay at Tysoe is here. You can help or you can go. What's done is done. We have to think of the children.'

He turned, as if to leave her, but a thought struck him. 'Do you still have the child inside you?' How could he know? – but she remembered that John had prayed on the hill for the child

60

he would never see. 'Take what is offered. Don't let the child die, not when the father took blame on himself to save its life.' He walked away, without looking back.

She was not part of their 'cause', had never been angry about her position in life. As a family, they had always had just enough. They had been hungry, but never starved; they had always managed somehow. Her mother had begun and ended every meal with a prayer, 'This is a house of love, Lord, and we thank You for Your bountiful goodness.' Whether dry bread or mutton broth, it had always been 'bountiful'. And though they could always have eaten more, when one by one they were asked by their mother, 'Are you satisfied, child? Have you eaten sufficient?' they had known well enough to reply, 'Yes, thank you, mother. I have had just enough.'

Cath crossed the bridge, and looked out over the land which the people of Otmoor were fighting for. It was a large shallow basin of flat ground, always wet and often flooded, where moorhens, herons and wild geese lived more easily than men. A cold place. She and John might have huddled together there, but would not have stayed long.

There were other places, more welcoming than this. At Dame School they had warned her not to waste time dreaming of such places, but to remain where she belonged. Where was that? They had told her that she was not to try to imitate her betters, but to fit herself for the station in life into which it had pleased God to place her, and since she had never wished to wear a fringe on her spencer, or pantalettes which were too long in the leg, or to trim a hat too gaudily, she had pleased her betters as well as God, and been praised for knowing her place.

She sat down on a stone. A mist was rising; it would be dangerous to walk further. They had told her at the inn of those who had walked too far, lost their way in the fog, perished of cold or drowned in the marsh. They had taken some pleasure in telling her. In the centre of the moor were two large rocks called Joseph's Stones, which had once marked the entrance to a giant's tomb. One unfortunate fog-bemused traveller had lost his wits and been found next day clinging to one of those stones; he could not speak of the night's adventures, but howled like a dog when they tried to move him.

She did not belong here, was no more part of the place than the cause. If they wanted this cold moor, let them fight for it. She could not imagine her own people of Finstall blackening their faces and dressing up in women's clothing to go out by night to pull down fences, all to regain a piece of wet land which only caused the beasts which pastured there to go sick of the flux.

But if it wasn't here, where did she belong now? She was walking back towards Charlton, the palms of both hands over her stomach, stroking it. She had told John not to build up his hopes for their baby, but that was because she had wanted nothing to come between the two of them. Now John was dead, and had died thinking of the child he would never see, his only child. If it were to survive, and were not already dead inside her, she would have to find a way of making sure she could give it more than 'just enough'.

She could help or she could go. *What's done is done. We have to think of the children.* Well, since she had no wish to think of herself, she would think of her child and John's. Since she did not belong anywhere, and had nowhere to go, she would stay. For a while, at least.

Bevil was to be found at Higg's Beer-House at the sign of the Crown. She was directed to climb a narrow flight of stairs and knock once only at the door at the top. But Bevil himself opened the door as she approached it, and held it wide for her to enter.

'I'll help if you want. What do you want me to do?'

'Can you read and write?'

'My mother taught me.'

Bevil handed her a letter. 'Read this, and start making copies. We shall need fifty or sixty: I will give you paper. But write clearly for those who read with difficulty.'

She took the letter. Bevil said, 'Let me hear you read it aloud.'

'The bearer of this letter is carrying the child of the young man hanged at Tysoe for conspiracy and firing hay. He was innocent of both charges, as the bearer has good reason to know, for she was there.'

Cath looked up from the letter, and said, 'And if I had decided not to stay?'

'Then I should have destroyed the letter, wasting paper and ink.'

She continued reading. 'He was guilty only of being poor and of having no work, and was hanged by the rich, who feared that their wealth and land were threatened by you – the people.' She remembered the crowd of villagers surrounding the cart which had carried John up Sunrising Hill. None had been rich, no great landowners, as far as could be told. 'They killed him to try to scare us into starvation. Will you let his death go unnoticed, and forget his sacrifice? The child this woman carries will have no father. The rich landowners have seen to that. Will you allow those same landowners to tread you underfoot while they steal the land of your forefathers, the land which is rightly yours, the poor people of Otmoor?'

'Very well.'

'It is not finished.'

'You have shown me that you can read. Now write.'

Cath sat on the floor, and began to copy the letter, which was not short. It reminded the poor people of Otmoor that the rich landowers had built a channel to divert the river, which would drain their own fields and flood the land grazed by the poor. Some of the poor had broken this channel, and the law of England was on their side, for they had been acquitted by a judge. Since ancient right and the law supported them, the poor people of Otmoor must now act again to enforce their rights. The action was not specified, but Cath assumed that the poor people of Otmoor would know what it was to be. The letter ended with the words, 'Otmoor For Ever'.

As Cath wrote, neatly and clearly as she had been instructed, Bevil explained what she must do with the letter. Starting next morning, she must visit all the hamlets, villages and towns within a day's ride, and present copies of the letter to the men whose names were written on a list Bevil had made. Bevil himself had already been to these places, and the names were of men with whom he had spoken, and whom he judged to be sympathetic to their cause.

By the light of two rush-lamps, which made the small room smell of roasted pork, Cath wrote, while Bevil studied his list, and planned her itinerary.

'Convince these people that they must come and stand with

us, so that one day we may stand with them in their fight. In unity is strength.' The pork fat melted and dripped from the rushes to the floor. The smell reminded Cath of the kitchen at Warwick and of the cook's words: *Young people travel too much, that's my view. I hope you're going to last, Nose.* 'Unless there are at least two hundred people on the moor when we possess it, our men will be collected up by the Yeomanry, and we shall have lost the moor for ever.'

The room contained a bed of straw in one corner, a small table and a stool. Bevil Blizard rose from the stool, and began to pace the room.

'Is the letter right?' She did not know how to answer. 'Will it make them come? If too many fear failure, then we all fail.' He paced, and paused, and paced again, then stopped before her, staring down at her. 'I think you can make them believe that we shall win.' He squatted beside her. 'Do you have enough light to see?' She nodded. 'When you began to speak to the court at Warwick, your voice was frail, and trembled. But that was most important to you, and this is not. Am I right?' Cath was silent. 'I think you will speak with more assurance.'

He took one of the copies she had made. 'There will be many for whom you must read the words aloud.' He pointed to the words, 'The child this woman carries will have no father', and said quietly, 'When you read these words, you may find that you are distressed and tearful. That will do us no harm.'

He stood, and moved away to the window, which over-looked the moor, on which the light was fading. Cath had been told that the centre of the moor was called 'the loneliest place in the world'.

'They are good people hereabouts. You will not regret your choice to stay.' She watched him roll the stem of a long clay pipe between his fingers, and began again to write the words, 'The bearer of this letter is carrying the child . . .'

'How did the fire start?' He was lighting his pipe with a rush from the lamp.

'I lit a match, and threw it down when it burned my finger.'

'Into the hay?'

'No. Away. As far away as . . .' She pointed to a spot between herself and the window, and in pointing remembered that only a wind could have carried the burning match as far as the hay. But there had been no wind, not even a breeze.

'But the grass where you were was dry?' He took from his pocket the glass from a telescope, and used it to study the map of his own making.

'Yes.'

'And the sun very strong?' She nodded. He looked up at her from the map, and spoke again. 'If a magistrate should detain you for any reason, you will conceal this list, will you not? The letters are less important, since they do not say when we plan to act.'

'How are the people to know when they should come here?'

'They will be told by you, and you will be told by me, just before you leave. Do you find it strange that I should place so much trust in you?'

She did not reply.

A Journey

Bevil had said, 'It is not always safe for a woman travelling alone. Yet you have come this far alone. Are you frightened?' He had looked up at her sitting on the horse they had provided, and she had shaken her head. He had handed her a riding-crop, saying, 'Dismount only when you are sure it is safe to do so, and if anyone tries to stop the horse or rob you, don't hesitate to use this in your defence. We have very little time. You must not be delayed.' As Cath had begun to move away from him, he had called after her, 'Never use the whip on the horse.'

Away from the town, she had looked more closely at the whip. Secured to the end of each of the five leather thongs, there was a small razor-sharp piece of flint.

Cath's experience of horses was limited to those her father had tended, which had been docile, sometimes stupid, but always affectionate. Special food had been stolen for them to make their coats shine. Their manes had been plaited and their tails trimmed.

The mane of the horse she now rode had never been plaited, its tail never trimmed. No linseed or molasses had been secretly given to it, since the appearance of its coat was not important. The horse was a mare, named Cloud. She had been used for breeding, and other odd jobs, and was now too old for farm work. When she died, or was butchered, every separate part of her carcass would be put to use. Even her shoes would be taken off, and fitted to another horse. She went at her own pace, which was for most of the time a walk. The only instructions

66

she was prepared to take from Cath were those concerning the direction in which they should travel.

They were to go east as far as Wotton Underwood, by way of Piddington and Ludgarshall, then south as far as Brill, Oakley, Worminghall and Waterperry, west to Kidlington, north to Bletchingdon, Wendlebury and Bicester, and back to Charlton by way of Ambrosden and Merton.

She was to tell the people on the list that she had come directly from Bevil at Charlton, and that he begged them to meet him there at six in the morning of the sixth of September, bringing as many trusted friends as they could persuade to make the journey.

It seemed to Cath that a great deal of trouble was being taken to persuade people who had nothing to do with the moor to come and fight for it, nor did it seem to her that the letter she carried would be sufficient persuasion. She had asked Bevil why he did not accompany her, and had been told that he would be occupied at Charlton.

She would be alone. That suited her best. She would have proper food and somewhere warm to sleep. A small purse, in which coins had been placed, hung around her neck, and marks had been made on the list to indicate those people who might give her shelter. A quartern loaf, six apples and half a pound of cheese were in a bundle which hung from the saddle, and before she had begun the journey, Bevil had given her a tankard of milk, and watched while she drank it. He had said, 'For the health of the child.'

Seven children watched in silence as Cath dismounted outside a row of tumbledown cottages. Soil had dried on their faces and hands, hiding sores and blisters. Their clothes were thin and torn, and their eyes red from lack of sleep. Around them small stones had been set out in straight lines on the ground to mark the walls of a make-believe house, and in each of its six make-believe rooms crouched a child. The eldest, a girl of nine, sat on a pile of earth in her room, nursing a baby which sucked at the dry nipple of her flat and unformed breast. From within the cottage came the sound of a woman screaming.

Cath crossed the small front garden, in which cornflowers, michaelmas daisies and golden-rod had been overgrown by

67

bindweed and pennyroyal. The door of the cottage was open, and she could just make out the profile of an old man, sitting motionless by an empty fireplace and staring at a bare wall. The earthen floor of the one-roomed cottage had been strewn with straw. Lying on this in one corner, with her skirt rolled up and her legs wide apart, was the woman who had screamed. An older woman knelt by her, wiping the sweat from her forehead with a bloodstained cloth.

'Does Mr Kirtland live here?'

The older woman turned, and stared at her. 'He's not here.' The woman in labour screamed again, and reached out towards her companion, who had left her, and was moving slowly towards Cath, staring her up and down. 'If he's got you with child, you'll have to wait your turn.'

'Can you tell me where I might find him?'

The older woman went on past Cath, and leaned against the rotten wood of the door jamb. 'I've done all I can, and she still won't let it drop. Flinching and bawling like as if it was her first.' She looked across the overgrown garden to the children sitting in their make-believe house on the dirt road. 'Look at 'em. Poor as rats, and twice as hungry!' The woman stared into Cath's eyes, and Cath looked away, remembering the food she carried. *For the health of the child*. 'What do you want Crowy for?'

'I have a letter.'

'He's over at Chilling Place. Trying to get the boys set on.' The woman indoors screamed again, even louder and longer, causing the girl who held the baby to stand, and look towards the cottage. The older woman said, 'Her womb's so hotted up, might as well be on fire.' She wiped her hands on the bloodstained cloth, and held it out for Cath to take. 'If you're waiting for Crowy, you might as well sit with her. I'm needed at home.'

'I'd be no use. I wouldn't know what to do.' Cath backed away through the tangle of bindweed towards the road. The screams from indoors had become more regular and more violent.

'Bout time you did, then.' The older woman followed, still holding out the bloodstained cloth, and shouting, 'How'd you fare if folks ran away when it come to your turn?' Cath had reached the horse, and was trying to mount. 'Least you can do is get Darkie Kimber to bring her something for the pain. She can't be left. It ain't Christian.'

Cath was sitting on the horse, with all the children standing in front of it, looking up at her. One of the youngest stretched a tiny hand out towards her, and wriggled its fingers. She closed her eyes. She and John had laughed together at the noises made by their own stomachs. Hunger had been laughable then.

'Here's a good strong boy, sir.' The father made his son turn round on the spot, so that the boy could be inspected from all sides. 'I should want two shilling for him.'

'That's not a two-shilling boy. Not that one. Turn him again.' The father touched his son on the shoulder, and again the boy turned, his eyes looking straight ahead of him into the middle distance and avoiding those of the farmer's son, who stood watching him.

'Hmm!' The farmer pointed to the father's other son, who was two years older. 'What about this one? You could have two shilling a week for him.'

'Surely he's worth two and a half, sir. He's got more growth than his brother.'

'You ask a lot for a lad with no shoulders to speak of.' The farmer felt the older boy's upper arm, inspected his hands, and bent down to place his own two hands around one of the boy's thighs, pressing his thumbs and fingers into the flesh until the boy flinched. 'He's got no muscle there at all. Does he never run? You've not brought me a sitter, have you, Crowy? I don't pay boys to fatten their arses.'

'He's a runner before anything, sir. He's always at it.'

'Whenever work is threatened, I expect. I might give him a try for two shilling, if only for the sake of his health. That boy needs exercise bad, Crowy. You've been too soft with them.' He waved a dismissive hand towards the smaller boy. 'That one ain't worth a shilling until he can break a sweat. Look! Even my dogs don't take no interest in him; he's got no smell. Unless he gets a stronger smell about him, how do I know he ain't going to turn into a woman?'

The smaller boy stood motionless and blushed as the farmer's son, who was even smaller than he, circled round him, twitching at the nose, sniffing, and repeating the words, 'Ain't worth a shilling.'

'Give him a try as well, sir. Just for a few pence.' The father began to plead. 'I swear he's stronger than he looks.'

'Now, Crowy, I get a lot of boys offered me; you know I do. I'd be a right fool to take the weaklings.' The farmer moved closer and became more confidential while his son continued to circle. 'Look at the width of his neck. I wonder it's thick enough to support his head. You've bred a runt there, man; admit it. He might improve with a little more meat, but he'll never work here.' He shouted to the younger son. 'When did you last eat meat, boy?'

The boy could not remember. The effort of keeping all his muscles flexed against their being felt again, together with the small grinning face moving faster and faster round him, combined to make him giddy. 'Don't know, sir.'

'My men must look as good as the cattle. You know what I do with a runt, Crowy.'

This time the boy heard the word 'runt' and angered by it as well as by the spinning malicious face, cried out, 'I'm not a runt. I can work hard.'

The face ceased spinning, and shouted also. 'Speak when you're spoken to, runt. You've got no smell about you.'

'Better than stinking rotten.'

Kicks were directed against the shins of Crowy's boy by the farmer's son. The boy put out a hand sharply in self-protection, and the farmer's son landed flat on his back on the stone yard.

Angrily the farmer pulled his howling son upright, hit him about the face, and sent him running towards the house. Then he turned on Crowy. 'You're a grasping lot, you are. You breed children like rabbits, and expect someone else to feed them. Don't your woman know when to stop dropping runts, man? Well, someone else can feed that.' He pointed at the smaller boy. 'I'll take the other for two shilling.'

The two boys and their father bowed to the farmer, and walked away towards the gate.

Twenty-seven rag dolls, tied with straw and supporting cob-webs, dangled from one of the walls. Another wall was

70

covered with skins of animals – squirrels, rabbits, foxes, stoats, badgers, hares, moles. Even a cat and a dog had been flayed, stretched out, and nailed. Many of the skins were shrunken, dusty and very old.

Outside a young vixen prowled around the crab-apple tree to which she was tethered, snuffling among the henbane, foxglove, vetch and mallow. Inside a jackdaw jumped about from perch to perch in a cage of osiers, muttering words which Cath could not understand.

'Answer him.' Darkie Kimber stood at a table. She had slit the belly of a grey squirrel, and was now easing each of its flesh-pink legs from their covering of fur.

'What did he say?'

'He says, "What's you got wrong wi' you, then?"' The answer came from by the fire, where Waggle Ward sat, her large posterior almost burying the three-legged stool beneath it. She was stirring handsful of animal fat and wood-ash into a cauldron of boiling water. Both door and window were shut, so that the air was heavy with the stench of rancid animal fat, which she was turning into rancid soap.

'It's not for me. It's Mrs Kirtland. Her womb's too hot to let the baby out.' The jackdaw cackled, and began jumping about his cage more quickly. He did this whenever a stranger spoke.

Cath had been reluctant to pass the snarling vixen in the garden. The animal had bared its teeth and rushed to the end of its tether as soon as she had set foot inside the garden gate of this cottage, two miles from the village. Until now the conversation of Darkie Kimber and Waggle Ward had been concerned exclusively with the comic aspects of Cath's approach, but the jackdaw recalled them to more serious matters.

'Do she bleed greatly?' Darkie's eyes seemed to watch something just behind Cath's left shoulder.

'Yes, I think so.'

'Tell them if she bleed greatly, I want some of it.' The soles of Darkie's bare feet scraped along the clay floor. Her shoulders bent forwards, and her thick black hair, parted in the middle, hung down around her pale, pale face. Such pallor was not seen in country districts in the faces of cottagers. If Darkie

71

walked past a field where men were working, they would run into the next field, or put down their tools where they were standing and go home for the rest of the day. Yet their wives came to her when they were sick, would lie on the table now slick with the squirrel's blood, and beg her to cure them. And sometimes she did, just as she had cured Waggle of a violent red rash, which Waggle had developed when Menzil Child, her husband for only four days, had gone missing. He had gone out, and not returned, and no one had seen him; it was as if he had been spirited away. Waggle had appeared at Darkie Kimber's door, complaining that her husband had gone and her body was on fire, and, questioning having revealed that she was still a virgin, had moved in, and stayed.

'Tell them I want a pint. A pint of what she bleeds.' She handed Cath a jug. 'Half is no good to me.'

'Can you not come to her? She's in great pain.'

Darkie stared over Cath's shoulder, and almost smiled at something only she could see. 'A woman who's borne nine children has no right talking of pain.' She turned to Waggle. 'No more ash, I said. Do you want it to rid the skin off their hands?' She dropped the skinned squirrel into a bucket under the table. 'We don't gad about when we're busy. Waggle's got the soap to make, and I'm doing these creatures here.' She held up a mole to the light, and studied it carefully before making an incision. 'I dare say those children of hers could eat this one here as meat, if someone knew how to make it tasty.' Cath looked away as the knife parted the fat mole's skin.

'The woman is screaming for help.'

It was Waggle who replied. 'Babies have been dropping out of that woman ever since Crowy got his aim right. Ain't no wonder it got hotted up, with all them comings and goings. Besides, stopping soap halfway through turns it rancid. No more than creatures like being left with their coats half on and half off. Makes 'em dry and okkered.'

'Can I have something to take to her for the pain, then?'

Darkie shuffled over to an old badger-skin, and, lifting it like a curtain, revealed three shelves on which stood rows and rows of pots and boxes. She sniffed at five of the pots before deciding on one, from which she emptied some Good King Henry into the palm of her bloodstained hand. 'I don't reckon as how I could stomach this, if my womb was hot enough to boil a kettle.'

'What you giving her?' Darkie shuffled over to Waggle, who sniffed at the rotten-fish aroma of the herbs in her hand. 'That should stop her screaming.'

'If I gets my pint, we can call it a bargain. Otherwise I wants a halfpenny.'

Cath nodded, holding out her hand for the herb. 'What do you want the blood for?'

Darkie smiled, displaying a mouthful of rotten teeth. 'Well, it ain't for me, young missy, so don't you go fretting yourself. It's for Ember out there, who you got so frit of. She's too shy still to get that kind of drink herself, but she do like it all the same. Shines her coat up a treat.' She moved back to the table, picked up the mole she had skinned, and threw it towards Cath for her to catch with her other hand. 'Tell those children to put an onion in with it. Takes off the taste of the earth.' She saw that Cath's gaze was towards the squirrel in the bucket under the table. 'No, missy. That's Ember's.'

Darkie opened the door. Holding the stinking Good King Henry in one hand and the skinned mole in the other, Cath ventured out into the garden to circumvent the tethered vixen.

'Keep well downwind of her. If Ember smells that creature, she'll have the tree down to take it from you.' Cath walked in a wide half-circle to reach the gate, watched by Darkie from the door.

'That there horse is pretty old, ain't she? Don't you want to sell her?'

'She's not mine.'

'Lot of good items to be got from a dead horse, if you knows how.'

'She doesn't belong to me.'

Mary Tooth sat on a bench outside the back door of Higg's Beer-House at the sign of the Crown in Charlton. The small room inside was packed to overflowing, mostly with men whose faces had been blackened with soot, and who were wearing women's clothing. They were gathering to go out onto the moor, there to break the enclosure fences. Mary's husband, Tom, was among them. He had borrowed her oldest skirt and a bonnet. They had stood behind a gravestone in the church-yard across the road, while he struggled into her skirt and she smeared his face with the soot carried in an old glove. Tom was a small man, a shepherd, not much bigger than his wife, but even so there had been difficulty in fastening the skirt, and they had giggled together in the dusk, almost like two children.

Usually the men came for the company; they did not bring their wives, but she had insisted, saying, 'I'm not to be left at night, Tom.' She could accustom herself to being alone in the cottage by day, though even then there were sometimes strangers peering in at the window – moochers begging water or a slice of bread. Even the branches of the crab-apple scratching against the window made her flinch at night, and she would lie awake listening to the screams of a dog-fox doing his courting.

She and Tom had been married two years, and there were no children, perhaps never would be. He had said, 'I need the company. I sit on that hillside sometimes, and if the dog don't bide with me, I wonder if I'm really there. Cos if he don't see me, who else is there? That feeling I get does damage to my stomach, girl. I need the company.' She herself had had company before, that of her own family and the village, and now had only his, and that only at night. Their cottage was five miles from Waterperry, three from the nearest neighbour. Shepherding was the only work Tom could get. He had told her it was stupid for a country woman to be afeard, but she could not help it. He told her it was all in the mind, bound to be, and she had agreed.

Until two nights ago, and she alone. A face pressed against the window, eyes wild, hair and beard wild, nose pressed flat against the glass. She was not to be left at night. It had been real, and not a ghost. Folks spoke of ghosts, but that was nonsense to her mind. The good wouldn't want to come back, and the bad wouldn't be let to. She was not to be left alone at night.

A horn could be heard blowing from over near Moorcot. It was time for the men to leave. The landlord stood by the back door, breathing in the night air, and rattling the Otmoor Fund box close to her face.

'Tom's my husband. He's going out tonight.' She had no coin to place inside the box. The landlord moved the box away, and patted her on the shoulder. 'Good man!'

She knew that what money in the box didn't go to provide 'cuffs' to protect the men's hands from the thorns, went on beer. She hoped Tom would not get drunk; he was unused to strong drink. And so pleased to have joined the company. The ten-mile walk had seemed easy with Tom in such good humour. She would not spoil enjoyment, would not fret if he wished to start back before it was light. It was stupid to be so frightened. The man at the window could have been a moocher, looking for food.

The next name on Cath's list was Tom Tooth of Waterperry, but the tiny shepherd's cottage was shut up. Nobody answered her knocks and shouts, and already dusk was turning to dark.

Bevil had marked Mr Tooth's name with a cross. This was where she had hoped to get shelter for the night. The next name on the list was at Elsfield, many miles away. Cloud needed water. There was a well, but no bucket that she could see.

Cath walked round to the other side of the cottage, where an old crab-apple tree leaned towards the house and scratched its branches against the window. Here there was a shed, with its door slightly open, and beside it a dead crow hung upside-down from a hawthorn. She called again, but there was no answer, so she moved towards the shed door, opened it further, and went inside.

She allowed a few moments for her eyes to get accustomed to the darkness, before deciding that there was nothing which could be used as a bucket. She moved some sheepskins covering a stone trough, then jumped back suddenly as two eyes stared up at her. The mouth below the eyes was drawn back, baring teeth as it hissed and spat. A wildcat leapt out of the trough and onto the side of it, arching its back, and snarling. A half-born kitten hung, half in and half out of its mother's womb. Cath backed away, and the cat dropped to the floor and pursued her, its half-born kitten still dangling from its rump.

But it could not spring in such a state. It stopped, stood rigid for a moment as if in pain, then stretched its neck backwards, extended its tongue, and licked at the half-born kitten. With an audible sigh of relief, Cath released the breath she had been holding, and turned towards the door. Then she saw the man.

He was dressed in a collection of rags which had been knotted together. His straight steel-grey hair hung down and passed his shoulders. His beard was matted with grease and dried saliva. He barred her way, staring at her.

'You're not her.'

Cath shook her head, not knowing why. She said, 'I was looking for Mr Tooth.'

'I'm not him either.' The crevices of his face were filled with sweat and dried dirt. He took a step towards her, and the wildcat behind her snarled. 'That's my lady. Come with me all this way.' He spoke with an accent, one she had not heard before. 'Come from as far north as a man can walk. Don't tell me your name. You can be Mary for me tonight. That's her name. I heard him say it. Can't give her a baby. That's where I sleep now most nights.' He pointed towards the tattered thatch of the cottage roof. Did he mean that he slept *on* the roof? 'So I'll be ready when she wants me.'

Did he mean that he slept on the roof and listened to what went on below?

Mary Tooth sat outside Higg's Beer-House, and shivered. Inside, in the warm, an old man was singing.

> '*An outlandish knight came from the North Lands,*
> *A-wooing came to me.*
> *He said he would take me to the North Lands,*
> *And there would marry me.*'

Tom Tooth stood unsteadily, shivering, between two other men. Beads of sweat ran down the sides of his face, making white lines in the soot. Had the pistol not misfired, he would be dead, for he had been standing directly in line with the barrel. The pistol had been waved about in a threatening way, then held steady, and the trigger pressed. And had misfired. The young landowner, Wentworth Croke, had continued to hold the pistol limply in his hand, looking down at it, hardly able to understand what he had tried to do.

Now one of the other men was wrenching the pistol from

that limp hand, and was beating Croke about the head with the handle of an axe.

And now Croke lay senseless on the ground.

Down into the damp grass, scratching and kicking as she went. The moon tumbling and racing in the sky. The smell of stale urine and wild garlic. A hoarse raw breathing, rasping like a hunting-horn through fog.

'I saw her face.' Once begun, never to stop. Should she submit? Could she retreat? 'I saw her undress herself. That's why I stay. I could give her what he can't.'

Then the stars. Winking. Knowing. Not to submit. Struggle. Struggle, bite, push away. Kick. Kick into nothing, into air, into the night, against the stars. Bite. Kick. Scratch. Not submit. Until one large hand is gripping two thin wrists. The hand has fingernails like black crows' feet, bent and curved.

'It's nothing to you, is it? Soon you'll forget all about it. Do you ever watch foxes do it? Cats! – have you ever seen them, heard the noise? Foxes, it's almost evil. Stoats – they're hard to catch at it. Birds, it's nothing at all. But horses! There's a coupling! They have a rare old time. Should I like to be a great black stallion! Think of the horses, Mary, and lie still.'

Moon gone, stars gone, and only the branches of an elm tree, as her hair is grabbed and tugged, pulling her head back for another mouth to be pressed against hers. The memory of a different mouth. 'Do you love me?' A different mouth, a different breath. John had tasted of life, and was now dead. This man was alive, and tasted of death. 'Say it! Say it! I'm fifty-three, and no one has ever said it to me. It's nothing for you to say it. You'll soon forget. You're not Mary either. It's just that I'm lonely, you see. A lonely black stallion.'

Then more wet kisses, covering her neck and face, more dry fingers stroking up and down her arms and legs, more talons trying to reach inside her and destroy all that she had left of John, the only thing she cared for in the world. Anger, building inside her, against his person, against herself, against the horse chomping grass at the other side of the cottage with the riding-crop tied carefully to its saddle, against the whole world. She had twisted her head sideways to avoid the person's reechy kisses, and her face was buried in wild garlic and cow

77

parsley, and towards even these weeds she felt a deep and personal anger.

'It won't take long.' She went limp, heard herself saying, 'Alright', and knew that she was taking a risk. For a moment the man did not move, did not speak. Slowly Cath released her hands from his, and, lifting them up to her neck, began to unfasten her dress.

The man sat upright, still holding her to the ground with his legs. 'You're not her.'

'No.'

His right hand came down again, sliding inside her clothes, squeezing her breasts. 'She's plumper.' The black crows' feet fingernails scratched and nipped at her skin, and, without being able to see, she knew that the fingers of his other hand were struggling to untie some of the knotted rags about his waist. Gently, and giving murmurs of pleasure, she placed both hands around his right wrist. Then she jerked his wrist away, and brought her knee up into his groin, sending him rolling onto his back.

She scrabbled quickly to her feet, and ran to the other side of the cottage where she had left Cloud. She could hear the man stumbling after her, blubbering and weeping with frustration and self-pity.

'I only wanted a friend to talk to. I don't want to go mad. Tell me I'm not mad, Mary. Promise me. I only want something soft to touch.'

Somehow she was in the saddle. She had the riding-crop. But the man had Cloud by the reins, and was pulling her towards the cottage, back towards the ground where they had lain. Cath waved the crop above his head, warning him to let go, or she would strike him. He grabbed her ankle, trying to pull her to the ground.

'Please . . . Please stay with me . . . I'm only human.' He had pulled her off the horse, and she was beating him around the head with the crop. Then he was backing away from her, with his arms up, trying to protect his face, still weeping and begging her to stay with him, still crying, 'Please!' and asking her to tell him that he wasn't mad, while she lashed at the knotted rags wrapped around his body, and in the moonlight saw the lines of cuts made by the sharp flints at the end of each thong, marking the arms, the legs, the throat, the face.

Snarling and hissing at him, to make him know that she had a baby inside her. Spitting and screaming at him that she wasn't Mary; she was Cath. Cath! that was her name. She was a widow with a child in her belly. A widow whose name was Cath.

Blood ran from the lines of cuts. The man backed into the shed. From out of the darkness of the shed, the wildcat ran past him, carrying the newly born, but now dead, kitten in her mouth. Outside it stopped, as if confused. It dropped the dead kitten, sniffed at it, then scraped earth over it, as if burying its own shit. Cath ran back to where Cloud waited.

She did not see the wildcat return to the shed, did not see its nostrils dilate as it scented the new blood, running down from the deep lines of snatches, did not hear the whimpering cries made by the man, or see the terror in his eyes as he stumbled away from the cat, or watch him fall backwards over the stone trough to the sound of a steady and relentless purring.

Incidents During a Repossession

Six am
The black and white mongrel bitch, sleeping between a rose-mary bush and a bay in Mary Savin's garden, opened its eyes. Its ears had already been alerted, first to the sound of a distant horn, then to another closer, then by a whistle, by the crying of a baby, more blowing of horns. Then there was shouting, mostly of the words 'Otmoor For Ever!' repeated too many times for a mongrel bitch to count, and mixed up with other shouts of a more personal nature, such as 'Where's Jack?' and 'Jenny, come here when I tell you.'

The senses of hearing and of sight gave message upon confusing message to the mongrel bitch, and to these were added the messages conveyed by her sense of smell. The individual aromas of hundreds of pairs of feet marched upon the moor and approached Mary Savin's garden and cottage, which it was the bitch's duty to protect.

The multiplicity and confusion of the messages alarmed her, but the mongrel bitch knew her duty. It was her custom and practice, whenever anyone walked along Otmoor Lane from Charlton towards the moor, that she would begin barking when she first heard footsteps, and would then rush to the end of the garden and out into the lane, by which time sight and scent would have confirmed the presence of a traveller. She would then continue to bark until the traveller was out of sight. She ran, therefore, into the lane, and began to bark.

There were more feet and legs than she had ever seen before. They approached and passed, and then more approached and passed, and still more. It was a forest of legs, with hardly space between them to run and jump. Among the feet, the handles of pitchforks were dangling, and hatchets and knotted sticks were swung from marching arms. Feet all around her, ignoring her, and all moving in one direction, onto the moor.

She barked. Several times her own feet were trodden on, changing her barks of threat and protest into squeals of pain. None of the feet attempted to enter the garden, but at any moment they might; she could not let up. Sometimes in the past she had chased and snapped at the feet of those solitary travellers on whom she could smell fear, but none of these feet smelled of fear, and there were always as many feet approaching as retreating. It was inhuman to present a mongrel with such a responsibility at six o'clock on a Monday morning.

Seven am

Cath was wearing a stained linen smock and trousers of coarse canvas tied below the knees with straw. She had a pair of good boots, given by a farmer of Noke who had told her that they must walk for him in the Repossessing, because his wife was sick, the children below working age, and he could not leave the beasts. Inside each boot was a layer of dried grass, which made them more comfortable to wear. Her hair was tucked up under a round hat of woven straw. She went on foot. Bevil had said he had a use for the horse.

Everyone was on foot. Carts and horses had been left nearby, filling the narrow lanes of Charlton and Fencot, Moorcot and Oddington.

They walked at the edge of the moor, on ground they called The Flits, where peat had been cut for fuel, and sedge and rushes grew. Four old women, who scraped up cow-dung to earn a pittance from its sale, stood wearing their best clothes and waving as they passed. Soon close to a thousand people would be gathered together at 'the loneliest place in the world'.

Cath walked beside a group of folk from Bicester, who continually laughed and shouted. A little way ahead of her walked Bevil with a gentleman who kept his face turned away from her. Later she recognised this gentleman as Mr Bradshaw, the man who had conducted the hearing at Tysoe, and who had spoken to her outside the Assize Court at Warwick.

'Does she still grieve for her young man?'

Bevil shrugged his shoulders.

'Will she be of any more use to us?'

'Let's wait and see. Will they summon the militia?'

'They may be intimidated by your numbers.' Mr Bradshaw surveyed the vast crowd. 'You may have done too well. Did they come because of her example or your persuasion?'

Bevil Blizard smiled. 'They came because they were promised a show. Let's hope they get one.'

'No resistance. Leave that for later.'

'When?'

'When there is enough of a disturbance to effect an escape. Sydenham Welchman will be in Oxford. He will see to it. The more people involved, the further the word will spread. I must go now.' He glanced over his shoulder towards Cath. 'A man has been found dead near Waterperry with his face cut. Striped cuts all over him, as if a beast had clawed him. The rats had been at him too. Parts of him eaten away. Still, I should get rid of that riding-crop of yours if I were you.'

Seven thirty am

Mary Tooth walked beside her husband, Tom, holding his hand and carrying cold potatoes wrapped in a cloth for their midday meal. He wore his own clothes, not hers, and had no soot on his face. Disguise was unnecessary. There was safety in numbers. As for company, he had enough of it, almost a thousand people, quite enough to reassure him of his own existence. Some of them had even remembered him from the night he had 'gone out' with them.

It was Mary who had discovered the body of the moocher, had recognised the staring eyes, and felt only relief at the discovery. His death would not stop her imaginary terrors, but at least she had not imagined him; she was not going mad.

There had been no trace of a wildcat. They were extinct in these parts.

Eight am

The hedge was of hawthorn and hazel, sixteen years old. Clumps of nettles had established themselves in front of it like defensive patrols. Birds had nested in it. As the group of repossessioners approached, with cries of 'Otmoor For Ever!', a blackbird chattered angrily at them. 'Bugger Otmoor', it said. 'You keep your thieving hands off my nest.'

Too many people rushed forward to pull up and destroy the hedge, getting in each other's way. The blackbird flew out, and remained at a distance, watching. Arms and legs were scratched, and small children covered their eyes against the thorns, as men and women both, some with and some without hedging gloves, tore up roots, loosening them with rails and hatchets, and flung whole bushes into the air with shouts and cheers.

Cath had visited some of these people, and been taken into their homes. Now she found that she had nothing to say to them. Some did not seem to recognise her. Others who did were watchful of the girl who was carrying the child of the young man who had been hanged at Tysoe. No one asked her why she was dressed as a boy herself, and she did not tell them.

Nine am
The black and white mongrel bitch sniffed between the legs of the small boy walking beside Crowy Kirtland.

She was lost. She had been carried along by the crowd so far away from Mary Savin's garden. Perhaps she could have found her way back, but her senses now all played her false – sight, sound and smell all confusing instead of informing her.

Wagging her tail, she encircled the legs of the boy, trying to keep them clear in her mind from all the other legs which surrounded her. Her anxious eyes peered up into his eyes. She jumped, and tried to lick his hand. Almost it seemed that she had found an owner.

'Leave that dog be!'

The runt of a small boy folded his hands beneath his armpits and hugged them tight to hide them, so forcing the mongrel bitch to jump higher.

Ten am
The osiers had been cut to make baskets or eel-traps, and had left sharp stalks sticking out of the mud. Cath, wading knee-deep amongst them, heard a voice shouting her name, turned, and saw two arms waving. The owner of the shorter arm had

straw-coloured hair. Suddenly she had lost the sadness brought about by the sight of Mr Bradshaw, and was waving and shouting in return. 'James! William!'

'We thought you was a boy, Miss Cath. Then we noticed as how you were frowning. I'd know that sad look anywhere. Is life treating you that bad?'

She grasped their hands, and pressed them. 'No, James, I'm well. How are you both?'

William's deep amber eyes were fixed on her while his friend did the talking. 'Fair, miss, only fair. We come all this way on a cart, and Boy here never stopped fretting lest the wheels should drop off, and he might have to walk. Now he've cut his hand on a bit of hedging, just to give him something else to fret about.'

Boy William held out his left hand for Cath's inspection. She kissed the hand, and wrapped her handkerchief around it to stop the bleeding, while he turned his eyes away from her, and blushed.

'We prayed we might see you again. So we never stopped looking, just so as to give Jesus a chance to answer our prayers. Now that he has, I feel so full of happiness, I could kick all them fences over just by myself.' There were tears in James's eyes. 'We heard tell as you came as near as Bletchingdon, yet you never came to see us.'

'I didn't know where I might find you. All I know is your first names.'

'James and Boy William would likely have done around Poyle and Hampton.'

'I'm sorry.' She took their hands again, William's right and James's left, and walked between them.

'Will you be staying here on Otmoor for good now?' Cath shook her head. 'Till the baby's born, though. You must rest up a little until he's strong.'

Cath smiled. 'Or she.'

'Will you?'

Cath shrugged. 'My work is done here. I shall have to find other work.'

Boy William made one of his rare contributions to conversation. 'Why are you dressed like a boy, miss?' And Cath remembered why. Bevil had told her that Joan of Arc dressed as a soldier for the same reason. Bevil was a learned man, no doubt of that.

A cry went up, and the crowd pressed them back. A tree was falling, a ten-year-old sycamore, a tree for the cause. They were all part of the cause. Cath said, 'It's easier to walk through mud', and she lifted the boys' hands, and held them to her face. These hands gave warmth. They had been kind to her.

They stood in silence, listening to the noise and laughter all about them, watching the men and boys hack down a fence, while the women talked or scolded their children, warning them not to get lost in the crowd. Had there been sideshows or music, they would have called it a fair. The folk were happy, and determined to be so.

'You're much too pretty to be taken for a boy, miss.' Cath stuck out her tongue, and placed a clenched fist gently against Boy William's cheek. What the two boys shared was not unlike what she and John had shared. Their happiness seemed to include her. They made her smile, and watched her for those smiles. Perhaps, given time, she could do some repossessing of her own, forget her aloneness and regain a little of what she had lost.

'Will you two still be friends when you're as old as I am?'

As usual, it was James who answered. 'We will if he haven't cut himself up into slices by then.'

Eleven am
A gang of boys chased the horse, brandishing pitchforks and fence-rails. Each time she turned, people blocked her way, forcing her to turn again, running backwards and forwards, round and round, until sweat poured from her.

Horns were sounded and whistles blown, as Cloud reared up on her hind legs, pawing at the air with her forelegs, and neighing. All she could see around her were humans' faces, stretching across the moor. Below her was a black and white mongrel bitch, which darted, barking, in and out between her legs. Surely they could tell that she was too old for such a game?

The boys had formed a circle round her, and were coming closer, waving their sticks high above their heads. One of them had a rope. Cloud lowered her forelegs to the ground, and shook her head, scratching at the earth and snorting in protest. She hoped that they would be warned off, would take fright and leave her alone. But the boys laughed at her defiance, knowing her to be too old to fight, too old to be brave.

She moved round in a circle on the spot, kicking out with her legs, trying to watch all sides at once. Then suddenly she rushed forwards, and two of the boys gave way, so that she was out of the circle. One of the boys threw a fence-post at her as she went by, which struck close to her right eye. She ran on, the dog beside her, jumping and barking. Parents pulled small children up into their arms, and gave way before her.

The vision in her right eye became blurred. Unable to see, she stopped. Before her there was a barrier of faces, hundreds of them, swaying, each seeming to be connected to the one next to it. A field of swaying faces, mouths wide open, shouting words she did not understand. 'Otmoor For Ever!' Was it a command? Cloud had always been a biddable animal. And behind her the boys with sticks, still running.

Turning quickly to her right, she felt the wrenching of a muscle in her side. Then there was a sharper deeper pain, as she cut open her belly on the jagged end of a broken sapling.

Then she was going round and round in circles again, with the dog snapping at her heels, telling her to run, and the boys throwing wooden rails at her head. She saw a section of fencing which had not been pulled down, but beyond it was a smaller field in which there were fewer humans. Once there, she would find room to outrun them. There was only the fencing to jump.

She rushed at the fence, pulled her forelegs as high as they would go, and made the jump. Pain shot through her belly. Her hind legs dropped. She was caught on the fence.

Sinking down on top of her forelegs, she rolled over onto her side, struggling and kicking to get her hind legs free. In the distance she heard the sound of a falling tree. Every sound was clear now, and distinct. The horns, the whistles, the cheers, shouts of 'Otmoor For Ever!' The sharp final click of a bone breaking.

There was no pain. Just the noise. And stillness. The people who had been in movement all about her were now still and watching. The dog no longer barked. There was birdsong, and somewhere the sound of a small child asking to be allowed to ride on the horse's back.

She lay on her side, and waited. Some of the boys who had been chasing her stepped out of the watching crowd. There were broken fence-rails between her legs, and one of the boys pulled them free. He performed this operation with great care, so that the pain lasted for no more than a few seconds. Another boy made a leash of the rope, and secured the dog. Then they stood back, and watched her, waiting, and she knew that they were waiting for her to stand. But she could not stand.

After some time, one of the boys commanded her to get up, and waved his pitchfork. She watched him, but remained still.

A sharp knife was offered by a man who possessed a knife and kept it sharp, but confessed that he had no stomach for this particular task. Another man, who claimed to be used to such matters but had not brought the tools of his trade, took the knife, and advanced towards her. At that moment, the sun appeared from behind a cloud, and was reflected from the blade of the knife, so that she saw it, and knew where her death would come from.

Some of the crowd had edged forward to see what was to be done, but were told to move back, unless they wished to be covered in blood. Cloud's forelegs were tied with a leather belt, taken from around the waist of the man who claimed to be used to such matters. The man took a handful of her mane between his fingers, lifting her head higher and further back, and he talked to her, telling her quietly that she was to be a good girl, and not to be afraid, because he was used to such matters, and would not take a minute to do this job. If she were sensible, and did not struggle, he would take away her pain.

With her right eye all she could see was a blur of faces looking down on her, and above them grey clouds, moving fast. The clouds raced across the sky; it was reckless to move so fast. No one was shouting, 'Otmoor For Ever!' The only sound besides that of the man's soothing voice was the sound of her own heart as it pumped and thumped inside her.

The man's arm moved quickly, with a piece of glittering metal at the end of it. There was a stinging at her throat, then choking, coughing, gurgling. Dark liquid spurted from her into the air, and fell on the grass and the hedge around her.

87

Her heart pumped slower. Greyness drifted down on her, pressing her downwards into sleep. The racing clouds seemed to be lower and lower in the sky. There was a smell which was strange to her. Perhaps it came from the clouds. They were too low; they had turned the weather. She could feel the cold, and began to shiver. The blurred faces of the people turned away, as they began to collect wood for a fire.

Almost before Cloud's last muscular spasm was over, an iron bar had been chosen as a spit. The man who claimed to be used to such matters had not waited for the horse to be still. Another man, used to other matters, had taken his place, ready to remove the hide, and carve the flesh into pieces suitable for roasting. This man's skill would lie in making sure that nothing of the valuable carcass would be wasted.

The rope had been removed from the neck of the black and white mongrel bitch, and was being used to drag more wood towards the fire. She crouched down, watching the man work, swinging her tail from side to side, and grumbling because she had been threatened with a stick.

None of those lucky enough to get close to the pieces of horsemeat roasting over the fire, and to consume some, raised the question of the horse's ownership. Some questions are better not raised, since the answers may not find general approval. It was assumed among the people that the horse had belonged to one of those rich landowners who were trying to take away the people's rights, and was therefore a justified casualty of the battle.

A small boy may be more nimble in a crush than his betters. Boy William, seeing a crowd round a bonfire, had slipped through legs to find out what concerned them, discovered roast meat, and returned to share it with Cath and James.

'What is it?'

He shrugged and smiled. 'Meat.'

All round them, people were shouting, 'Meat!', and pressing towards the fire, with arms outstretched, trying to grab a piece of roasted horse flesh.

Arrest

Towards the end of the morning, a troop of horsemen, led by a reverend gentleman in bands, approached the people on the moor. The horsemen stopped at a distance, and the reverend gentleman began to read from a piece of paper he took from his pocket. Most of his words could not be heard, and the rest were not understood. The reading was of as little interest as it might have been in church. Someone said, 'Parson's reading the lesson', and there was laughter, as they continued to break down the fences. The reverend gentleman stepped aside, and the Yeomanry drew their sabres.

Suddenly, as if from nowhere, Bevil Blizard was at Cath's side, pushing her forward towards the militia. James and Boy William tried to follow, but were carried by the press of people away from the drawn sabres. Cath struggled, but Bevil gripped her hard.

'Was the man at Waterperry dead when you left him?' Cath stopped struggling, and stared at Bevil, who collided with a child which was screaming for its mother, swore, and brushed it aside. 'Keep your head covered until you are in court. Make sure they are watching you when you untie your hair and let it down. Tell them why you came to Otmoor. Tell them what happened at Tysoe, and that you are carrying his child. Don't try to escape from the wagons when we do. I have to be further north very soon. It's best my name isn't known, not by the courts. Your fine will be paid. After that it's up to you. I am the only person who knows you went to Tom Tooth's cottage.'

The soldiers were picking out men from the crowd, collect-

ing them and herding them into a separate group. The men
went peaceably, and others laughed and shouted to the soldiers to help them break the fences. Bevil said, 'Just let them
take you for a man until you are in court. Then your job is
done.' He pulled her towards one of the young soldiers, and
shouted, 'We'll go.' The young soldier pointed to where they
should stand with the other prisoners. There were sixty-six of
them.

'What are they doing now? I can't see.'
'Still asking questions.'
Cath was standing beside an old man with white hair and
glazed opaque eyes. They had been marched to a barn at Islip,
and were waiting to be questioned. The hands of the old man
were clasped in front of him, one thumb rubbing the knuckle
of the other. He shuffled his feet, shifting his weight from one
leg to the other.
'I've walked a good way today. Good long way for me. Once
you start, you have to keep up with the crowd.' His head
moved from side to side, as if he were looking for someone. 'I
do see some things, you know. I'm not stone-blind.'
He was an old man. They had told him of what was to
happen on this day, but not this part of it. No one had told him
there would be this part. 'Emmy said nobody would come.
Only the troublemakers. Did you see them roasting that old
horse? Just like a fair, it was. Poor old mare! I didn't see it for
myself, but I was told, and I smelled her, roasting. Have to be
very hungry to eat that. Wait till I tell Emmy. Will they have
done with me soon?'
Emmy had told him not to come, but he had seen the routine
of his days stretching ahead of him, just as they stretched
behind. For the last twenty-odd years, he had got out of bed at
sunrise and retired at sunset, and frequently nowadays Emmy
had to remind him which was which. He needed something to
show her, something to talk about. In summer he went to bed
when he was tired, whether the sun had set or no. He was tired
now, very tired.
Two magistrates, the Reverend Theophilus Leigh Cooke
and the Reverend Vaughan Thomas, sat at a small table,

questioning each prisoner in turn. Some were released to go home, others kept back.

'Where are you from, young lad?' the old man said. 'I'm from Woodeaton. Got to get back there. Don't know why the soldiers chose me. Must have been walking the wrong way. She'll be wondering where I've got to. Said I'd be back to help her. Is it still light outside?'

'There'll be a few more hours of light. Don't worry.'

'You're a young man, aren't you? Only my eyes are going. I've tried the waters at Charlton and at Oddington. Does no good. I'm a half bit excited by all this, that's what it is. Am I being silly?'

'No.'

'Just wait till I tell her how many folk she missed seeing. She'll ask me for everything that happened; I must retail it. I hope she don't think I'm dead.'

The old man was pulled forward by a soldier, questioned by the two magistrates, then led to one side. Cath was next. She coughed, and concentrated on trying to make her voice deeper.

'That old man is nearly blind. His wife is waiting for him at home.' She coughed again. The voice didn't sound right.

'My wife is also waiting at home. Name?'

'William . . . Boy.'

'William Boy?'

'Boyd. With a "d".'

'I think I know how to spell, young man. Age?'

'Fourteen.'

'Old enough to be hanged, then. Why is that hat still on your head?'

'It's where I keep it.'

'You may find that remark somewhat expensive.'

What he saw now, from the cart as it bumped along, saw between the heads of the men pressed tightly around him and beyond the heads of the escorting soldiers on horseback, what he saw were fields. He saw fields and small hamlets which he had not seen for many years. It was early September. He knew so, had been told so by Emmy, and anyway knew it, could smell it. He saw reds and browns, golds and sun-scorched

91

yellows, everything blurred, everything melting into every other thing.

His left eye hardly worked at all, and the right showed him a world always in steam, a steamy misty world, as if November fog had settled long ago, and never since cleared. When the real November fogs came, he would grope his way to the bottom of the garden, and know that this was his boundary, and that beyond it he would not survive. Within it, held in by the oncoming blindness, held within the garden and within the house in which he could still plait withies and make baskets, he might safely wait out the years until death.

Today was to have been his last excursion, his last look at the world beyond the garden gate. He had ventured out, just a couple of careful steps, and had been pushed along by the crowd. He had heard the shouting of 'Otmoor For Ever!' and known what was happening, for there had been talk of it, and Emmy had said nobody would go. He had glimpsed a hare being chased, watched it rise up, gasping and catching for breath, eyes wide and heart thumping before a log had been brought down on the back of its neck. He had seen the log. Was it a log? Was it a hare? But he had seen something, had felt part of something.

Now, standing on a cart among strangers, holding onto this boy who spoke like a girl, and trying to stay on his feet, he felt frightened. Here, among the blurred September reds and browns and yellows, in the low warm evening light, once so reassuring and full of memories, he felt only fear.

'Are they taking us to the Castle?'

'They said so.' He had asked the question before, and received the same answer.

'I never seen the Castle since I was . . . twenty odd . . . I must have . . . Never did go inside. Emmy will want to know everything. She'll ask me. I must keep it in my head. Everything that happens. I hope she don't think I'm dead.'

One of the promises he and Emmy had made to each other was that they would go out screaming. They would not lie quiet and accept death, as some folk do. They had made this promise because they knew that, if there were pain, they would certainly scream, and preferred to scream in the fulfilment of a vow than because they could not help it. But now he was among strangers. They would not know why, and would think him cowardly.

'I'll scream. I told her. I'll kick up such a fuss, you'll wish you'd never made me promise.'

Cath squeezed the old man's hand. 'They'll only keep us there a few days.'

'I wonder what she'll do.'

She was standing on a cart, just as John had stood, except that her hands were not tied behind her back, but were gripped tightly between the old gnarled hands of a near-blind basket-maker. *'Hold him upright. He has to be seen.'* *'He'll be seen alright when his own eyes have been taken.'* The old man's eyes were constantly moving, searching between the heads of the other prisoners for some place or person he recognised. John's eyes had refused to look at her until the end, when they had been full of puzzlement and wonder and fear. *'I pray for the baby that I shall never see.'* This old man had promised his wife that he would scream his life away. John's life had ended with a sigh and the chink of a coin against keys.

The wheels of the cart on one side mounted a boulder, tipping everyone sideways, and she released one of her own hands from those of the old man, clutching at a pair of legs to steady herself, as someone simultaneously clutched at hers. In a gaol full of men, how could she disguise the fact that she was a woman?

'What's happening?'

'It's the road. It's very rough.'

The old man gripped her hands even tighter, lifting his face to the sky, and closing the lids over his opaque eyes to rest them. 'I've seen many like it. The first five years we were married, we walked from one parish to the next. Summertime it weren't so bad. We'd stop and rest, laying side by side in a field, touching each other's hands, and looking up at the sun. We dursen't do more. We was so innocent, we thought even kissing might lead to a baby, and we couldn't have fed one of them, not a baby; we couldn't feed ourselves. Other folk had babies, but mostly they died. We were saving ourselves till I could find work, then, after, we saved ourselves until we had something put by, and when we did, it was never enough. Or

I'd lose the work and the tied cottage, and we'd have to move on. We were into our thirties before we'd looked around, and that was the funny part, for it turned out we couldn't make babies anyway. We'd saved ourselves for nothing. We might just as well have been at it like rabbits for all it could have done. Thirty-nine, and still no baby.' He rubbed Cath's hands gently between his own. 'We was made very sad by that. We still think of it. We'd have great-grandchildren by now, if we'd been like other folk. Wonder what she'll be thinking's happened to me.'

Time passed. There were men now (as there had been men, and women and children too on the hill they called Sunrising), walking and keeping pace beside the two carts. At first they walked, and the soldiers glanced uneasily at them, but could not quicken the pace of the horses or the carts would have been left behind. So the soldiers sat bolt upright, and their officer put his hand on his sword, and threw quick hard glances to left and right at the walking men, who were, after all, doing no more than walk, and quietly, and there were not so many of them, so that it seemed unlikely that there would be any breach of His Majesty's peace.

Except that the men were joined by others, more and more men, walking beside and behind the two carts as they drew nearer to Oxford. The men were no longer silent. They began to hoot and jeer at the soldiers, and when they were jostled by horses, did not give ground, but began to jostle back.

Then they began to throw stones at the legs of the horses.

The horses reared, and the soldiers lost all dignity in trying to control them. There were shouts of 'Unhorse them! Unhorse the buggers!' 'Down with the bloody officers.' The officer drew his sabre, the sergeant his. Stones and bricks, now much more wildly aimed, at the horses, at the soldiers, many into the carts themselves. Just like the hare, the old man did not see what hit him on the back of the head, so that his knees buckled under him, and pulled him down to the floor of the cart.

More stones and more bricks, as the crowd grew, and the soldiers tried to keep their horses steady. They had entered the outskirts of Oxford by the road from Kidlington, and were hardly more than a mile from their destination, the Castle. But people seemed to be appearing at a great rate, far more than so

94

small an escort could hope to overawe. The people had set up a chant, 'They shall never go to gaol.' A soldier's head was cut open by a stone. Another fell from his horse. Sticky dark blood dripped from the end of his nose, and he lay in the street, curled up in a ball, his small young hands covering his head. The two carts jerked, stopped, then started again, as their occupants shuffled and staggered, those of the first cart trampling on the near-blind old man who lay on its floor, still clasping Cath's hands.

'Sir?' said the sergeant, his sabre still drawn. The captain sheathed his. 'Going for help', he said, and galloped away in the general direction of the Castle. Cath saw Bevil shouting and waving from the second cart, saw the rich-looking farmer standing, arms folded, at the corner of Beaufort Street and Saint Giles, heard him shout, 'Unhorse them! Unhorse the soldiers!', saw some of the soldiers ride away, and the prisoners jump down from the second cart to disappear among the crowd of drunken, catcalling men and women. She saw Bevil, bareheaded, stand alone on the cart like some hero from a chapbook, waving at the people and crying, 'Otmoor For Ever!' before he too made his escape.

The ten soldiers surrounding the first cart tried to hold their ranks, but their captain had fled. The sergeant used the flat of his sabre to hold back as many of the crowd as he could. His ear was split open, and a tooth had been knocked out. He became concerned about the tooth, ceased his defence, and bent his head to the hand holding the reins of his horse, feeling inside his mouth with a finger. The mob shouted to the prisoners on the first cart to escape as the others had done, and pressed forward, throwing sticks and clods of earth as well as bricks and stones. Most of these hit the prisoners, providing an additional inducement to leave the cart.

Five more soldiers rode off. Men at the back of the cart jumped off, and ran into the crowd. Those at the front pressed towards the back, not wishing to be left behind or wounded by the flying missiles. Heavy boots, thick with the mud of repossessed Otmoor, trampled the face of the old man lying on the floor.

Cath tried to pull the old man to his feet, and was struck on the base of the back by part of a brick. The force of it sent a knife of pain shooting from her groin right through her stomach and into her chest. A different pair of hands wrenched her own from the old man's grip, and pushed her towards the back of the cart.

Robert Smallbones, cornet of horse in the Oxfordshire Yeomanry, had not followed his captain in flight. He dismounted and climbed into the cart in order to avoid having his uniform ripped off his back, and found an old man lying on the floor. He was not dead, and had not screamed. He had a broken nose, a fractured rib, and had wet himself. He was also now totally blind. His eyes had been taken.

Saint Giles Fair

Once free of the cart, Cath ran, dodging the stones and bricks and mud, dodging those who threw them and those who merely shouted encouragement to others to throw them, dodging and bumping into revellers and knocking their purchases, mementoes of the Fair at St Giles, out of arms and hands. Some laughed at her, others shouted angrily and grabbed at her arm, but she shrugged them away with more strength than she knew she had. She was angry, very angry.

She was running away from politics and intrigue, from troublemakers and those who followed them. The world had gone mad, and she was in the thick of it. The man whose child she was carrying had been used by such people, and she, who had burned the hay at Tysoe, had been used also, used and deceived. She had been forced to kill once, and would kill again if need be. Who were these people to put her life, and her child's life, at risk? A brick! They were fools, all of them, lying fools and cheats. Let them starve, let them rot in their cottages, waste away, become consumed with horrible diseases – what did she care? A brick! By God, she could kill them all.

She ran. Her angry tearful face was lighted by rag flares, spluttering and smoking, set in shallow dishes filled with lumps of melting tallow and hanging from poles. She passed rows of red, blue and green beer-tents and gypsy caravans, passed a shabby donkey trudging round and round in a circle to pull a construction of wooden horses. The horses were white, painted with alternate spots of red and blue. They had roughly carved bodies, and their heads, fashioned out of half-inch boards, could have belonged to any beast. Their stiff round legs never moved. Children sat astride these animals, hugging their board necks or tugging at the strips of rabbit skin intended to represent their manes. No man who was used to such matters would ever slit the necks of these horses, which moved very slowly, and would not jump, in spite of the encouragements uttered by the children. *'Go to it, my boys! Unhorse the buggers! Unhorse them!'* Fools!

The Cheap Johns were shouting, 'Fun for the little ones! Buy them a nice toy here!' Anything and everything could be had at a price, and was going cheaply. Just so, she had been bought, paid for with a few small coins, some milk and cheese and apples, 'for the health of the child', that child which might now be lying dead inside her – John's child. She could die herself, she was so angry.

She ran on past a stall selling tripe, chitterlings, pettitoes, trotters and chadron. She held her stomach, and felt sick. The next stall sold Plum Jack and fig cake. She had eaten horse, the horse loaned to her, and in whose company she had travelled all the villages of Otmoor. Inside her stomach, with the child, there was a piece of Cloud's flesh.

She stopped by the next stall, holding her stomach still and gasping for breath. Glittering statues and flowers had been formed out of sweet breads of every kind. Gingerbread and brandy snaps were piled high with peppermints, peardrops and rock. There were dolls made of wood, with painted eyes that stared out lovingly, each wrapped in a skirt and shawl of vividly clashing colours, and illuminated by dozens of flickering candles thrust into the necks of bottles. These flickering, dancing, multicoloured flames were reflected on glass, on the shiny surfaces of the sweetmeats, and in the eyes of those who stopped to stare and wonder. All around Cath, small arms thrust upwards, and tiny fingers wriggled in anticipation. *'Look at 'em. Poor as rats, and twice as hungry!'* One of the children stretched out a tiny hand towards her, while indoors the dying woman screamed in labour.

'Sweet breads, lady? Buy some sweet breads. How about a pretty doll for the little one?' The children around her turned to look at the person the stall-holder was addressing and to wriggle their chubby fingers towards her, but when they saw

Cath's expression, the tears on her face, her long loose hair and the boy's clothing, the chubby fingers were withdrawn. Oh, she was learning; learning fast. They had taught her. They had robbed her of everything she cared about, and now, no longer caring, she would be hard. It was the only way. Now that she did not care, she was free.

'Attention, attention! That wandering teacher of Natural History, the great Mr Wombwell, has brought his Travelling Circus to town, ladies and gentlemen. And it is his intent to play for your delight the overtures and marches, the immensely popular, gigantically popular melodics of our time. Roll up, and see the animals, hear the music. Be educated and entertained in one and the very same breath. A mere coin, a small trifle will purchase the experience of a lifetime, not to be missed. Can you afford to neglect the opportunity your little ones have been waiting for? "What's a reindeer, sonny?" "I know, sir, cos I seen one with Mr Wombwell." There is a future for the enterprising; but for the neglected mind – only ruin. See it all with Mr Wombwell. Hear the music, listen to the hyena. "What's a hyena sound like, sonny?" "I knows, sir. I heard it with Mr Wombwell."'

And on it went. The education.

Everywhere she turned, there were people and loud music. There were giants and dwarves out of all numbering, an equestrian troupe, a troupe of performing dogs, and street-acrobats dressed in Eastern pantaloons or loosely fitting tights with holes. There were peepshows, where twenty-six people could sit down at a time, and look through optical glasses where tallow candles were regularly snuffed and trimmed by an attendant, beyond whom were presented six drawings of 'The Latest Scenes From Paris'. If you squinted, you could see the guillotine drop, and a head roll towards you. 'It's an education. Bring the baby. See how a civilised country does it.'

Yes, she had learned finally. No more mistakes now, no more being deceived. She would trust nobody. Here was 'The Crocus', pointing to a large worm, pickled in a jar, and informing all who would listen that this worm was two hundred inches long, and had been extracted from the intestines of a lady of quality, by means of a medicine prepared by his very own hands. 'I watched her daily, and when this enormous object wriggled out from within her, she got up from where she was reposing, and kissed me. So passionately did she fall upon me, ladies, that I quite forgot my calling.' The dandy doctor wore the gown of a university don, and claimed to be a town councillor of Newcastle upon Tyne. His bottled brown liquid would cure the toothache, lumbago, corns, pimples, bunions and any ailments of the eyes, since it contained a powerful extract of the herb celandine. For deafness there was another bottle, invariably efficacious, provided that the drum of the ear was not already broken.

It was an education. Everything could be had, and was going cheaply.

Cheap jewellery, cheap caged birds, cheap fruit, coconuts and hedge-nuts. Cheap tools for the husband, cheap baskets for the wife. Cheap inkles, cambrics and cheap lawns. Cheap ribbons, tawdry lace, and pair upon pair of sweet little gloves to fit tiny plump wriggling fingers. She wished she could grab every tiny glove and burn it.

'You're werry out of breath, young lady.' She was standing away from the main parade of revellers, close to a line of gypsy caravans. 'Your heart will suffer something cruel if you don't sit down.'

The voice came from somewhere near the ground. She had closed her eyes, and had no wish to open them. She could hear the snarling of a lurcher dog at a little distance, and, much closer, the crackling of dry twigs being burned inside a tin bucket.

'Now I looks proper, I know I seen you at Cheltenham last Michaelmas.' Someone was cooking red herrings and snail soup. From somewhere else, there was the distinct aroma of dead pig. And here beneath her, a man's sweat, old sweat, seeped and dried into old clothes. 'You vos wearing a bunch of paper flowers that showed me the colour of your eyes.' Large warm spongey fingers were rubbed against her own. She opened her eyes. 'They're a lot less pretty now, from all that crying. You'd need to wear orange to match those now.'

The top of the man's head came level with her waist. It was balding, and on it a once blue, now faded and threadbare velvet beret leaned to one side. His chins, of which there were many, wobbled as he spoke, and his heavily hooded eyes blinked and stretched themselves wide, as if he perpetually encountered the most wondrous of sights. His hands, one of which was now gripping her own fingers, were like warm pieces of damp rubber. On his barrel-chest, bright red hair poked from beneath a faded shirt, once emerald green, decked with shiny buttons and mother-of-pearl beads.

'Why you been a-weeping and a-wailing so?' His large feet were bare and very dirty. 'Tell Ernest the Able.' She stared at him. 'Do tell him, cos he has a big heart.' The eyes blinked and were stretched wide. 'What now? Do tell him.' He waited. 'He's known as big-hearted all over the country. Big-hearted Ernest the Able. So tell him why you been squalling and running your breath all out.' She turned away, looking towards the half-doors of the caravans and the flickering light from inside them. The crackling of twigs had stopped. People were eating.

'Did Ernest see you at Cheltenham?' She shook her head. He had lifted her hand, and was pressing the back of it to his lips, which were also warm and damp. 'Do you know vot he'd like now, better than mince pies? To take you to the dancing.' She looked down at him, first at the eyes, which were again stretched wide above a nose which he was wrinkling and twitching in an attempt to transmit encouragement, and then past his face, down to his feet. 'Vose feet are a trial to Ernest. He just don't know to turn vith 'em. He searches high and low for shoes, but they never fits as comfortable as vot his skins do, vich, as you can see, gets them a great deal less than clean. And vot with sharp fings, and vot the animals leaves behind, Ernest's feet have a pretty poor time of it, he can tell you. Vot he likes best, my dear, ven those feet have been vashed clean, is to have someone pretty dry them for him. That's better than mince pies any day.'

His hand was tugging at hers, indicating the way they should go. Cath said, 'I've no strength for dancing.'

'Then you shall sit, my dear, until you has.' It seemed less trouble to go with him than to resist. They walked back the way she had come, past the Snuffbox Gypsies, at whose stalls snuffboxes and cheap knives were balanced on top of tall ash rods. The gypsies proffered livets to throw at the boxes, with cries of, 'Knock 'em down! Knock 'em all down! Win a prize now; knock 'em down!' Bricks and stones had been thrown at the cart, and had knocked the soldiers and the prisoners down, had knocked down an old man, sand-blind, to be trampled on the floor of the cart. Snuffboxes and cheap blunt knives!

She was sipping root-beer, which tasted of dead horse; it could only be stomached in small doses. The large tent in which she and the dwarf were now sitting contained perhaps five hundred people, many of them dancing or bobbing about to the music of a fiddle and a drum. On a sign nearby, Cath read, 'THIS BOOTH HAS BEEN BROUGHT ALL THE WAY FROM VAUXHALL GARDENS AND FREE-MASONS' ASSEMBLY ROOMS, LONDON. KINDLY DO NOT SPIT OR URINATE AGAINST THE CANVAS.'

Groups of the young and unattached of both sexes, some in fancy dress, paraded around the edges of the dancing-space, as though it were Otmoor, and they about to repossess it. Swaggering girls, on holiday from work in service, walked with their arms linked, singing. Pimply boys with splashes of colour daubed on their faces carried wands, decorated with streamers of coloured paper, to shake into the faces of oncomers. They had pockets filled with rice or hemp-seed to pour between the collar and neck of anyone who seemed less happy and hopeful than themselves. For happiness and hope, like everything else at the Fair, were readily to be had, and were being offered free.

Ernest the Able tapped his large feet to the beat of the drum, beaming and nodding at those who passed, and waving a large hand at other show-people, and even to revellers whom he thought he might have met at Cheltenham last Michaelmas. One of the show-people (who seemed to be on excellent terms with Ernest, and waved back) was either a very large man or a slightly undersized giant, with an enormous pot-belly, a long dark-brown beard and greying hair. This man was dressed in the skin of some animal, now stained and shabby, and had a shawl draped over his shoulders. He was dancing with a woman whose eyebrows had been combed upwards to mix with the hair of her head. Long strands of hair grew out of her ears and nostrils, and her beard and moustache were also long. All this hair was the colour of dressed flax.

Ernest noticed the direction of Cath's gaze. 'She makes good money. Werry popular attraction. German. She plays the harp and writes poetry.' The hairy woman's partner waved again. 'Friend Frederick is happy vat it's warm tonight. He don't like the cold. His blood get werry weak and give him all sorts of aches of pains ven the frost come. He sit before the fire and sleep the vinter away if Ernest let him – don't venture out after October until April come, or even May. He does sewing to keep himself together.'

'Himself together?' Cath imagined the large man coming to pieces, and having to stitch bits back on.

'Body and soul.' Ernest leaned towards her, pressing his mouth against her car. 'Never say Ernest told you, but he can sew such a good stitch, and such a small one; he do all his best vork for a fine lady's shop in London. Mustn't be known, Frederick the Fearless stitching French lace on fine ladies' smalls. It don't pay as good as being Fearless, but he likes it more than throwing cannon balls and lifting bullocks in the air. Specially if the veather ain't so varm, and he has to wear only his skin.'

It was dark. They were walking. Their faces passed through shadow into light, then back again. The spluttering flares and the illuminated stalls and booths coloured them green one moment, then purple, then orange. All the colours of the rainbow made attempts on their dejection, and all failed. Their feet hurt.

Had they not walked so far, they would have been excited by the flickering colours, the unusual smells, and the noise which passed for music. The fiddle, which they could hear being energetically scraped inside the Dancing Booth, needed tuning, and one of its strings had snapped during a quadrille. They could not enter the Booth, having no money, and it was most unlikely that Cath would be dancing.

They walked side by side, James holding Boy William's sleeve to make sure they were not separated in the throng. Around them the revellers were laughing, in shrill empty high-pitched cackles, desperate to be happy and to have something to remember for a whole year until the next St Giles Fair. The revellers giggled insanely at nothing, ripped and destroyed their finery and paper hats, pulled faces, breathed out fumes of beer and gin, leaned over the two boys, belching and breaking wind in all directions, each one competing with his fellows to make louder and longer noises in proof of pleasure. It seemed to James that the fumes were actually visible and of different colours, depending on what kind of alcohol had been consumed, with what in the way of food it had been mixed inside the revelling stomach, and from which orifice it was now escaping. There was no doubt in his mind that the champion of the competition was a large fat girl, who achieved a fart which seemed to attack all his senses, and who appeared to him, even with his eyes closed, to move in a thick mauve mist.

In Boy William's amber eyes were reflected the glittering piles of sweet breads, as he seemed almost to drift towards the stalls.

'We're not here to stuff ourselves, Boy. You just use those eyes for trying to find Miss Cath.' They had refused a ride on the cart back to their home, and had ridden on another cart some way towards Oxford, but had walked the last five miles. Since they had also walked a considerable distance while helping to repossess Otmoor, their feet and legs had been severely affected.

'How do you keep going, James?'

'I tell myself there ain't no such thing as pain, Boy. It's all a matter of thinking right. If we'd no thoughts inside our heads, we'd feel no pain at all.'

'Not even if we was burning to death?'

'Not even then. Makes you think, that does. How are your feet now?'

'Sore.'

James sighed. 'They're not sore, Boy. I just told you. It's your mind what's sore. Trying to make out it's your feet what's complaining. Passing the blame. You tell that mind of yours to stop telling lies, and give you an idea of where Miss Cath might be.'

'She could be anywhere.'

'Wrong, Boy. There's more places in the world she couldn't be than those she could. If that mind of yours had told you to say she could be anywhere within twenty mile of here, that there ain't no arguing with. She couldn't be in London, nor yet Japan. See what I mean? That mind ain't doing its job proper.'

They had reached the end of the stalls and booths, and turned to walk back again. 'I'd have that mind taken out, and a nice piece of suet dumpling put there in its place.'

'Why do you always mock me when you're getting upset?' The boy with the amber eyes had begun to feel frightened. They had no money, had walked through the Fair four times, and now James was beginning to lose patience, which was rare in him.

'Your mind telling you now that I'm upset, is it, Boy?'

'Yes.' Tears were pricking behind his eyes. They had refused a ride home, and would be out all night. When he returned, he would be beaten. James had let his sleeve go, and now stood facing him, raising both arms, then letting them fall against his sides with a thump. He did this three times. He was upset.

'Course I'm upset, Boy. It's got too dark now. We'll never find her.'

'Ain't my fault.'

'Well, walking faster and running like I told you might have got us here sooner.' James was shouting. Yes, he was upset.

'My feet —'

'Your feet, your stomach, your head! Is there any part of your whole body, Boy, that ain't just about to drop off?'

'Some bits I ain't hardly had a chance to look at lately.'

Suddenly Boy William discovered that he was laughing and crying at the same time. Surely it would be alright. He was with James. It was always alright when he was with James.

'Now that'll do. I don't want any of that kind of talk.' An arm was placed around his shoulder, and his laughing tear-stained face was pushed against the chest of his friend, James. 'Your mind is blacker than that gypsy's eyebrow, Boy. I'm sure a lump of suet would be much more of a friend to you, and twice as nasty.' Then they were walking again.

'All in to begin! Now we positively commence.' James and Boy William sat down to rest on the wooden steps which led up to the platform on which seven actors stood in a semi-circle doing their Sally.

This was the third Sally, the third time they had announced to the people passing by that they were about to positively commence. After the first and second times, too few of those people had followed the actors into the booth to make positively commencing economically worthwhile. Nine paying customers had, therefore, been left already seated to sit longer (six of them having already sat a fair while), and the seven actors had sallied out again. Since each Sally was longer than the one before, and contained more extracts from the show, some of the paying customers of the first Sally had already risen in their seats and requested their money back, explaining that they had already waited thirty-five minutes, and that the folk outside were seeing more of the show than they were. Their request had been denied, and they sat on resentfully.

'Well, now, Master Makepeace, what would these good people see if they stepped inside?'

Someone from inside the booth shouted, 'Nine more good people, waiting to see a show.' There were, in fact, apart from James and Boy William, only two other good people near the steps of the booth, and these were a young couple, who hugged and kissed, and seemed to be not at all interested in the prospect of seeing a play.

'For the merest two pence, Master Marchmain, they shall see the wondrous drama entitled *Bluebeard and the Eastern Princess*.' A man stood on the lowest step for a moment, looked around him, then mounted another step, and sat down beside Boy William.

'But what of comedy, Master Makepeace? What have you of more mirthful matters, to transport these good people into forgetting the trials and troubles of their daily lives?' All the actors wore wide smiles, but it seemed to James that their eyes were still enduring those trials and troubles, and had not yet discovered the pleasure their mouths so widely expressed.

'What indeed, Master Marchmain? We have the most splendid and gorgeous pantomime ever to delight the heart of man. It is called *Silly Billy and the Evil Fairy of Old Cheapside*, and has been played before the Duchess of Whitchurch in Her Grace's private apartments.'

One actor chased another across the platform with a besom, and another fell, getting his head stuck in a bucket. The man sitting next to Boy William leaned over and spoke quietly to him. 'Are you too sad to smile?'

Boy William shrugged his shoulders, and smiled shyly,

avoiding the man's eyes. He felt sleepy; his own eyes were heavy. James was watching the actors.

'Are there no songs in this here show, Master Makepeace?'

'There are songs, Master Marchmain, and we'll sing one for you now.'

The actors, including Master Marchmain, whose question was thus shown to be solely for purpose of plot, began to sing:

> *'I'd be a butcher's boy,*
> *Born in the Borough.*
> *Beef steak today,*
> *And mutton chops tomorrow.'*

The man said, 'That's better. If you have good teeth, you should always show them when you smile, as they do.' He nodded at the actors.

> *'I'd be a butcher's boy . . .'*

James continued to give his attention to the actors. Boy William's head nodded forward on his chest.

> *'Born in the Borough . . .'*

The man did not move, but continued to watch Boy William, his expression as gentle as his words. James would talk to him if talking were to be done. Boy William's eyes closed.

> *'Beef steak today –'*

Just across the parade from the actors' booth, a man began banging a drum. He had pan-pipes stuffed down the front of his coat with a muffler, and as he banged the drum, he blew into the pipes. The tune was of a waltz, 'Marriage of the Roses', and its time was incompatible with the song the actors were singing. They were altogether defeated by the loud and rhythmical banging of the drum. Four of the actors gave up, folded their arms and sulked.

A Dancing Bear joined the man with the pipes and drum, and the young courting couple, enjoying a rare moment of disentanglement, descended the steps to cross the parade and watch. Hugging and kissing could be practised almost any day, but a Dancing Bear only came to Oxford once a year. Only Master Makepeace finished the song.

'*And mutton chops tomorrow.*'

'And do the ladies favour us with a dance, Master Makepeace?'

'They favour us, Master Marchmain, with the most enter-prising agility.' The ladies of the troupe stepped forwards, smiles securely pasted on their faces, and proceeded to execute an energetic jig to the rhythm of the waltz across the parade, where the Dancing Bear was doing somersaults. A stick had been planted to remind her that rolling sideways was no sort of accomplishment for an accomplished bear, and she somer-saulted round it, muzzle first, then head, back, and finally rear legs which landed with a satisfying thump to much applause.

'Are you together, boys?' Boy William had given up the fight to remain awake, and James, who would rather have been giving his attention to the actors or the bear, was required to answer.

'Yes, sir. We're resting.' James had noticed this man earlier, walking along the parade.

'Most wise! The little one is clearly tired.' The man wore blue tights, a short tight-fitted waistcoat of red velvet over a white loose-sleeved shirt, and a purple cloak. Tied to his wide leather belt was a purse containing coins which he jingled. 'I expect you've spent all your money here today.' The voice was deep and almost cultured.

'No, sir. We didn't have any to start with, so it has cost us nothing.' It seemed to James that the man's clothes resembled those of the actors, except that they were of much better quality, and he was not in want.

'That doesn't seem right. Are your parents not with you?' The coins in the purse jingled.

'No, sir. We're looking for a friend.' Thus reminded of their mission, James patted Boy William on the head, and tugged at his sleeve. William, still with his eyes closed, repositioned himself more out of reach, and pleaded for just a few more minutes.

James told himself that Boy William was younger than he, and much less strong, as well as being easily led. He blamed himself for bringing the boy here instead of allowing him to ride home on the cart. Let him rest for a while. James turned his attention to the Dancing Bear and its audience. On the platform above them, the jig reached its spirited if disorganised climax, with the ladies of the company doing the splits and the men clapping and cheering.

'All in to begin! Now we positively commence.' Folk were laughing, but the laughter came from the other side of the parade, where a monkey, wearing the cocked hat and red coat of a soldier, was swinging on the bear's chain, and trying to reach her head and sit astride her muzzle. The bear was resisting, waving her arms in the air as if agitated by wasps, while continuing to lift and lower her feet slowly in time to the music.

'Are you hungry?' Boy William, who was leaning sideways, supporting his weight on one elbow, kept his eyes closed, and nodded, while James shook his head. The man did not speak again, but he continued to clink the coins in his purse one against another, and his eyes never stopped watching the boy with amber eyes.

He was a well-built man, his thighs muscular, and sunbronzed arms showing through slits in the sleeves of his loose white shirt, which was open to the middle of his deep-brown chest where dark blonde hairs glistened. The hair on his head was of the same colour and also glistened; it was thick and curling at the base of his neck, but thin and receding at his temples. He had long fingers, and his nails were clean and neat, and on the smallest finger of his left hand he wore a ring of gold in which was set a dark-green stone. James noticed that the man also had a smell about him, a sweet heavy scent of almonds.

'All in to begin! We are positively about to commence.' Two people, who had given up any hope either of seeing the show or getting their money back, stamped noisily out of the booth and down the steps, leaving only seven inside. The man offered James money, and suggested that he should fetch some food.

'Thank you kindly, sir, but we won't take a stranger's money.'

'I'm not a stranger.'

'Is there no tumbling, Master Makepeace?'

'We tumble till we fall from grace, Master Marchmain.' Two men of the company, dressed as clowns, ran towards each other, alternating somersaults and back-flips, while the rest of the company clapped their hands to provide a rhythm which would drown out the sound of the bass drum across the parade, where two more dogs had joined the dog and the bear, and were waltzing on their hind legs, wearing conical hats and frilly collars.

'I'm not a stranger, am I?' The man appealed to Boy William, placing his long fingers under the boy's chin and turning the face towards him. 'Tell your brave young friend not to insult me by calling me a stranger.' The boy's amber eyes stared briefly into the stranger's eyes, then down at the flittering green stone on the man's little finger.

'Why are you dressed like that?' James heard his voice coming out higher and sharper than he had intended. The man had done them no harm. Nevertheless they must go soon, even if it meant carrying Boy William on his back.

'I'm an actor. I don't suppose you've spoken to a real actor before.' James shook his head. 'We make friends everywhere we go. It's one of our principal talents.'

'Shouldn't you be acting somewhere now?' James indicated the actors on the platform. One was trying to persuade a small snake to enter his mouth, while another scooped up forksful of fire to swallow, and invited his colleagues to join him in a light meal.

'They're very poor specimens. I doubt they'll have a herring to share between them tonight.' He jingled the coins in his purse. 'I've finished for today.' The fingers which had turned Boy William's head now rested on the boy's knee. Boy William concentrated on stopping that knee from trembling. His own right hand was now resting against his stomach, where the piece of roasted horseflesh had begun to give him pain. He had known what he had been eating, had seen the horse's head lying separate from its body, and had marvelled at how wide and bright the eyes were, staring upwards and reflecting the fast-moving clouds. Now he was being punished. He needed sleep, needed it badly.

'Our little friend is hungry. Look!' Boy William was trying to rub away the pain. 'I can't go and get food for him. It's you who knows what he likes.'

William looked at James, who returned the look, saying, 'We should go, Boy.'

'We won't find her now, James. I'm not well enough.'

'We have to find her.' James held out his hand.

'He's too tired and hungry to go walking about, searching for a friend who may not wish to be found. He's shivering with the chills. Look!' The man took off his cloak, and placed it round the boy's shoulders, then pulled Boy William closer to him. Wrapped in a purple cloak, the boy with amber eyes leaned against the man's chest, with his arm resting on the man's thigh for support. The warmth given off by the man's body made sleep even more difficult to fight. He was too weak to fight. James fought for him, and for them both.

'We must go, Boy. We should go right now.'

'Let him rest a while. There's no harm.' William breathed in the sweet sticky scent of almond oil and listened to the man's heartbeat, felt it against his ear. It was moving quickly, helping him to forget the pain in his stomach and the eyes of the dead horse staring up at him.

The actors had retired inside the booth, positively to commence their performance. It would be a brief version of *Bluebeard* and their shortest account of *Silly Billy and the Evil Fairy of Old Cheapside*, after which the booth must be taken down and the takings placed upon a drum, and somehow divided. The manager's wife, who had been issuing the few tickets, was already folding up her canvas cubicle.

James felt his anger grow. It was an emotion he feared and hated, and it coiled itself around the inside of his head whenever he had allowed a situation to get out of his control. He was angry with himself for not having taken William by the hand and walked away directly the man had spoken to them, and angry with William for not sensing, as he did, that the man was dangerous. He did not know in what way the man was dangerous, but only that danger was very close, and he must be careful.

'You wouldn't like for to have to climb up red-hot chimneys, Boy, I'll tell you that, with your feet and hands a-burning and your throat choking from the soot, and then be cruelly beaten for being too slow.' James had heard that there were men who kidnapped small boys for just such a purpose.

The man had his arm around Boy William, holding him close. He laughed. 'It's cruel to make him walk when he needs to sleep.'

Boy William's eyes remained closed. If he were just to be allowed to sleep now, he would climb any chimney, hot or cold, tomorrow. An hour's sleep. Two hours. Then he would walk or climb anywhere with James.

'I want you to come with me now, Boy William, or I might take it into my head to leave you here for lost.' His voice now was very near to shouting. The Dancing Bear was being walked back to her cage. He watched the owner drive her in with a pole. She sat on the floor, and waited for her muzzle to be removed.

'What will your folks do when I tell them you were lost because you couldn't keep your eyes open?' The Dancing Bear had been unmuzzled, and a pail of water and a quartern loaf had been placed just inside the door of her cage, which had been locked. She was alone. 'What would your folks do?' The only music now was from the Dancing Booth further down the parade. People were leaving the booth, swaying out into the night air, arms around each other's shoulders, making their ways home to supper and sleep. 'You tell me, Boy. What would they do?' The Dancing Bear sat tearing the stale loaf of bread with her decaying teeth, while the brightly dressed monkey danced around his master, begging for nuts and apples and gingerbread.

Then a dwarf came from inside the Dancing Booth, followed by three other people, and shouted to the owner of the dancing animals that he would see him at Leamington. One of his companions was a large man dressed in an animal's skin, another wore a skirt but seemed to be bearded, and the third was a young woman dressed as a boy.

James jumped to his feet. 'Miss Cath!' The group was moving away from him in the opposite direction. 'Miss Cath!' He jumped up and down, and waved his arms above his head.

'Over here, miss! It's James and Boy William.'

'So that's the friend you were looking for?' James ignored the man, and continued to shout.

'Please, Miss Cath! We've been trying to find you.' The group could not hear him. They continued to move away, talking among themselves. At any moment they might turn into one of the lanes, and be lost to sight. 'Wake up, Boy! Quickly!'

'I told you she might not want to be found.' James grabbed the front of William's shirt, to shake him awake, but the man gripped James's wrist with one hand, and tightened his hold on Boy William with the other. 'Leave him to sleep. Why don't you run and fetch your friend?'

The man released his hold on James's wrist, and James ran as fast as he could, shouting Cath's name as he ran.

The man waited no more than a moment before standing, pulling the sleeping boy up into his arms as he stood. The cloak was used to cover the straw-coloured hair, and the boy with amber eyes was carried off through what remained of the Fair in the opposite direction to that taken by James.

Shortly afterwards, the man turned into a side alley, and after that into a narrow lane. Boy William, only half-awake, imagined that he was four years old, and being carried by James to play in the meadow below Hampton Poyle.

They were all asking him questions at once. 'What did he look like?' 'What was he wearing?' 'Describe the man. What did he say to you?' James tried to remember exactly what the man was wearing, but his thoughts were spinning around inside his head. He remembered the blue tights and the red velvet waistcoat. He remembered the purple cloak in which the man had wrapped Boy William. And he remembered the sweet sickly scent of almond oil.

'How old was he?'

'Older than you, Miss Cath. Younger than . . .' James gestured weakly towards the dwarf. In the country, folk were aged by weather at much the same rate, but this man had had a soft skin. 'He said he was an actor.'

'Where? At which booth?'

'He said he'd finished for the day.'

'What was his voice like? How did he speak?'

'Like a gentleman, but not quite. Deep. He wasn't from hereabouts.' But so few of the people of the Fair were from hereabouts.

'And he offered you money?'

'He had a purse full of coins. They kept jiggling.'

'Not a real actor,' said the lady with the beard sadly.

'He said the actors at the booth wouldn't have a herring to share between them.'

'But knows the trade.'

They had returned to the actors' booth, and were standing by the steps. From inside a shortened and very rapid version of *Silly Billy* could be heard racing to its conclusion. James tried to make himself believe that at any moment the man would return with William, having gone simply to get them something to eat. It was wrong to think ill of folk before they had harmed you. It was un-Christian to look for evil where none existed. Yet if one waited too long, then evil got a head-start, as the man might have done with William. James had sensed that the man had wished to separate him from William. He should never have left them alone together. He sat down on the steps, covering his face with his hands.

Cath sat beside him. James said, 'Why did he take him?'

'I don't know, James, but we will find him. We have friends now who will help us.' She placed an arm around his shoulder, and he began to whisper. She bent forward to try to hear him, then realised that he was no longer talking to her, but was telling Jesus what had happened, and asking for His help.

The night was growing cold. Frederick the Fearless shivered. Ernest the Able was running up and down the parade, peering into alleyways and asking all he met if they had seen a man carrying a boy wrapped in a cloak. Frederick hoped that Ernest would stop by their caravan, and bring him something warm to wear.

The Bearded Lady took Cath by the arm, and led her a little way from James. 'You know this young boy who has been taken?' Cath nodded. 'What does he look like?'

'He has blonde hair. He's eleven years old, not very tall, about this high.'

'What else?'

'His eyes. They're very . . . very bright. Like amber stones. Clear amber. Very bright.'

'He is, would you say, a beautiful young boy, then?'

'Yes, I think he is very beautiful.'

The Bearded Lady sighed. 'That is a pity for him. Maybe he will prove very difficult to find. If someone wants him so very bad, much money will change hands. I will find Ernest, and talk with him. He knows, I think, of such things.'

Almond Oil

'The important thing is not to cause a stir.' They had entered a house, Number 7, Summertown Lane. It was tall and narrow, and was held upright mainly by the support of Numbers 6 and 8. The main feature of the interior seemed to be stairs, and all were to be climbed. 'I can be exceedingly kind, or I can be just as exceedingly cruel. In this respect you hold your future comfort or discomfort in your own hands, and that cannot be said of everyone.' The man paused for breath. 'Your nabs is heavier than he looks. Quite a lump of beauty, aren't we?'

Tears had been wiped from his eyes, and a dock-leaf held close to his nose for him to blow into. Another dock-leaf had been plucked, and was being rubbed against his knees. He watched his own small fingers gripping tight hold of James's shoulder, while the top of James's head moved backwards and forwards as he rubbed, chasing the nettle's sting away with his magic. Then the head moved back as far as it would go, and the face of the kneeling James looked up at him, smiling. 'Is that sufficient magic, my Lord?' He lowered his own head, touching James's chin with his forehead, hiding his eyes and wishing he had not cried, for he was Lord and Master. Soon he would be lifted onto his faithful servant's back, and carried home.

'I can hurt you in ways that no one else will notice. But if you obey me and be my friend, you will find me very kind and generous.' The man paused again. He had counted seventeen stairs so far. Next year he would reckon up the stairs before renting the house.

'I have many men working for me. They are very hard men sometimes. I often feel that they do not like little boys. Little boys upset them. Consequently they become angry and violent.'

They had reached a small landing at the very top of the house, where two doors faced each other. Still holding Boy William wrapped in his cloak, the man felt in his purse for a key. 'Twenty-five stairs! That's ten stairs too many for this kind of enterprise.' The door was unlocked. 'What was I saying? Oh yes, I was going to tell you about the little boy who tried to run away.' The bundled boy was placed on the bed, and the man turned to relock the door. 'Two of the men of whom I spoke found this boy hiding under a caravan. It was at Bideford Fair, if my memory serves, three years ago.' The man sat on the bed to remove his boots, and as each was removed, he sniffed inside it. 'I remember the details well, for the affair preyed on my mind just a little. They dragged him out, as one might have expected, but do you know what they did then?' Having removed his waistcoat and shirt, he scratched at his armpits, and then smelled his fingers. 'I arrived too late to save him. He was a pretty little boy, not unlike yourself, except that his hair was black, and he had very pale-blue eyes. Large and pale-blue, most unusual, almost the colour of these.' He was squeezing himself out of the blue tights. 'Well, by the time I arrived, all that pretty black hair was gone, you see, because these men had become so upset that they had pulled it out by the roots.' He stood completely naked, pouring water from a large jug into a basin. 'The kicks and the cuts, even some quite deep wounds they had given him with their knives, all healed up in time, but that boy was never any good to me, in spite of all the trouble I had taken to find him, because his hair refused to grow again. He was completely bald at the age of thirteen. It was so vexatious.' The man applied a lather of soap to his armpits and such other parts of his body where sweat, if neglected, might give off an unpleasant odour, particular attention being paid to the feet.

'Hair is most important to my clients.' He poured a minute drop onto the palm of one hand from a tiny flask, rubbed both palms together, and passed them over the hairs on his chest, then massaged the oil into the receding hair of his temples with his fingertips. The room began to smell of almonds.

'Hair and skin! Your complexion, my young friend, will be your fortune. From this day forth, you are to forget sweets and fried foods, and cakes are no longer for you, unless, of course, a client buys one for you, and wishes to watch you eat it. HEALTHY BOYS ARE WHAT THE OLD MEN LIKE, Boy William. Your mind may be as black as a gypsy's eyebrow, but your face must be that of an angel.' The man laughed. He was clean and naked, oiled and scented. 'Your friend James has, I'm sure, kept your body pure.'

He crossed the room to the bed, and unwrapped his bundle, peeling back the purple cloak gently from around his treasure. Boy William was asleep. The man loosened his boots, and carefully removed them. 'This is what I take pride in, little friend – doing my job well.' The child's smock and trousers were eased off him, without his even stirring in his sleep. The sleeping body was white, and as it began to feel the cold, it curled up and rolled on its side.

James had said, 'I'll do it first. Then if it's safe, you can try.' But that was what James always said, and this time he hadn't listened. He was wet and shivering, had climbed the hollow willow tree until the two round eyes of an owl had blinked at him from her nest, and had fallen backwards, rolling from the bank into the brook. He was cold.

A blanket was placed over him, and slowly the warmth returned. The man washed his hands again, before wrapping himself in another blanket, and sitting down at a small table to drink red wine and nibble at thin slices of cold pork, which had been left on a plate for him, covered with a cloth.

'You're too tired to eat now, I think. It would lie heavy on your little stomach. Tomorrow you shall have a large breakfast before you leave.' While he ate, he watched the sleeping bundle on the bed. 'I think you may turn out to be a real catch, William. Finding boys who don't fart and swear and put the gentry off is getting harder all the time.' When he had finished his supper, the man moved to the fireplace, and ran his right forefinger along the grate. Then he placed the finger in his mouth, and rubbed soot into his teeth.

All he could see above him was a narrow black tunnel reaching high up into the sky. The tunnel smouldered, and red

and orange sparks flew about, pricking and burning his eyes as
he tried to blow them out. The sides of the tunnel were hot, as
James had warned him they would be. Blisters bubbled and
burst on his knees and elbows. But here there was no magic, no
dock-leaves. Above him was a circle of pale-blue sky and
racing clouds, below a man's muscular legs, clothed in pale-
blue tights, and a thick leather belt with a heavy iron buckle
swinging from side to side like a pendulum. He could not see
the top half of the man. Suddenly the black walls of the tunnel
began to crumble and fall on top of him, and he fell beneath the
smouldering weight of them, screaming for James.

A hand tasting of soot was placed over his mouth. His eyes
were open, and he saw that the blanket was being lifted and the
man's strong brown body sliding itself into bed beside him.

'I shan't sing for you now, boy; it's too late. I'll sing for you
in the morning, I promise. I always sing for my boys when I
take them under my care; it calms them so.' Boy William felt
the warmth of the sun-bronzed body pressed against his own,
felt two arms encircling his waist, and smelt the sweet sickly
scent from the glistening hair on the man's chest. He was not
climbing a chimney, but lying in a bed. The bed was in a small
room, with a table, a chair, a jug and a basin. Some clothes
were hanging behind the door; they were his clothes. He was
naked, and lying in bed, with a man's warm body pressed
against him. The man's arms were holding him. He was safe.
But where was James?

'Tomorrow you will be taken to London by a man named
Chamberlain. He will take you, two other boys, and a girl by
the morning coach. You are to call him "Uncle Samuel". He
will not molest you; he knows the rules. Should he even try to
touch you, you have only to say, "Virgins fetch more", and he
will know what that means. Now will you repeat what I just
said?'

'Virgins fetch more.'

'Good. You will be taken to a house in Chelsea, appropriate-
ly close to the Barracks. The address is 71, Philbeach Gardens.
Refuse to be taken anywhere else beforehand. I stress this
point, William, because it has been tried, and boys have
reached Mrs Crabtree in Philbeach Gardens at second hand. I
do not introduce second-hand boys to my clients, William. Go

119

only to Mrs Crabtree, and she will look after you. No one else must touch you, understand?' Boy William indicated that he did, since, although he did not at all understand the man's meaning, he could understand the words, and would remember them. 'Good! You sit tight on that bottom of yours until you shake hands with Mrs Crabtree, and riches may not escape us.'

The man fell silent. He was reviewing the list of his clients' names. The enjoyment he felt in striking an imaginary line through the names of those he considered either unsuitable or not rich enough to enjoy the favours of this new prize was too great to be hurried.

'I think your first benefactor should be a duke or an earl. Castelford was very civil when last I saw him. He's certainly prepared to pay for the best, and that's what you are, William, the very best. You're moving into another world.' Boy William watched the man get out of bed to snuff the candle. Then there was darkness, and the voice of the man as he climbed back into bed, bringing with him the scent of almonds.

'You're not unapproachable, are you, William? I don't have to teach you everything, do I?'

William did not know how to answer this, and therefore made none.

'To me you're just something to warm the bed. Little boys are not my pleasure. Go back to sleep now.'

Boy William thought about James. He shut his eyes, and saw him, wandering through the Fair still, calling out William's name, while he, William, lay here warm in a bed, and was to be sent to London in the morning. There William was to be presented to a duke or an earl, and be paid money for making a good appearance, and not picking his nose. He would not be forced to climb chimneys, or be beaten for being too slow.

'I'll sing for you in the morning, Willy. I always sing for my boys. They become so afraid that they might not have found the friend they have been looking for. Singing reassures them.'

William closed his eyes. The man's voice was sleepy, deep and sleepy. 'They all want singing, and some want other things. Ten, twelve or thirteen, they always want the same – singing or other things. It fair wears me out.'

When Ernest the Able had listened to the Bearded Lady's speculations as to why Boy William had been abducted, he became silent and thoughtful, and entered a state of deep contemplation. First he contemplated his fingers, then, with his head tossed back dramatically, he contemplated the night sky, and finally, wearing an expression of sorrow and pity, he contemplated James's face. Then he spoke.

'Ernest believe vis may be true. It upset him to his werry bones. He lose a werry good friend when he vos young, cos vis friend vos taken in the same way. Many years vent by before Ernest meet vis friend once more, but hc vos old now, and nobody's favourite no more. He had made lots of money, vis friend of Ernest, but it vos gambled away. Now they vos sending him out collecting, finding nice young healthy boys, and taking vem back to London. He ask Ernest to help him, cos children like Ernest, and trust him. Yes, Ernest vos Big-Hearted Ernest ven.'

He sank down onto the steps of the actors' booth, and turned his face away from his four listeners. They waited.

'It vos a werry long time ago. London is for selling vot you can get a living by. Everyfing and anyfing has a price vere. Pretty young boys make money for us to tour our Mischevious Giant. Ernest vos werry much applauded at Norfhampton.' The dwarf took a red handkerchief covered in white spots from his pocket, and seemed for a while to be counting the spots. Then he said, 'People are as different from each other as Brighton is a werry long way from Scotland. In London is even ladies who like to pay Ernest to sleep wiv them, but he could never charge, or give short measure.' He wiped his eyes with the spotted handkerchief, blew his nose, and stood up. 'Ernest remembers now. He vill look.'

'Blue tights, Mr Jacob. Blue tights, red welwit weskit, and smelling of almonds. A man like that does not go unnoticed.'

'An actor, you think, Mr Ernest?'

'An actor vith money? No! Someone who puts oil on himself, Mr Jacob. A slippery customer, who has a young boy vith him.'

'I don't know anything, Mr Ernest. I truly don't.'

The little man stood shivering in his nightshirt. The five

people who had crossed half Oxford to find him, and who now stood confronting him, seemed to fill his tiny room. It was the room of a methodical bachelor, with one of everything, and nothing out of place. Even in the dim light provided by Mr Jacob for his guests, it was evident that all the furniture of the room had been evacuated from a much larger and grander setting.

The small table was set ready for Mr Jacob's solitary breakfast. He straightened the silver-plated knife and fork, and addressed the largest of the five. 'I don't know why I go on living in this world, Mr Frederick; I really don't. There is so much violence and evil.'

'Do you still do your verk, Mr Jacob?'

'What work is that, Mr Ernest?'

'Looking after other folks' houses ven they be empty, Mr Jacob.'

'Oh, that work! It comes and it goes with the seasons. I don't get much from it, as you know, Mr Ernest, and there's an awful lot of cleaning and carrying of other people's property. And the stairs! They do have such a lot of stairs, these old houses. It takes it out of me when I'm as poorly as I am at present. I've been very sick, Mr Ernest. I hardly like to speak of it.'

Mr Jacob's face resembled a jug with two large handles. The jug was the colour of yellowed fly-blown parchment, and the handles – his ears – did not match, since one had a piece missing and the other was bent over at the top. The lids above his shifty eyes were vermilion and heavily veined. Sparse tufts of hair hung from his jaw. His shoulders dropped away from his neck like the wings of a crippled hedge-sparrow. He was small in stature, though not a dwarf, and looked as if he had been kicked and spat on for many years.

It seemed to Cath that probably Mr Jacob had been bullied by everyone he had ever met, but that there was much in his manner to invite it. He said, without the slightest conviction, 'I like to please a friend whenever I can; it is my only pleasure.' He bobbed towards the Bearded Lady. 'And to assist artists of such eminence would have been a privilege. But you can see how I'm situated. I don't get about any longer to hear the news as I used to.'

'Do you tell me, Mr Jacob, vat you have not allowed a

youngish gentleman, wearing blue tights and smelling of almonds and a-collecting of young boys, to stay in one of your empty houses?'

'They're not my houses, Mr Ernest. I merely look after them. Allowing people to stay, gentlemen or not, would be more than my neck was worth. Letting your good self and that friend of yours stay the one night, that was a special favour, never to be repeated. After all you were appearing in the real theatre then, and that *Mischevious Giant* of yours was such a good piece. I have always considered it a fault in even the greatest dramatists that they have never considered dwarves when composing their best roles.'

Ernest the Able's large and dirty feet, which had flapped backwards and forwards, cleaning themselves on Mr Jacob's colourful oriental rug, now moved as restlessly among the refuse and animal excreta on the cobblestones of the street outside Mr Jacob's door.

'Vy?' Waving his arms in the air above his head, as if sword-fighting with a giant, he pleaded for an explanation of his friend Frederick's passivity. 'Tell Ernest vy.' He appealed to James, Cath and the Bearded Lady, who stood watching his feet collect filth. 'Do you see vis man here, who say he is Ernest's friend?' He grabbed Frederick by the sleeve of the enormous greatcoat he had collected from the caravan, and pulled him into the centre of the street. 'Do you see vis big man, who turns ve uvver cheek, while Ernest, his friend, is slapped in the face vith insults, and made to look small.'

Next to Frederick, Ernest did look particularly small, but made up for it by jumping up and down. The Strong Man stood where he had been placed, his head lowered, his feet neatly together. 'Take a look at this Fearless Frederick, who Ernest nurses froo bronchitis, vith hot milk and rubbing on of goose fat! Vis good friend who is no use ven Ernest himself need help! Vis Strong Man, who cries with pain when he gets too cold, but don't cry ven a small boy is going to be werry hurt!' Ernest was close to tears, pushing and prodding at Frederick, and flicking the back of his hand against the Strong Man's greatcoat. 'Ernest fink it's time he looked for a new friend. He fink it time Ernest met someone who can love him.'

Covering his face with both hands, Ernest began to move slowly away from Frederick towards the other end of the street. Between sobs, they could just make out the words, 'Vat vos ven Ernest vos in real Theatre. Pity about dwarfs!'

Frederick the Fearless stood motionless until Ernest the Able had almost reached the end of the street. Then he walked forward, unfastened and removed his greatcoat, ceremoniously handed it to the Bearded Lady, shivered, folded his arms, and prepared himself to approach Mr Jacob's front door, shoulder first. Ernest, who had expected some such action, turned, and was running back down the street, so as to arrive — as he did arrive — at the very moment at which the door, splintering in the middle, departed from its hinges on one side as the bolt was drawn from the other, to reveal Mr Jacob, still in his nightshirt, backing away from the collapsing door at which he had been crouched listening.

Mr Jacob's one chair was the first item of furniture to be lifted high in the air by the man who laid paving stones across his chest and invited members of the public to break them with a sledgehammer. The chair was a fine piece of craftsmanship and said to be Louis Quatorze. It had been evacuated from one of the better houses which had at one time been in Mr Jacob's care.

The chair was lifted, and was lowered, and was considerably the worse for the lowering. 'I don't know if I can endure much more of this life, Mr Frederick. I'm sure if I were a bigger man, I shouldn't behave so inconsiderate to those less fortunate.' Mr Jacob picked up a leg of the chair, and ran his bony fingers over what was left of its varnished surface. 'This chair was my best and only true friend, Mr Frederick; I called him Pierre. Truly I had rather you had taken off one of my own legs than his.'

'Take off his own legs, ven, Frederick. Don't vaste time making firewood.' Ernest waited with James just outside the door to the front room, while Cath and the Bearded Lady watched in the street, lest anyone should be disturbed by the noise, and come to investigate.

'Hit me, Mr Frederick sir, if you must. Break my spine, but spare the furniture; it's irreplaceable.' The small table at which Mr Jacob served himself his lonely meals was a lady's boudoir table, hand-painted and gilded with lovebirds and peacocks.

'This is Marie, Mr Frederick. She and I have been together such a long time. I beg you not to part us.'

Even with Mr Jacob stretched full-length across Marie, clinging to her with his feet in the air and snivelling, Frederick found the table so attractive that he paused and surveyed the room for something less resembling a work of art to demolish. 'My dear mother would weep salt tears if she were alive and knew how the world treats me so cruel. It would break her heart to see the scars and bruises I have about my own body, let alone these delicate objects.' While Frederick was examining a porcelain statuette of Aphrodite, it slipped from his grasp to the floor. Frederick stared at the fragments, worrying at his own clumsiness. If he were to be as clumsy as this when he performed, the public would jeer at him.

'Kill me, if that pleases you. I shall expire anyway, without my friends to dust and polish.' Still prostrate across the table, Mr Jacob breathed heavily onto a peacock's tail, and rubbed at the paint gently with the cuff of his nightshirt to remove a blemish of dried broth.

'Vat small boy is being molested many times over, Frederick, vile you discuss spit and polish vith vis monster.' Frederick turned away from the gilded cupids cavorting around a mirror. It was unlucky to destroy one's own reflection. Thoughtfully he bent Mr Jacob's fork and spoon, before ripping down the hanging tapestry and brocade curtains. After that there seemed to be little else he could usefully do.

'Tear my tongue out if I tell a lie, Mr Frederick. Gouge out my eyes, and slice off my ears; it's all the same to me. I don't know who you're looking for, and I couldn't tell you his name if my very manhood depended on it.' Ernest the Able rushed into the room, followed by the Bearded Lady, who had become impatient with her passive role in the street. Together they prised Mr Jacob's fingers loose from Marie, the table, and stood him on his feet, so that Ernest could climb onto his shoulders, there to proceed to bite his good ear, pull his hair, and twist his nose around so that his nostrils pointed at the ceiling, while the Bearded Lady stamped vigorously on his bare feet and belaboured his posterior with one of Pierre's broken legs as if she were beating a flea-ridden carpet.

'Alright, alright! I'll tell you where he is.'

Mr Jacob was persuaded to do more than that. After further encouragement, he volunteered to take them there.

The bell of a church clock somewhere in Oxford was striking the hour, first the chime, then two separately tolled notes. He counted them. It was two o'clock. Boy William was wide awake. His clothes were hanging on the back of the door. He could not see them now, for the room was too dark, but he remembered. They were hanging no more than five feet away from the bed.

Somewhere outside this room, outside this house, in some street or alley or lane somewhere in Oxford, James would be walking and calling his name. James would still be looking for him. He would not have given up, wouldn't leave William here, lying in bed with a man he didn't know. James would never do that. He would keep trying.

He had been dreaming, but he had also been awake; he must try to separate what he had dreamed from what he had seen and heard. He remembered certain words spoken and instructions given by the man, and he had been awake then, but the words and instructions had nothing to do with him, and must have been meant for someone else. They had not been words about finding Miss Cath and helping him and James to get home, but about being taken to London by a man he must call Uncle Samuel, and not letting anyone touch him until he had shaken hands with a Mrs Crabtree. They had been about a rich benefactor, and a boy whose hair had been pulled out, about not having to be taught everything and not being unapproachable. And the man had promised to sing to him.

Staring out into the darkness of the small room towards the door where he knew his clothes hung, listening to the slow steady breathing of the man who lay beside him, feeling the man's hands rest limply against his buttocks, Boy William heard the bell of the church clock strike the quarter. That chime would carry through the stillness of the early morning, and somewhere James would hear it.

One after the other, and very slowly, he moved the man's hands. His own hands were sweating. He lifted the arm which lay over him, and placed it down between them. He edged his way gently along the arm lying under him until he was free of it. Then he waited for the man to move or wake. There was no movement, and the man did not wake; there was only the renewed scent of almonds. Slowly, almost without breathing, he reached out and felt for the edge of the bed. Again he waited. Nothing. He slid from under the blanket to the floor, and crouched there.

As the blanket moved, the man stirred, but did not seem to wake. Then William was at the door, carefully lifting his clothes off the hook, and trying to turn the door-handle. The door was locked.

Since the man was naked, the key must be somewhere in the room. Again he became aware how dark it was, and he could not remember where the man had left his clothes. Moving slowly and feeling his way like a blind man, he discovered a piece of velvet – the man's jacket. Then he found the tights, and then the wide leather belt, which swung as he lifted it, and the large buckle struck the back of the chair. He drew in his breath, and held it. He heard the man turn over in bed, but did not see the man open his eyes, and keep them open.

Still as a statue, his fingertips feeling the shape of the key through the soft leather of the purse, he allowed the breath held in his lungs to be released slowly through his mouth. Then he slid the key out of the purse, and moved back to the door.

Turning the key in the lock without making a noise was impossible, but the man lying in bed did not stir. The door opened, and Boy William passed through it, and was descending the stairs as fast as he could in the dark. One, two, three, four – he counted them. Somehow, he didn't know how, he remembered that there were twenty-five. Eight, nine, ten, eleven! A landing. Did that count? Was it a stair? Fifteen, sixteen! Then, darkness or no, it was two at a time, jumping down clutching his clothes and boots. Twenty, twenty-two! He was almost there, then *was* there, at the door to the outside, pulling back the bolts, of which there seemed to be dozens, all making a clatter as they were released. His clothes and boots had fallen to the floor as he struggled with the bolts.

Then the scent of almonds, mixed now with the sweet scent of the early-morning air in the street beyond the door, morning air seeping in and around and through the cracks in that old ill-fitting door, but not strong enough to drown the scent of almonds, as no noise of opening bolts could drown the noise of deep hollow laughter, ringing like the bell of the church clock, yet not to be heard by James.

'You're not very clever, are you, little Boy Willy?' The man was sitting on the stairs behind him. 'Not very much foresight about keys?' The man laughed again. Boy William looked down at his own naked body. The early morning air was cold. He began slowly to put on his clothes.

'If you had thought to lock me in up there, we'd both have been confined, but I should have been separated from you, and I shouldn't have cared for that, not with you banging and shouting down here to be let out. For that door needs a key also, and if you had a few hours to spend in the looking, you might find it.' The man smiled, and shook his head slowly. 'You have disappointed me, William. Bringing me down all these stairs in my skin, to watch you scratching and clawing at that wooden door like a rat leaving a sinking ship.' He stood, and moved forward. 'Did I not warn you, William, of the vast difference between my cruelty and my kindness? Perhaps you were not paying enough attention.'

The man placed the fingers of his right hand beneath Boy William's chin, lifting it gently into position before striking him hard across the face with his left hand. The green stone of the man's ring made a hairline scratch across Boy William's cheek. 'Now look what you've done. You have caused me to mark you.'

There was no struggling, no dodging or running, no fighting. Even with boys of his own age and size, Boy William had never fought. On the rare occasions when it had seemed that no other course of action would do, James had always managed to involve himself, and fought for both of them.

Partially dressed, Boy William climbed back up the twenty-five stairs ahead of the man. 'If I should feel the inclination to cause pain, Willy, I do so upon those parts of the body which other people don't see. Those are the sensitive parts. As I told you, I dislike pulling out hair, because hair is important in our business. Large bruises are long in healing, but you would be surprised at what pain can be caused by a red-hot darning needle applied to the more private parts of your body, and it makes no more than a pinprick of a scar. The art lies in finding the right nerve, and teasing it into life. Most boys realise that they have made a mistake in crossing me even before the needle is applied. They beg to be forgiven; they promise anything; it's pitiful to hear them. I've had great muscular lads of fourteen, threatening me with murder one minute, and crawling to me on their hands and knees the next.'

The key was taken from Boy William, and used to re-lock the door. Then the man began to wash his hands. 'I require so much convincing once a boy has tried to run away, Willy, so much reassurance. Sometimes I do believe the promises, but at other times I fear they will be broken, and often I cannot make up my mind, so I use the needle anyway, just to be sure the dear lads know what's what. When I'm extremely undecided, I leave the needle inside them for quite a long while, and I sit and watch them in comfort, and often I sing. Singing helps me to decide whether to believe the promises made to me by these unhappy lads or no.'

The flame of the candle flickered, and the darning needle was twisted and turned in its centre. Boy William lay naked on the bed. He had been told to remove those clothes he had only just put on, and he had obeyed, without protest or pleading. It was clear to him that there would be no second chance to escape. The door had been re-locked, and the man had the key.

He watched the light playing on the shiny surface of the darning needle as the flame danced around it. His jaw ached, and the scratch on his cheek stung. His feelings of emptiness and sadness frightened him more than the thought of pain.

He had known these feelings before. And he remembered that yes, he had fought then, in a way, but it had not been real fighting.

'No tears, Boy Willy? No begging and pleading?' The man was watching him, waiting for what was usual.

He had begged that other time with that other man, begged and pleaded. Last summer they had been standing on top of a hay rick, waiting to stack the next load of hay when it arrived. The man had pulled him down, and wrestled. At first he had laughed, telling the man to leave him alone, telling him that he didn't fight, but the man had gone on, moving his hands inside Boy William's clothing and covering Boy William's face with kisses as if he were a girl, and Boy William had felt sad, and begged the man to stop. Then the man had given a kind of gasp, a kind of sigh, and had pushed Boy William away, and lain there a short while on top of the rick, and the men with the next load of hay had arrived. The man had watched Boy William out of the corner of his eye as they had continued working, and tears had formed in Boy William's own eyes, and he had pretended that dust from the hay had caused them.

He had told no one of the event, not even James, had not been able to think of words which would describe it. James would have said that it was in his mind, would not believe what the man had done to him or that he had been treated as if he were a girl, and would not understand why he thought so much about it that it had made him feel sad and empty.

'You've been far away, Boy Willy. What have you been thinking?' The man sat down on the side of the bed, holding the red-hot needle by a cloth between the finger and thumb of his left hand, close to the green stone. 'And still no tears?'

The man leaned forward, bringing the needle close to Boy William's face. 'It's always best to see what's going to hurt.' The man's right hand was lowered onto Boy William's right thigh, and moved to find the nerve he intended to tease into life, but at the very moment at which the point of the needle touched his skin, Boy William fainted.

With the assistance of Ernest the Able and the Bearded Lady, Mr Jacob had insinuated himself into clothing more suitable than a nightshirt for traversing the streets of Oxford in the early morning. When they reached the front door of Number 7, Summertown Lane, he protested for the eighth time that he was not involved in their dangerous business, and must beg to take his leave, and for the eighth time his protest was ignored. The keys were removed from his pocket, and the door unlocked.

Much to Mr Jacob's surprise, it opened, since the bolts drawn back by Boy William had not been replaced. The procession of six began to ascend the twenty-five stairs, led by Ernest with Mr Jacob, still protesting but *sotto voce*, hemmed into second place. Ernest had suggested that the two ladies should wait at the bottom of the stairs for fear of what might be encountered at the top, but both Cath and the Bearded Lady had resolved to spend no more time walking pavements or hiding in doorways: Frederick the Fearless had, however, restated his dislike of physical violence and offered to stand guard by the front door, but one glance from Ernest had persuaded him to change his mind and follow the rest.

At the top of the stairs, they were faced by two doors. 'Vich?' said Ernest to Mr Jacob.

'Believe me, Mr Ernest, I know nothing more, on my very life. If you have any pity, you will allow me to go home now, and secure what is left of my own door against the terrible vengeance this man will seek. He has associates who will hunt me down and murder me slowly.'

Ernest chose a door, opened it with a key from Mr Jacob's collection, and entered. The room within was dark, and seemed to be empty even of furniture, but after a few moments, the pale faces of three young children, huddled in a corner, could just be seen.

For a long while, no one spoke. Then the eldest of the children, a girl of outstanding beauty, aged perhaps ten, stood and moved forwards slowly. 'Hullo, Uncle Jacob. Have you brought us some food?'

'On my life', Mr Jacob said miserably. 'On my very life.' The others left the room, to try the door opposite.

Unlocked and opened as slowly and quietly as possible, this door also seemed to disclose only darkness. But again, as their eyes grew accustomed to it, it could be seen that the room was not empty. There was the outline of a bed, the sound of steady breathing, and the sickly scent of almonds. Something was on the bed. Cath discerned pale straw-coloured hair lying as if draped on the chest of a man. She turned to look for James, and discovered him by her side, staring intently at the two figures on the bed, close together, both naked, only half covered by blankets, both, as it seemed, asleep.

'Boy was very tired, Miss Cath.' They had made almost no sound at all until James whispered, but now suddenly the naked man sat bolt upright on the bed, pushing Boy William's head off his chest as if it were an insect which, at any moment, might bite, so that it landed heavily on the pillow beside him. Then the man lit a candle which stood by the bed, lifted it, and saw Cath, James, Ernest, the Bearded Lady and Mr Jacob, with

Frederick the Fearless standing beyond them on the landing with the three other children.

He stared at them coolly for a while in silence, and then said, 'If ladies are to be present, I think a fellow should be allowed a moment to secure his person against the chills of early morning.'

No one moved. The man had pulled a blanket from the bed to cover himself, uncovering the naked body of Boy William. James saw a thin trickle of blood on the boy's thigh. He grabbed the clothing from the back of the door, and moved quickly to the bed.

'Dress yourself, Boy, and be smart. There are all sorts of people watching you, and we've found Miss Cath.'

Boy William's eyes were slow to open, and when they did, and he had regained enough consciousness to be able to focus them, the first face he saw was that of the Bearded Lady, smiling down at him. He closed his eyes again. Then there was the voice of his friend, James, once more, and the hands of James and Cath helping him to dress, and it was safe to look again.

'Question the boy. You'll find him quite unharmed. Not a mark on him.' James had seen a mark, but said nothing in contradiction, since his only desire was to get Boy William dressed and far away from that room and that man. 'Little boys are not to my taste. They cling about me, like blowflies at a picnic, pestering me to introduce them to those who will make them rich. What can a fellow do?' The man pointed to James. 'Ask that young man. Did the boy not fall asleep in my arms? Did he not go with me willingly?' He addressed James directly. 'And then you left us to find your friend, and so we waited until we could wait no longer. How could I know you would return? I have to have my own rest, you know. Was I to leave the lad to freeze to death?'

James said, 'We should go, Miss Cath.' Cath had found the man's blue tights and red velvet jacket and was ripping them into small pieces, watched calmly by the man himself. The Bearded Lady said, 'And the other children? The girl?'

'The girl was offered to me by her mother, for twopence. I have a receipt. Please leave me a shred or two to wear; it's past summer, you know. The girl is almost eleven, and already a young woman. She informs me that she lost her virginity two years ago, and many times since. She is known very well in these parts, as I discover. Twopence may have been an over-payment, for she is of very little use to me, unless I can cleanse the foulness from her speech, and repair her maidenhead.'

The man had told the truth about the girl. Her beauty had enabled her to work for some time as a child-prostitute in and around Oxford, but she had become too well known, and now wished for somewhere new, where she might find a larger clientele and a more regular income.

The older of the two boys, who was nine, knew little of what plans had been made for him, but begged not to be sent home, where he was frequently beaten. He requested to be taken to London, since Ernest, Frederick and the Bearded Lady were bound that way, but on reaching the street and the fresh morning air, he made a bolt for the freedom of the alleyways, and was never seen by them again.

The smallest child, a seven-year-old boy, wept. He was hungry and frightened, and understood nothing except that he had been sung to and promised pork and eggs and as much rice-pudding as he could swallow. He was taken by Ernest and the Bearded Lady to the Poor House, where his parents, if they were interested, might find him.

There was nothing they could do to the man, so they did nothing.

PART THREE

The Christmas Child

The Hide

His feet felt as if the soles had been flayed with a withy branch, and then a branding iron forced against the raw flesh. Were his mind really a lump of suet, as James so frequently suggested, it would now be cooked and sizzling, for the sky was cloudless, and the sun seemed to have concentrated all its heat onto his forehead, giving him a headache. His right thigh itched and stung, where beads of sweat had broken out around the thin trickle of blood (now dried), and he had rubbed it.

They had been walking for over an hour, but were now resting. Below Boy William's head was a clump of scorched and dusty grass. His eyelids, which were sore from the sun and from lack of sleep, had closed. He would sleep now, as he was, if left, sleep though the sun burned through his forehead and his eyelids were on fire. He would sleep though his feet were red raw and probably bleeding (he lacked the strength to look), and in spite of the stinging high on the inside of his thigh, which no amount of scratching or rubbing seemed to cure.

Left alone, he would sleep, but he would not be, could not be, left alone. Soon they would start walking again, and take him with them. He could hear their voices, Miss Cath and James, talking quietly, murmuring words he could not make out. Why were they whispering? There was nobody to over-hear. The empty road stretched before and behind them, and to either side there were only fields, unoccupied even by cattle.

'It's no good walking all over the place, and only sleeping where you can find a dry ditch.' James's voice was fatherly, but stern, as Boy William had so often heard it.

'I don't intend that any more. I promise.'

'You must drink milk every day, and eat meat once or twice a week if you can get it.' He paused, trying to remember what else. 'Bread is a deal good for babies, so I heard.' Cath nodded. Bread was a deal good for babies. 'Neglecting yourself is an insult to Jesus, but that's a matter between you and Him. But for neglecting . . .' James gestured towards Cath's stomach, and Cath nodded again, this time to indicate that she understood, even if she were not quite so much in agreement about insulting Jesus as about bread's goodness for babies. 'It's cruel to my mind', said James.

For a while Cath let the stillness settle about them, looking first at the dry sun-baked earth on which they sat, then at the empty road ahead, finally towards Boy William, lying beside them with his eyes closed, one hand on his right thigh and the other now covering his forehead. Then she said, 'Life is cruel, James. It would be more cruel to bring a baby into the world with too much in the way of expectations.' Again they fell silent, and watched a yellow Brimstone butterfly examine a clump of clover in the grass before deciding that it had little to offer, and moving on.

'There are good things in the world, Miss Cath. You can't say as how life is all disappointment. It frets my aunt not having the things she's used to, but she don't allow herself to stay fret.' He smiled. 'I sees to it she don't, anyhow. 'Tis worst at Christmas, when she wants to help others.'

James explained that his aunt had once lived on her father's farm, with servants to look after her. But the farm had been lost after three disastrous harvests, and she had moved her father (now sick with some wasting illness) and herself into a tiny cottage with what was left from the disaster. Now she and James lived in that cottage, neither having any other kin.

'What happened to your father and mother?'

'I don't speak of them, Miss Cath.' He picked up a lump of earth, and crumpled it into dust. 'Miss Frances Lentloe is the only kin I have now, as far as I know of. She is my real aunt, and blood kin, and she would take to you just like what me and Boy have, if only you'd give her the chance.'

Cath shook her head, and the argument continued, as James tried to extract from her a promise at least to visit his aunt.

'If I go back to Warwick, I can work there, I know. I have friends there.'

'Friends like me and Boy?'

'No. Not like you and Boy.' She took his hand, whose fingers had been scratching the ground. 'Not like you at all. You are my real friends. You know that.' She pressed the hand tightly between hers. 'I want to have John's baby now. I want to live to see it grow. And you've done that; you've made that possible. No one could ever be more of a friend.' James's fingers squeezed hers, and Boy William slept on. 'But, James, I don't want my baby to start its life by taking the bread out of other people's mouths. If you don't start right, you never do any good.'

'You could work at Poyle.'

'Doing what?' James realised that he should have thought of the answer before making the suggestion. He attempted to think quickly, but no thoughts came at all. 'What would I do there?' Cath said. 'Is there a hotel, with a kitchen? That's what I did at Warwick. I was the cook's Nose.' She laughed at the memory, and puzzled him. 'You've hardly enough work for yourselves. Night-grazing for old women who haven't the money to pay you! Look at the grass. If there's no rain soon, every blade of it will be guarded.' James did not look at the grass, but he looked away from Cath. 'I'm sure your aunt is a good Christian lady, but it would be hard for her to bear the gossip of the parish, if she were to take a stranger into her house to bear a fatherless child.'

'We could explain. If we told them its father was hanged for a mistake. We needn't say you weren't married.'

'No.' Cath's voice was firm, and its strength and certainty surprised James. She stood up, and he scrambled to his feet also. 'No one must know that now. And no one must know I was the young woman helping Bevil Blizard at Otmoor. I can't tell you everything that happened, but there was an accident. If they know where I am, they might come looking for me. Do you trust me, James?'

He nodded. It was not enough. She held his eyes with hers until he spoke. 'You know I do, Miss Cath.'

'What happened wasn't my fault. This time, it wasn't my fault.' She woke Boy William, and helped him to his feet. 'We must go on,' she said, placing an arm under his shoulder to support some of his weight.

As they walked, feeling the heat of the day grow as the sun rose higher, their eyes searched the fields around for any sign of a brook which might furnish them with a drink. Boy William continued to think of his feet, the itching place on his thigh, and his headache. Cath and James continued a desultory conversation, in which he learned nothing of her life, and she much of his.

His aunt had a little cottage, and there was a small garden in which they grew vegetables. James did day-labouring, when he could get it, on the farms about Poyle and Hampton. One day might be spent picking out stones or pulling couch grass with a group of field women, who coarsened their language when they spoke to or about him, and teased him for being no longer a boy, nor yet a man. 'Tis all about men and women lying together to hear them talk. Don't have another idea in their heads.' The next day, he might be hoeing or carting and spreading manure. 'Don't bother me none, but Aunt Lentloe won't have me stand upwind of her. She reckons it's a good healthful smell in the right place, but standing in her kitchen don't mix well with the food.'

Sometimes he was put in charge of small children, who were supposed to be bird-scaring with wooden rattles, but ran away from him to hide in the ditches and long grass, and when found would often be fast asleep. 'Tis like having ten or twenty Boy Williams to look after, only they be a deal smaller, and some of them female. If I cast them so much as a black look, they run off squalling to their mothers, and then the father comes at me with his fist waving. It is a fretful way to earn a crust, Miss Cath.'

Occasionally he would be put to work with the men, and charged to work as well and as fast as they did. 'Which on some of them farms is well and fast when they're being watched, and slow and ill when no one's looking. But I match their pace, never do less and never more; going too fast, that makes them real mad. It ain't easy, but we manages, with Jesus's help. Aunt does her lace, and takes in gloves to be sewn.

Folk round Poyle don't rightly starve, even if they don't get too much meat to wrap around their bones.'

Close to Peartree Hill, Cath noticed a small group of willows, two fields away on their right, and told the boys to wait while she went to find out if there was water.

It was a spring, only just trickling out of a low bank, but water, and from underground, and therefore more likely to be pure. When they had each in turn drunk several times from cupped hands slowly filled, and James had warned Boy William against becoming bloated by over-indulgence in the water, the boy pulled James aside, and whispered to him. James began to laugh, and then made a gentlemanly courtesy to Cath, and spoke in an exaggerated accent. 'I beg the lady's pardon, but would Miss Cath mind taking in the view over towards Yarnton, as Master William wishes to wash his wound, and would not offend your ladyship by exposing his nakedness. I've told him you've already seen him lying about without either stitch or button, but he's such an old woman when it comes to modesty.'

Cath and James gravely turned their backs on Boy William, who removed no item of his clothing, but by pulling here and pushing there contrived to bare the top of his right thigh, and hold it under the trickle of water. James said, 'You must forgive the gentleman, ma'am, but it is his nature. He behaves just like this when we go to our country seat in Frogsnest Wood.'

'A wood?'

James dropped his imitation of a gentleman, and became more serious and a little sad. 'When there's no other work, we goes off to our hide in the woods, Boy and me, to make brooms and catch songbirds. We don't care for it, Miss Cath. It ain't very Christian, I know, for wild creatures don't thrive in cages, but we get to eat. When the birds is scarce, we just cut the birch, and make brooms for Kidlington Market. Tuppence a broom we get at good times, but folks don't want to buy brooms every day of the week.' He shouted over his shoulder, 'Mind you don't drown there, Boy, with all that water,' and spoke to Cath again. 'We might stay there for two or three days, maybe a whole week, working all the time the light lasts, trying to net the birds or making up a pile of brooms to raise a few shillings. And Boy's always the same. Hiding in the bushes to make water, though there's nobody for miles to see.'

Boy William had finished his washing, readjusted his person, and was sitting by the low bank with his eyes closed again. 'Now just you look at that. There's some might think Boy Shiltern was the only body didn't see no sleep last night.' He pulled the boy to his feet. 'Up you jump, young master. There's miles to run yet.'

'Would it be safe for me to stay in your hide?' The two boys looked at her. 'Just for a few days rest before I go on over to Warwick. If you wouldn't mind, of course.'

James swung Boy William's arm into the air, and jumped into the air himself, uttering a yelp of happiness. This was followed by other yelps and a short dance, with considerable jumping up and down on the spot. Boy William sat down again to rest his feet.

Cath felt for the purse which still hung by a string around her neck. 'I have a shilling left from my work at Otmoor, and the Bearded Lady made me accept this for the baby.' She showed them a half-sovereign. 'She said it would be unlucky for her if she didn't give the child a present for Christmas.' Boy William's eyes were completely open now, gazing at the shiny yellow coin.

'But it's only September.'

'I know. Wasn't she a werry kind person? And all the vay from Germany. A werry popular attraction. Makes werry good money.' They laughed together, and Cath put the two coins back into her purse. 'I don't understand how she knew about the baby. It doesn't show yet, does it?' She looked down at her stomach, then back at the boys, who moved their heads solemnly from side to side and then burst out laughing again.

So they returned, refreshed, to the road, and soon James, glancing over his shoulder, noticed a small cloud of dust behind them, which grew into a larger cloud of dust, and then separated itself into an undernourished donkey pulling a small cart which, though badly in need of repair, contained seven passengers, the driver and another man, two women and three girls of roughly Boy William's age.

The donkey, which seemed to have a greater sense of the

courtesies of the highway than its driver, slowed down to pass the three walkers, now standing in a line. One of the young girls took a particular interest in Boy William, and commanded her father, the driver, to stop.

The donkey cart, its occupants, and the cloud of dust, moved on a short way, while the young girl continued to demand a halt and a proportion of the cloud settled on the persons of Cath, James and Boy William. Then the cart stopped, and a conversation began, which was concerned with the size of the cart, its general state of repair, and the number of occupants it already contained. Nothing was said of the donkey. The conversation was ended by one of the women, who could be heard to exclaim, 'Oh, let the child have her way, Abel, or she'll witter all the way to Woodstock.'

The three travellers were taken on board. The small girl, her demand satisfied, squeezed herself next to Boy William, turned bright pink, but did not speak. The adults in the cart were also silent, and seemed to be morose, a consequence perhaps of having had too much to drink at the Fair the night before. James asked if they would pass the Cross at Thrupp, but received only a nod in reply, and since all heads were nodding anyway because of the roughness of the road, could not be sure whether his question had been answered.

The spectacle of ten bodies pressed together in uneasy silence, all holding onto a piece of cart or to some graspable piece of each other so as not to be thrown out, appealed to James's sense of the ridiculous, and made his already high spirits difficult to contain. Cath, gripping his upper arm, felt his body shake with spasms of internal laughter. Boy William, crushed upright between two pink young girls, caught no pleasure from them, no laughter from James, no content from Cath; he felt only depression and dread. He had been away from home two days without permission, all household duties neglected. His father would be waiting for him, waiting to grab him by the hair, strike him about the face, thrash him with a leather belt as an example to his younger brothers, who would be required to watch the edifying sight of their naked brother bleeding and crying for mercy. He would weep, he would scream, and the more he did so, the more angry his father would become.

'It were as good as a feast to watch the blood spurt out all over him.'

'Same colour as ours. They think theirselves different when they gets into uniform.' The two men on the cart resumed a discussion of the rescue of the Otmoor prisoners.

'I felled one with a stone. Right to the back of his head, it flew true from my hand. Down he went like a field of barley.'

The two women resumed their own conversation. 'It weren't nothing special, were it, Stumper? I reckon last year had a sight more novelty.'

'They takes your money alright, but don't give you nothing for it. That old play, so-called, that weren't no better than what we could do. By the time they got started, 'twas nearly over.'

James looked towards Boy William. His eyes were closed, his face pale, and his head lolled forward, bouncing and bumping against the shoulder of the pinker girl.

'This boy be dead, pa.'

'No, Petal. They'm never bounce so easy if they be dead. Poke him awake if he frets you. You was the one what come over all Christian to save his feet. Can't take the feet, girl, and leave the head by the side of the road. Succour the one, you'm bound to have the other.'

'Don't he have a good head of hair, though? 'Tis a crime that colour be wasted on a boy.' Boy William's head bumped against her shoulder again, and a curtain of hair washed against her lips, and fell away. The tongue of the pink little girl flicked out and licked those lips, and James saw something in her eyes which disturbed him.

'He must have had a fair good time last night, if he's too dead to notice you, my pet.' The girl's mother coughed, clearing her throat of dust, and spat over the side of the cart. 'No, if it ain't no livelier next year, we shall save our money, and do our drinking at home, my dear. 'Tis all for the children these days.'

'It were better ten years ago.' Perhaps, James thought, you were younger ten years ago.

'You didn't bag no soldiers then, though.' The driver of the cart was determined that his bravery should not be forgotten,

144

and his companion agreed. 'No, boy. Now that is something to remember.'

One of the women pressed closer against Cath, and whispered in her ear, 'He never went near the military. He was in the booth all night, filling his belly.' She turned to shout at the driver. 'You'd be better holding your tongue about such deeds, Abel. It's likely they'll come looking for you if you go about telling folks what you done. They'll have to search for them prisoners, that's the law, and you might find yourself amongst them.'

It was four miles from the Cross at Thrupp to the edge of Frogsnest Wood, and another two and a half from there to Hampton Poyle, where James and Boy William lived. The wood itself covered some two hundred acres, and was extremely dense, with bracken, elder, dogwood, guelder rose and bramble forming a profuse undergrowth beneath the trees.

'This is Western Path. We've given all the paths names. This is the west side of the wood, so if you know the name, you know where you are. That oak tree has our mark on it. Boy was always getting himself lost before we made our mark.' The mark carved into the oak was a wavy line on a flat line, with a vertical line descending from the flat line, and ending in a twiddle.

'What does it mean?'

'Don't you know letters, Miss Cath?'

'You know I do.'

'Down beneath – J for James.'

'But its tail points the wrong way.'

'That's our artfulness, Miss Cath. The tail always points into the wood. Tells you which way you're heading if we be lost. J for James. That gives direction.'

'Where's the W for William?'

'On top. Don't you see it?'

'That's a crown on top. Or an M.'

'W turned upside-down. We did that so's folk couldn't tell who it meant. There's no end to our artfulness when it comes to keeping secrets. But it's easy when you know. There's a path along here, name of Stonepit North Path. One way points north, towards Stonepit Hills. But we turns south now, towards Gosford. "G. South" is our name for that. Saves time not to have all that to say.'

After twenty minutes, James stopped, and pointed to a small clearing ahead where the huge trunk of a dead elm lay on its side. Its roots, torn from the ground, formed a wall of eight feet square. Against the top of this wall, logs and branches had been laid, and covered with clods of earth, dead leaves and ferns. One side was closed in with more branches, the other draped with old sacks.

'No sense in building a hide too near the edge of the wood.' Cath admired the boys' work, walking round the outside, and peering past the sacking into the hideous black interior. 'Nobody except us comes here, and we ain't been here since summer.' James proudly held back the sacking. 'Welcome to Lentloe Shiltern. That's our last names put together, but mine first because I did the work. Boy stood there watching, and complained mostly.' Boy William was already sitting, and inspecting his feet for blisters. Since they had left the cart, much of the colour had returned to his face, and the dappled shade of the wood had magicked away his headache.

Inside, with the sacking back in place, the hide was completely dark. James scratched in one corner with his fingernails like a dog, scratching away first the dead leaves, then the soil itself. From the hole he made, he produced a tin box containing the stubs of three candles, five rush wicks, and a tinderbox complete with flint. He felt each of the contents in turn, assuring himself that nothing had been taken.

'That proves nobody else comes here, you see.' He lit a stub of candle inside the box, and held it up so that Cath could see the interior. 'The leaves is very dry, Miss Cath. Don't let Boy go lighting any fires without you by him.'

'But Boy's going with you.' The candle-flame was waist-high between them, lighting their faces from beneath.

'No, he ain't. He don't know that yet, but I've decided. Boy relies on me to keep him from harm. He'll get a beating when he gets home, bound to, and he's in no state, Miss Cath, to take more punishment. Let it come when it come. The beating he'll get later won't be worse for him being away a bit longer. He can look after you here – stay with you for the company, I mean – while I see to food and the like. Tomorrow about midday, I'll bring what I can.' He looked away from her, and said, 'It won't be cold tonight. Will you be alright?'

Cath nodded, then touched his face with the back of her hand, before taking the purse from around her neck, and giving it to him. 'Please try to bring some milk for the baby.'

'That's first on my list. If I can get over to Bletchingdon, where less folks know me, then there's fewer to wonder why I'm spending money.' He handed her the tin with the lighted candle-end, but she followed him out into the daylight, snuffing out the candle to save what was left. James squatted down to bring his own face on a level with Boy William's, placed an arm over the boy's shoulder, and said, 'Ain't no need for you to go back home just yet a while, I reckon. If I put it about that you're safe but afeard, that might satisfy folks for a while, and give your father time to get feeling bad about whipping you. Take care of Miss Cath. I shall be back here tomorrow, midday.' He ruffled the straw-coloured hair, stood, and began to move away. 'And you be on best behaviour here, Boy Shiltern, you hear me?'

Even as the now smiling boy nodded, James had gone, running back the way they had come and leaping upwards every few strides to touch the lower branches of trees, with Cath's purse tied securely round his neck. There was silence between Cath and Boy William. The boy looked around him at the columns of filtered sunlight stretching to the tops of the tall trees from the bracken at his feet. Those feet were so much less sore now, and, yes, his headache was gone. His mother never liked the sun. He remembered her, trying to thread a needle for sewing, sitting right close to the candle, blinking as it flickered, her eyes and the skin around them sore and red.

After the noise and bustle of the previous day, the quietness of the woods suddenly seemed strange to them both, and each began to move about uneasily, he to clear the area close to the hide of dead leaves and dry twigs by dragging his foot along the ground, she once more to examine the hide itself.

'Won't the smoke be seen if we light a fire?' She asked herself why she was whispering, and why did this whispering voice echo so?

'Not if the wood's dry. If it smokes too much, we do this.' He plucked the frond of a large fern, and waved it over the spot where he and James had lighted fires in the past. 'Spreads the smoke about.' He pointed to the tops of the trees. 'By the time it reaches up there, it's gone.'

Thick tree-roots protruded from the earth in humps, and the pale sun-starved tendrils of new growth were revealed as the side of his boot scraped away leaf-mould. There were violets and mosses among the bracken, but these were not spared either by Boy William's tidying boot. Not until the patch of cleared ground was some fifteen feet square did Cath allow him to prepare a small pile of sticks and dried leaves.

They had not waited for nightfall. They had lighted their first small fire, watched it burn and watched it die. They had not fed it with more fuel, since they had no food to cook, no water to heat. The fire was not needed for any practical reason. It was merely a gesture, to mark their arrival and their intention to stay, at least for a while. Cath had stamped out the dying embers, and Boy William had pulled up clods of earth and covered the remains.

Lying on dry leaves, with the wick of the last candle-end almost burned out and floating in what remained of the wax, they prepared themselves for sleep. Inside the hide the stillness and quiet of the wood seemed more natural. They had heard birdsong, of course, and once there had been a rustling behind some buckthorn, but whatever animal was the cause of it had not shown itself. Here, with the light flickering against the makeshift walls of their new home, it was easier to convince themselves that they were safe in the room of some house or cottage. The daylight outside would soon have gone. Until they were more used to their surroundings, it was better not to watch it fade.

She had walked through darkness many times, had looked for somewhere to sleep as the light had died, she and John at first, then she alone in Bevil's service. But then she had not cared, had been careless in her joy at John's company, then careless of her own safety when John was dead. Now she cared, would continue to care for the baby inside her, cared also for the boy with amber eyes who lay on his side watching her. The shadows about his face moved in time with the tiny flame which still clung to the wick in the last of the wax. Cath stretched out her fingers, and drew the fringe of straw-coloured hair to one side. 'What's worrying you?'

He lowered his eyes. 'I can't remember how we make brooms.'

A bubble of laughter broke in Cath's throat, as she wrapped both arms around the boy, and pulled him to her. 'James will show us.'

She was a woman of sixteen, and quick with child, but she placed her nose against his like a little girl, and rubbed noses. 'You mustn't fret so. How if I tell him that I want the very best broom-maker in Oxfordshire to show me his craft? That will please him, and he won't know that you've forgotten.'

The boy's head moved in agreement. His eyes were closed.

When Cath's eyes opened, they were drawn at once to a tiny chink of light. At first she thought it was a solitary star in a pitch-black sky, but then she remembered where she was, and that it must be morning. She moved Boy William's arm gently, stood up, and went out past the sacking.

The sudden brilliance of the daylight made her giddy, and she leaned against the roots of the dead elm to allow her eyes and ears to adjust. So much light and so much noise! Birds were singing all about her, from the branches of trees, from bramble and elder, raucous statements of territorial ownership, shrill enquiries as to the whereabouts of some errant spouse, generalised aggression, unspecified alarm. This was no sweet choir of dawning, but plain bedlam. If it were not for the probability of waking Boy, she would shout, and scare them off. Perhaps they would tire soon, and fly south.

It was certainly cooler. A thin layer of dew covered the top of the hide. The whole clearing looked different, perhaps because the morning sun lighted it from a different angle, and the quality of that light was sharper. This light came from the east, from Charlton and Otmoor.

She moved the clods of earth from the ashes, and set about building a fire, before she realised that they had no need for one. The sun would warm them soon enough.

Sitting on a log, and looking round at her new home, she told herself that her mind must attune itself to a new rhythm of peace and stillness – for clearly the birds could not keep up that noise all day. There was no longer any need for her thoughts to dart and race. They should be slow untroubled thoughts. She was safe here.

She stared into a tangled clump of elder and ivy, and found that her eyes met two other eyes, staring back. Cath felt no sense of alarm. They could not be human eyes, must be animal. Except that surely an animal, knowing itself to have been discovered, would move? She turned away, then turned back; the eyes had not moved. Could they be the eyes of a man lying flat? If so, they were not dead; they had life; they must be animal. She felt at the ground beside her until her fingers closed round a thick branch of ash. Then she stood suddenly, called Boy William's name, and took a step towards the eyes. A dog fox jumped from the tangle of elder and ivy, and moved away without haste. From his mouth dangled the remains of a nightjar. The birds in the trees above followed the fox in parallel, chattering angrily in complaint. She must get used to the peace and to the quiet.

When the sun was at its highest, James arrived with milk in a jug, a quartern loaf, four potatoes, a carrot, an onion and four candles. He had even thought to bring some salt in a twist of cloth. He returned Cath's purse, which still contained the half-sovereign, which had been intended, he said, for the baby, and must therefore be saved until its arrival. In any case it would be dangerous for him to try to spend such a coin anywhere within a radius of ten miles, since everyone knew his situation, and would assume it to be stolen. He accounted for the expenditure of the shilling in detail. Sevenpence halfpenny had gone on the quartern loaf.

Cath sat on her log like a great lady while James, her steward, made his careful accounting. She knew very well, she said, how expensive such items were nowadays, and very well that the candles must have cost more than had been stated. If a concern for her own and her child's welfare were to lead James into dishonesty, then the sooner the two of them moved on the better. She understood his reluctance to change the half-sovereign, but since her baby was still inside her, and unable to make its wishes known directly, she would take the liberty of being its interpreter, and would plainly state on its behalf that it preferred to have the food now, since otherwise it was more than likely to arrive in the world a weakling and quite unable to do any kind of justice either to milk or quartern loaves. Perhaps it was James's intention that they should supplement their food by trapping rabbits, but that was too dangerous, for, if discovered, they would be sent to prison, and she had only recently escaped from that prospect.

'We bury what can't be eaten, and if a fox digs it up again, then it's put down to him. Besides, who's going to come out here to see?' Their only disagreement, on that day and those following, was about food and how to get it, and after all the argument Cath had to accept that the danger of changing a coin with a value of more than most family men earned in a week was greater than the mere snaring and cooking of a rabbit in the woods.

Meanwhile James set about showing her how to make brooms. There was so much to tell and show, and so little time, for James could not stay long or else his aunt would become suspicious. As he worked at a broom, he spoke of their bird-snaring.

'For linnets and goldfinches we has to go out of the woods. Over towards Hampton Gorse, there's a fair amount of thistle and groundsel; that's where you find songbirds. We takes teasel or flax for tempting them.' He had gathered birch twigs and a handle, and now cut a thin strip of hazel. 'This here's to bind the twigs to the handle. It has to be real tight. I doubt a woman could do it.'

It seemed to Cath that whatever Boy William could do, she should be able to do, and she took one strip of hazel from James, and after several attempts, succeeded in tying it round the twigs.

'Most times you might bag the odd sparrow or greenfinch. Boy knows what to do with them. 'Tis only a mouthful, but as good to you as real meat.' Cath attempted to sweep leaves with the broom. The twigs loosened themselves, and dropped to the ground. The two boys laughed.

'Practice makes perfect.'

Cath dropped the handle of the broom, and said, 'How do you kill them?'

Both boys stopped laughing. She was serious. James looked

away from her. 'Boy knows how to do that. Don't you have to mind.'

She took him by the arm, and swung him round to face her. 'It's my baby, James, and my stomach they'll be going to fill.' Still he would not look at her, and stared at the ground. Quietly she said, 'Kindness is one thing, charity another. And my baby wouldn't thank you.'

'Then Boy can show you – that's if he can catch any. A rook has a size more meat on it, though it's a bit tough. Rooks are safe enough to kill, if you can hit one. Nobody cares for them.'

She had known it, heard of it, known that it was done by men and boys, carrying poles with nets tied to them. It was called 'spadgering', and was done at night. While the flocks of sparrows and other small birds were at roost in hedges, the nets would be lowered over them, and pulled tight. Then lanterns would be lighted, and the birds slaughtered. How the slaughtering was done, she had not known, or wished to know. *'Do you know how he chose his wife, Nose? He timed her, boning seventy sparrows for a pie.'*

She followed Boy William along the overgrown path to Hampton Gorse. They were to stop at a brook which Boy thought would still be in flow, in spite of the drought. It was a large brook, and fed the River Cherwell.

The brook was low, but still ran. From a large hollow tree, Boy took a home-made net, two leather slings, an iron pot for cooking and for carrying water, a yard of rope, a small knife and a basket with a lid in which to keep the birds. All was done cautiously, with much looking about. These objects were the boys' tools, which had to be kept in a separate place from the hide.

'Do you want to wash your wound?' He shook his head. 'Tomorrow you can show me where the birds sing. Today we have bread and potatoes.'

Everything but the iron pot and the knife was returned to the hiding place inside the hollow tree. 'Whose knife is that?' It was Boy William's.

'I could try for a rook.'

'Have you ever hit a rook?'

He smiled, and shook his head. 'But we could tell James that I tried.'

She filled the pot with water from the brook, drank, and then washed as much of her as she could, leaving her feet in the water to soak. The boy with amber eyes sat beside her, wriggling his toes and splashing them in the shallow water.

'What have you hit?'

'I hit a tree once, but it wouldn't lie down.'

And so the days passed.

At four each morning James made two journeys to draw water from the village well. Two pails full were needed for his aunt's use and two for his own morning bath, which was taken while his aunt was still asleep and before he began his tour of all the local farms to beg for a day's work.

Standing naked in the centre of the room, he would dip the soap into the first pail, and rub it vigorously over his entire body, reminding himself that cleanliness was next to godliness, and that the foul-smelling greasy substance was necessary to attain this state. Then, using a rough rag and more water, he would remove what he could of the soap, before lifting the pail of clean water above his head, tilting it slowly and wriggling beneath the flow, so that the water trickled down over him and reached the undersides of his arms and legs.

He would dry, and dress, and brush the water across the stone floor, through the door and out into the garden. In summer the door would be left open, allowing the floor to dry before his aunt came down. In winter he would have kindled the fire before going out to the well, since it was sometimes necessary to melt the splinters of ice before he bathed.

By five each morning he would be standing in the yard at Dale Farm with the other men and boys who were offering themselves as day labour. They would wait there in a line, so that each of them could be seen when the farmer came out to choose those he wanted. In winter there would be few chosen, or none. At hay-making or harvest, most or all would be found something.

On good days, James would be pointed at, and he would follow the farmer, stopping when he stopped, and following with his eyes the direction in which the farmer pointed, for the farmer never spoke to him. If the direction taken by the farmer's finger were towards the stables, then it was a very good day.

'Morning.'

'Morning, Mr Hopkins, sir.'

'Have you been set on to work with me, then?'

'Yes, if it please you, sir.'

'It will if you does a fair day's work at what you're told.'

'I will, sir. I promise.'

'Well said, then. That's what I like to hear, a man as knows his duty. You have a good pair of arms for fetching and carrying, as I recall.'

'I have, sir.'

'We'll do just a treat, then, I'm sure.'

This conversation, or something very like it, was a ritual. Ephraim Hopkins, stableman to the farmer, knew James well, knew him to be a good worker and liked him greatly. They had worked together often, and met and talked most Sundays at the Ranters' Meetings, for Ephraim was also a devout Methodist. The formality of their exchange was for the benefit of the farmer, who might be assumed to be hiding within earshot. Any job involving contact with the horses was too important to be given to an untrustworthy person: competition between the local farmers over the appearance of their horses was fierce, and a poorly turned out horse was a sure sign that a farmer was in trouble. Yet over-familiarity between casual workers and the regular men might lead to time spent in idle conversation. A balance had to be struck, and therefore, until Ephraim could be confident that the farmer would have tired of eavesdropping, strict formality would be observed. Later he would ask James for an opinion about the latest visiting preacher, and would bring out a small Bible he kept concealed between two loose bricks. They would take their midday snap hidden by a rail laden with saddles, bridles, harness, collars with bells and ornamental brasses (all gleaming, but still to be polished again), and they would eat bread together while James read the words of the Good Book quietly to this older friend, who could not read.

'Seen any good rustyback, James?' And James would try to remember whether he had noticed a wall in which that particular fern grew, so that it might be gathered and stored with Ephraim's collection of horse-medicines – elecampane, tansy, bearsfoot, crab-apples with mould on them, walnut leaves for worming, oil of vitriol to soften the mouths of horses which wouldn't pull, and oils of linseed, aniseed and rhododendron to draw and attract the horses to him.

Ephraim had been apprenticed to a groom at the age of ten, had lived on a farm twenty-two miles away, finished his seven-year apprenticeship, and remained there another eight years before walking off the job one day without a character, arriving at Dale Farm three years ago in the middle of harvest, to be taken on as a casual.

'He was a good master, and as near my own father as made little difference, but he wouldn't listen. If I'd chosen High Church, he would have blessed me dearly, but he feared we lot was too political for him. Here I can live out. They ain't got the room to house me anyway, and it saves them food. Long as I'm never late, that's all this master worries over. I don't talk religion, excepting to you, and he don't ask where I worships. Best that way.' Ephraim looked down at the brass he was polishing, the face of a lion, a noble independent face. ' 'Tis half a bit lonely sometime, until Sundays come round again.'

'Take a wife.' With the confidence which came from knowing he was liked, James became brisk and brotherly with this man who was twice his age.

Ephraim laughed. 'Not my line. I was betrothed once, plighted troth. We was only five and six years old. Parents spoke over us, them being old-fashioned like. Then I went for apprenticeship. She's most likely fat and close on forty now.'

'Twenty-five.'

'What?'

'If you was a year apart then, you're still a year apart. Women don't age faster than we do, and it ain't Christian for you to think they do.'

'And you're a bit too sharp for a young 'un, and not yet too big to ride the goafer, so see as how I don't put you on top of old Celandine.' James' hands and limbs suddenly became more energetic, moving at twice their normal speed. He had been put to riding the goafer at the harvest before last, and had no wish to repeat the experience.

Boy William was toasting sparrows, skewered on long saplings, and held close to the fire. The birds were headless. He had not killed them by removing their heads, but by wringing their necks, as was customary. The heads had been removed afterwards on Cath's instructions before she would agree to look at them. The birds' plumage had been burned off by the heat of the fire, and without either feathers or heads they hardly resembled little birds at all, and might be eaten without qualms or queasiness. Except that the feet remained birdlike. There was nothing to be done, however, about their feet.

He had tried several times for a rook, and each time the target had got wind of the stone's imminent arrival, and had shifted its position to make room. It seemed likely to both Cath and Boy William that all the rooks in the wood now turned out to watch whenever William ventured down one of the paths with his sling. Cath's own attempts had simply been a waste of stones, and since these were becoming harder to find, even by the brook, it had been agreed that she should stop practising.

Each evening, as James neared the hide, he began to whistle. This was to prevent the two hideaways from dashing into the undergrowth at the sound of his footfalls. This evening his whistle was particularly jubilant. He had decided to carry his own sling with him, and to hide it at the edge of the wood, and the decision had been wise and profitable. Now, swinging from one hand were the bodies of a wood-pigeon and a squirrel, while his other rested on his pocket, protecting two very recently cracked hen's eggs.

'Thought you was a good Christian, James.'

'Good as I can, but like to be better.'

'Stealing eggs ain't Christian.'

'Sinned twice, I did. First I stole them, then I cracked them. Poor old hen won't want them back now they'm injured.'

'Well, they're here now. Gone to the woods.' Cath held one egg out to William.

'They both be for the baby.'

'We share our food equally. Boy's still growing.'

'Not on eggs. Not when they're cracked, and has to be eaten raw. Boy won't go near 'em.' Boy William's facial expression conveyed all that could be said about his attitude to the eating of raw eggs.

Cath tilted back her head, and poured the contents of the first egg into her mouth. Boy William turned his head away. James watched approvingly. 'Does you more good like that, if you can stomach it.'

As the second egg was poised above Cath's open mouth, all three of them heard the snap of dried twigs, followed by a human cough. The egg splintered in Cath's hand, sending some of the liquid and shell into her mouth, the rest down her chin and front.

When Miss Lentloe stepped into the clearing, it was to find no one there. But there was a fire with a pot steaming over it, the burned corpses of two sparrows on the ends of sticks, a dead wood-pigeon, a dead squirrel, a small basket containing four live linnets, and six goldfinches, and twenty-seven badly made brooms.

'I know you're here, James. I've been following you.'

Ranters

'Have you felt it move, my dear?'

Cath said that she had not yet felt her baby move.

Miss Lentloe was on her knees, searching in a large press for her own christening gown. 'It was near a hundred years old when I wore it, so now it must be a hundred and fifty-eight. But you are getting bigger?'

Cath agreed. That truth was evident. She sopped her bread into warm milk to which honey had been added. There was a grumbling buzz from a fat and drowsy bee, climbing up from a corner of the window and unable to understand why its wings would not take it through the glass. Miss Lentloe took yet another cover from the press, and placed it on the bed. The bee fell back into its corner, and began another climb. When, that evening, Miss Lentloe herself joined Cath in the bed, Cath anticipated that they might both consider it a trifle too warm.

She had been asked many questions, and one question many times. Miss Lentloe seemed not to notice that she was repeating herself, and so continued to ask, 'How does it feel? What is it like, my dear?' It had only gradually become clear to Cath that by 'it' Miss Lentloe referred to the whole state of pregnancy. 'It' and all that concerned it was of such absorbing interest to Miss Lentloe that it was enquired about hourly, and sometimes between.

'A Christmas baby! In this house! The Lord's mercies are infinite.' Cath had already explained that if the baby were to arrive at Christmas it would be almost a month before its time. Miss Lentloe had ignored the explanation.

158

It was clear that, for whatever reason, so common an occurrence as one human being carrying another around inside her so entranced Miss Lentloe that, from the moment James had told her of Cath's condition, the worry, hurt and disappointment which she had felt at observing him slay two of God's dumb friends within the space of twenty minutes had been quite transformed into joy. She had said at first, 'I prayed for that poor little squirrel to turn and savage you, as David turned on Goliath, I was so angry,' and then, 'A bird, James! A winged messenger, a dove of peace, to put in your stomach! I'd rather you filled it with stones and horse-droppings, I really would.' And James had said, 'I did it for Miss Cath and her baby. They must have food,' and at first Miss Lentloe had been silent, and they had all three watched the transformation take shape in her face, and then she had opened her arms to Cath, and there had been no more talk of the squirrel, but only of how quickly they might bring her home.

Now she sat on the side of the bed, singing hymns to the child within Cath's belly, that child who had already digested its share of twelve roasted sparrows, two hares, three rabbits and a couple of finches, all God's dumb friends.

> 'There is a fountain filled with blood
> Drawn from Emmanuel's veins;
> And sinners, plunged beneath that flood,
> Lose all their guilty stains.'

and

> 'Can a woman's tender care
> Cease towards the child she bare?
> Yes, she may forgetful be . . .'

Here Miss Lentloe would bend a glance of reproachful tenderness upon Cath, continuing triumphantly,

> 'Yet will I remember thee.'

Cath had been travelling for so long, and had lain so seldom in a bed during that time. She lay contentedly and long abed, and allowed Miss Lentloe to take over the direction of her life, since that was the course which seemed to provide most pleasure for most parties. The cottage was small, consisting of only two rooms, but it housed them all sufficiently. The upper room contained a large bed, in which the two women slept; it had been rescued from the old farm, and almost filled the little room. Below was the main room, in which they cooked, ate and washed, and where James and Boy William slept on sacks beside the hearth.

Eventually, she supposed, Boy William would have to return to his own home, but this seemed to be a consummation desired neither by himself nor James.

Miss Lentloe, holding Boy William firmly by the hand, knocked on the door of the Shilterns' cottage. A full two minutes passed before the door was opened by William's older sister. The only light within the room came from a small fire in the grate, and by this fire Mrs Shiltern sat, trying to sew by its light. Five smaller children seemed to be asleep in a corner of the room.

'He's not to come in.'

'He's back safe, my dear, and very sorry for having stayed away.' To say this caused Miss Lentloe a little agitation, since it was not the truth: Boy William was, on the contrary, very sorry to be taken home. 'Surely you're glad to see him well?' Here she was on safer ground, since Boy William's recent diet and the outdoor life of the woods had brought colour to his cheeks.

'What I feel don't come into it. 'Tis his father pays the rent and he won't have the boy inside.' Useless to argue! Boy William's father had ruled that his son was not to cross the threshold. He had stayed away at a time when he could have been employed, to help the family budget. Now it was coming up to winter, when both work and food were scarce, and those who had had the joy of his company in good weather might pay for it in bad. ' 'Tis a disappointment to all, when one goes to the bad.' There were circles of dark red around the woman's eyes.

'This is very wrong, you know. At any other time, he could

sleep by my fire with James, and share what we have, but we're expecting a baby by Christmas, and like to need more house-room than there is.' Though some respect was paid by the folk of Hampton Poyle to Miss Lentloe's genteel origins and behaviour, she was known to be eccentric, so that they were unlikely to pay any more heed to her announcement that she was expecting a baby than to any other statement of intention to which she might give utterance. Meanwhile Boy William's sister still barred their way.

'Let him go back to whosoever's been feeding him up to now. Boy ain't no good at getting food for himself.'

Still holding his hand, Miss Lentloe walked a much happier Boy William back to her cottage. 'I blame James. He's older than you, and you're so easily led.' When Miss Lentloe moved fast, little boys had to run to keep up. 'I don't know what he learns on Sundays; I really don't. Well, now he must lead you into a job. We have five mouths to feed.'

Celandine moved round in a circle, rearing at one moment, plunging the next, and farting the moment after, while Boy William clung to her back. Three men, assisted by James, stood below, throwing heaps of corn beneath the large mare's hooves. Boy William had been chosen to ride the goaf, partly because of his size and partly because every other boy in the parish had performed the task at least once, and had made themselves unavailable on this occasion. Dust from the tram-pled corn rose and hung thick in the air, except when Celan-dine farted, when it whirled and danced briskly behind her. She was the most docile horse in the parish, but had an unhappy, and entirely deserved, reputation for flatulence.

Boy William had been on Celandine's back for over three hours, and the mound of loose corn beneath them had risen in height until now his own back almost touched the rafters. His head was thrust forward over the horse's neck, and his hair was covered in cobwebs. There was little room, little air, and a great deal of heat. The breath which hissed from Celandine's mouth as she panted was steamy, and just as foul as that trumpeting from her rear. The dust irritated her eyes just as much as his, and the more she blinked and shook her head, rubbing her mane against his face, the more his eyes watered and his nose ran.

He reminded himself, as he had done frequently during the long ordeal, that his payment for riding the goaf would be threepence farthing, and that, having done it once, he might be reckoned unavailable for next year. The threepence farthing would be given to Miss Lentloe for his food, and on Sunday she would return one farthing to him, though he would be expected to place it in the collection plate at the Ranters' Meeting. She had said, 'We are a family now. Every member of this family gives thanks on Sunday morning.'

'That's high enough, boy, or we'll never get Celandine off there.' The men had stopped throwing up the corn. What he had to do now was to catch a rope thrown up by the men below, to secure it around Celandine's ample body, and to sling it over a joist so that she could be lifted and lowered to the ground. The manner of his own descent had not been spoken of. What had also not been spoken of, and was a fact known only to himself and James, was that he couldn't catch. A ball, a rope, a stone, even a large crusty loaf, if thrown to Boy William would be sure to land on the floor.

The rope was thrown to him, and did land on the floor of the barn, some thirty feet below.

'Can the boy not see?'

James did not answer. He was already looking for a ladder. If bringing Celandine down were to depend on Boy William's ability to catch a rope, the horse would either stay put and waste away, or eat the corn and die of thirst.

'Come closer to the edge, boy, and grab the rope.' The farmer himself was now supervising proceedings. Below him Boy William could see the tops of heads. These heads were being shaken as the men walked about in disapproval and disbelief.

James had found a short ladder, and used it to begin his ascent of the side of the barn.

'Closer to the edge, boy. Don't you see we're waiting? Time is money, do you hear me? Is it a girl we've put up there? It's only a few feet, and there's a softish landing.'

' 'Tis a softish young 'un we chose, and all.' Celandine began to piss on the corn, farted, then dropped a large quantity of

162

steaming dung. Flies, which had up to that time been attracted to the horse's eyes and the sweaty faces of the men, shifted ground to this more attractive repast.

Fifteen minutes later, James edged his way along the beam over which the rope was to pass. He caught the rope from below, and threw one end of it so that it landed on Celandine's back. Then he instructed Boy William in the tying of it, before edging his way back and down, to help the men take the weight of the horse.

Celandine was hoisted, and lowered to the ground, where she placidly accepted approbation; she had done it all before. Boy William, after some time spent in deliberation, climbed down the side of the barn, and was docked half his wages for causing undue delay.

Together as a family, but in single file owing to the narrowness of the lane dividing the rows of gardens, the four of them walked, led by Miss Lentloe. It was Sunday, so there should be no running, nor would their purpose allow loitering. That purpose was to bear witness.

They walked past rows of bean poles, through the scents of roses, honeysuckle, woodsmoke and pigs. They heard the lowing of cows and, behind them, the single repeated note of the church bell; its call was not for them to heed. They walked out of the village and over fields, under yew and medlar, chestnut and larch. They paused at Ephraim's cottage, where James left the line to hurry past two hutches containing ferrets, and to knock and wait at the door.

Then they were walking again, without Ephraim, who had gone on ahead, and found him waiting outside the cottage where the meeting was to be held. There he greeted the people as they arrived, and held them for a while in the conversation for which he had waited all week.

'God is shining through your eyes today, Miss Lentloe. Are you in fever? If so, I would catch it from you, for you look mighty joyful.' Ephraim had words for everyone, and shook all hands in welcome. Cath, brought proudly to him by James, found his hand warm and dry, very much to be trusted. She could feel the friendship passing between James and himself like a presence in the air.

Such furniture as there was in the cottage had been brought out into the garden, and had been replaced by wooden benches. The preacher stood at the open door, and Miss Lentloe moved swiftly towards him.

'You look tired, Thomas.'

'They need signs, Frances; they always need signs. The rainbow and the snow no longer satisfy them. Each must have some special word from our Lord, peculiar to the time, to strengthen them throughout the week.'

'God's signs are on every hand, Thomas.'

He sighed. 'It is not enough. They require a peculiar vision. It exhausts me to conjure grace from a pair of boots. How shall I reveal the divine purpose to a twelve-year-old boy wearing his sister's dress?'

'Our Saviour wore robes.'

'It was a hot country, Frances. I shall wear robes also if this weather persists. You have a glow about you, I see. It is more than the pleasure our meeting affords. May I inquire the cause?'

'I am to have a baby for Christmas.'

'God moves in a mysterious way.'

'In my house. A child is to be born in my house.' Miss Lentloe blushed, and turned to indicate Cath, still in conversation with James and Ephraim, while Boy William sat on a cottage chair beside them.

'Who is she?'

'The boys found her, lying in a ditch half-starved, and brought her to me. A Christmas baby, Thomas, in my little cottage! The bud may have a bitter taste, but sweet will be the flower.'

The preacher's manner had changed. He was thinking fast. 'Is she modest?'

'Oh, yes.'

'Truthful? Sincere?'

'Oh, yes. Yes.'

'Then how . . . ?'

'The father is dead.'

'Well, she is not one of us, not yet. But a true Christian, you would say so?'

'I am sure of it.'

164

'The days of miracles are not past, Frances.'
'I have never thought they were.'

The meeting began with a short prayer and a long hymn sung without accompaniment. Then the thirty-one people present sat down to wait for a witness. The wait was short. A small rosy-cheeked old man rose to his feet, coughed joyfully, and opened his mouth to speak. But the preacher held out his arm, palm towards him, then lowered the arm slowly, and the old man sat down again, no longer joyful and with the roses in his cheek turned to plums.

'I know well it was thy turn to testify, Dagler, and that thou art right keen to do so, but the Lord speaks through me here today, and your turn will arrive next Sunday. God bless you, Dagler.'

'God bless you, reverend.'

'And bless all here.' There was a silence. The congregation waited.

Thomas Holyoake let his glance rove slowly over the congregation before him. The longer they waited, the more ready they would be to receive God's word. These were the people he saw before him on most Sundays, since other travelling preachers, unless known to him personally, were not encouraged. They came to hear him shout at them, to be told how wicked they were, and of how, without God's grace, they would roast for ever in the nethermost pit of Hell.

They were a drab lot, who took their Sunday punishment without response, only rarely speaking in tongues or falling down and frothing at the mouth, most unlike his previous congregations in Birmingham. But Mr Holyoake had perforce to leave Birmingham, city of Mammon, much as it needed his ministrations against damnation, to be sent into this country wilderness to sleep in a byre with cows as a kill-or-cure treatment for consumption. All the treatment had achieved was to increase his knowledge of cows. The Almighty continued to smite him (as Job had been smitten) with fevers and the emission of blood from the lungs. It would be counted towards his reward in the Hereafter, but was hard to bear meanwhile. And these people, these country puddings, were forever demanding a sign, as if the Almighty had nothing else to do but to minister to their appetite for marvels.

He closed his eyes, and began quietly. 'As thou knowest, Lord, our brother Dagler was about to remind you that the ground is getting mortal dry. He particularly wished You to know that this year the gleanings are hard to find. If it were at all possible for them to fall a sight more tidy, we should take that as one more sign of Thy ever-beneficent grace.'

Brother Dagler beamed. Though a little rushed, it was so far a fair summary of what he had intended to witness, and very elegantly put. Meanwhile Thomas Holyoake, having given God the local news, lifted both arms, stretching them wide to encompass the whole of his congregation, and began bellowing questions, none of which they were given time to answer.

'Dost thou believe in the Lord Jesus Christ, God over all, blessed for ever? Is He truly revealed in thy soul? Doth He dwell in thee, and thee in Him? Is He set firm in thy heart by faith? Is the Lord God the centre of thy soul, the summit of all thy desires? Is He? Dost thou, through His grace, fight the good fight of faith that thou mayest lay hold of eternal life?' Lowering his arms and his voice, he leaned forward. 'All the evil thou dost on earth will be recited before men and angels at that Last Judgement. Then will there be nothing covered that shall not be revealed, nor hid that shall not be known.'

So far nothing new, though welcome, and refreshing to the spirits of the chosen thirty-one. But now Mr Holyoake paused, gazing deeply into the eyes of one individual after another, and ending with Cath, and when he spoke directly to her, his voice was mild and gentle. 'For I was hungry, and ye gave me meat, thirsty and ye gave me drink. I was a stranger, and ye took me in, naked and ye clothed me.'

Cath could not meet Mr Holyoake's gaze, gentle as it was, and dropped her eyes. James placed his hand on top of hers, and gripped them tight, and when he looked towards his aunt, he received a radiant smile.

' "I was a stranger, and ye took me in." Yea, brethren! A young woman was found by two children. She was cold, and near to death. We do not know what thieves she had fallen among, or what they had taken from her, but those children did not pass by on the other side, nor did they run away. There was a voice, and it spake unto them, "Save my little ones." ' A shadow of worry crossed James's face. He didn't remember a voice, but there had been so much to do, and the horses to worry about; if it had been a very still small voice, he and Boy might not have heard it. 'And they took up that young stranger; they took up the unborn child she carried; they brought them amongst us, to be a sign. For this child, brethren, this unborn child, think ye, when shall it be born? When, but at that very time our Lord was born; it shall be a Christmas child.'

Mr Holyoake threw his arms wide again, and tilted back his head. 'Is this not a wondrous and triumphant occasion, brethren, is this not a reason for great rejoicing? God is your glory and your delight, and you shall love him in word and deed. Others might have failed His gift. I see here before me those – yes, those amongst you, those whose thoughts are filled only with the lust for riches and the ungodly pleasures of the flesh.' Brother Dagler shifted uncomfortably in his seat. 'Yet it has truly been said, "A little child shall lead them." These children did not fail His gift; they did not pass by on the other side. They gathered up two souls in one body, brethren, two souls they saved for Jesus. Thus saith our Lord God Almighty, "Thou shalt love thy neighbour as thyself." And who is thy neighbour, Brother Buffery – Sister Carp?' An angular lady in the front row opened her mouth wide, but whether in astonishment or to reply could not be known, since Mr Holyoake did not allow time for a reply. 'Every man is thy neighbour. The children of God are thy neighbours. The beggar at the gate, the poor shivering girl in a ditch, the very unborn child she carries, these are thy neighbours.

'All things are naked and open to the eyes of Him with whom we have to do. But too often, brethren, oh far too often, our own eyes are closed, our own ears are deaf to God's word.' Again Mr Holyoake's eyes met individually the eyes of his congregation in a lingering silent stare which seemed to probe to the depths of their uneasy souls. 'Truly it has been said, "A little child shall lead them", and again, "I come to call, not the righteous, but sinners to repentance." For I see sinners here, brethren. I see those who have turned their hearts against God's word, those who, on the Sabbath, on Our Lord's very day, have thought only of weather and the harvest –' A finger lashed suddenly out in front of him, and pointed at the unhappy Dagler, who shrank back on the bench, and was in some danger of falling off it. '– Have placed the lust for riches and the desire for earthly food above the wholesome desire for God's food, for the word which nourishes the spirit and refreshes the soul. "They shall be cast into a lake of fire burning with brimstone." But that *a little child shall lead them*. And so, by the charitable act of two children, has God's sign been brought amongst us.'

Mr Holyoake was a tall man, a thin man. The upper part of his body projected forwards, partly as a consequence of his illness, but largely as an occupational posture, brought about by spending many hours standing at this desk, on which a large Bible rested, and leaning over it to threaten the brethren with hell-fire. He bent now so far forward as almost to make a right-angle, and his voice was compounded of equal parts of sternness and love. 'Not this week, Brother Dagler, shalt thou give witness before the Lord. On this Sabbath Day, I say to this one amongst us, who was a stranger and is now our sister, who was lost and is found, I speak to her, and say, "Give witness, sister. Give us thy witness of God's love."'

They were waiting, old weather-beaten faces washed clean for Jesus and glowing, young clear-skinned faces shining, dull eyes and bright eyes, all watching her.

'The truth, sister. Testify.'

Miss Lentloe glancing proudly sideways, James anxiously looking up. This was her punishment, her payment for the last few days of peace.

'Tell us, sister. Tell us.'

'Speak to us. We love you.'

There was no help from Mr Holyoake. He had collapsed across the desk, half leaning, half lying, and now coughed a little, spat blood into a handkerchief, and held her once more with his eyes.

'Fear no one here, sister. We are all your friends.'

Very slowly Cath rose to her feet. She looked upwards, addressing God directly. 'Sir, if I may speak for a moment?' There was a silence. God had not refused permission, and whether it was by His inspiration, or by the pressure of James's body against her side, she found that she had the strength to

168

continue. 'My name is Catherine Rainstone. I was born sixteen years ago in the parish of Finstall. I am with child. The baby's father was hanged on the hill they call Sunrising, above the three Tysoes. They said he was political, but he wasn't. He was hanged for an accident, and he died to save me and the child. He took . . .' Cath's voice faltered. She hoped she would not begin to weep. 'He took my sin on him, and was hanged. The people wouldn't allow me to bear witness. They seemed to want him to be hanged. Why, Sir? He was innocent and loved everything You made, all Your creation, even woodlice. "Everything is put on this earth for a purpose", that's what he said. Great kindness has been shown to me by Your people here. I was found in a ditch, near dead, and given love. Will You not tell me why John had to die without seeing his only child born? I still love him.'

She sat down. Mr Holyoake allowed the silence to hold. This was not a witness such as he himself or any of the brethren had known before, but he had been right to call for it. He was surprised to discover that there were tears in his eyes. The brethren were watching him. Moved by the moment he had himself provoked, he must nevertheless turn it to their advantage in his never-ending war with Belial for their souls.

'His name was John, the name of God's messenger, John the Baptist. He was poor like us, a man of the people. He loved all God's creation, and perceived God's purpose even in woodlice. He was innocent, and they cried out against him, "Let him be hanged." He took the sin of another upon himself, and died to save her and the unborn. They took him unto a high hill, and there, in the sight of all, they killed him. Do you see the sign, brethren?'

The brethren murmured amongst themselves. They saw the sign.

'It is not a blasphemy to follow in the footsteps of Christ. "He that believeth in the Son hath everlasting life, and cometh not into condemnation." But it is blasphemy, brethren, to refuse the gifts of the Lord, to receive a sign, and turn away. To those who will refuse God's showing, there is lighted a fire in hell today, but "to as many as received him, gave He the power to become the Sons of God". Accept the sign, brethren. Cherish this child, and live in holiness for Our Lord has chosen his people, even the poor and the humble, to be a light unto the ungodly. Amen!'

He had never preached better. He was wasted amongst these rustics.

The fine weather lasted through most of October, browning their bodies and bleaching their hair. The boys swam naked in the river, and dried themselves by lying in the sun while Cath took in the view towards Yarnton. In the evenings, Miss Lentloe carried her Bible out into the garden, and read aloud.

'Until the day break and the shadows flee away, I will get me to the mountain of myrrh and the hill of frankincense.' People brought clothes for the baby, and some of them brought food for the expectant mother. Each present was handed over discreetly with a few kind words. The gifts were not of gold or spices, but they were luxuries both to the giver and receiver.

James and Boy William giggled as they shared with Cath the coltsfoot jelly, the smoked mutton and ham. They smiled with pleasure as she sliced the top of an egg or licked honey from a spoon. 'That baby is going to be so fat it won't need no dinners for a year nor more.' But they did not joke about the food in Miss Lentloe's presence, and all she herself would say was, 'No one is suggesting more than that the birth of a child is a gift from God, especially at Christmas.'

November was cold. Fires were lighted, and kept alight all day. Rags were stuffed into cracks to diminish the draughts. Large stones were heated in the fire, then wrapped in flannel before being placed on Cath's side of the bed. The baby must not catch a chill.

As Christmastide grew closer, and the faithful continued to arrive with gifts, Cath's swelling stomach drew their thoughts more and more to the Nativity. Those without sheep felt themselves to be shepherds, those without wisdom took on the attributes of Wise Men, and Miss Lentloe's downstairs room became their stable. Thomas Holyoake arrived one evening leading a donkey. He had sent word into three counties, but had been unable to obtain an ox.

The donkey was as reluctant to enter Miss Lentloe's down-stairs room as she to allow it admission. The garden seemed to her a perfectly good place for a donkey to remain. The faithful would see it as they arrived and as they left, and it would have more room to move about. Mr Holyoake adjured her to think of Francis of Assisi, who would never have left a dumb friend in the cold, but the Ranters, as a group, set no great store by saints, nor was the donkey particularly dumb. It expressed its resentment both vocally and physically at being pushed from the rear by a scrawny gentleman with a consumptive cough and a biblical turn of abuse. Boy William received a kick on the shin which kept him off household tasks for a week.

Once inside, however, well supplied with straw and tethered to a leg of the kitchen table, the donkey accepted its new accommodation philosophically enough, and even Miss Lentloe was persuaded that it made a fine picture. James, who was required to clean up after the animal three times a day, had his own opinion, but kept it to himself. The faithful visitors patted the donkey, and stroked it, and put down their offerings well out of its reach.

Punctually at nine pm, Miss Lentloe would remind any remaining visitors that both mother and baby needed their rest. The donkey would be stroked for the last time, and the visitors would step out into the frosty night, point to the brightest star, and swear that it was directly overhead. God had given them a sign of His abounding grace, and they could feel it abound within them. And the visitors who had brought meat, milk or preserves to the stranger girl would go home happily enough to a meal of thin gruel or cabbage soup. Their Lord was testing them, and they would not fail Him.

'Help me!' The pain had started. Her womb was on fire.

> 'The Son of Heaven how glorious shines.
> His love for me about entwines.
> Let me be true in all my ways,
> And keep me holy all my days.'

Miss Lentloe pressed the side of her face against Cath's, wrapped both arms around her, and the two women rocked backwards and forwards while she sang.

Cath remembered the woman lying on the earth floor, with her skirt rolled up and her legs wide apart. She remembered the

171

bloodstained rag and the children playing outside in the dirt while their mother screamed. She had hated the woman, hated her for screaming, had felt sick in her own stomach that anyone should feel such pain. She had said, 'I'd be no use. I wouldn't know what to do', and the other woman had followed her, and shouted, ' 'Bout time you did, then. How'd you fare if folks ran away when it was your turn?'

Now it was her turn, and nobody had run away. Miss Lentloe was holding her, rocking her. It did no good, but what else could be done? She screamed again, clawing at the bed with her fingernails as the pain tore at her insides. She imagined the baby struggling as she was struggling, saw it twisting and turning, its arms flaying wildly, its legs kicking, its fingers wriggling and grasping her, loosing their grip, then grabbing hold again. It was tearing her wide open, while Miss Lentloe rocked her, and sang hymn after hymn.

'It wants to be born, Cath. That's a good sign. We're tested even before we see the sky.'

She had asked for Good King Henry. Miss Lentloe had drawn in breath sharply, and clicked her tongue against her teeth. 'I won't give you herbs and potions, my pretty one. I won't give you witchcraft to take away what God intends. There's a reason for everything, and a mother's pain is what she pays for the enjoyment of God's most precious gift. I admit to the sin of envy, child. To have joined together with the man you loved, and made another life in God's image from your own, to make it and to watch it grow, that's not given to everyone. No, not to me.'

Miss Lentloe lowered Cath's head back down onto the pillow. 'There! Let me look at you. Everything must be right for his arrival. There is only one moment of birth, just as there is only one moment at the end. Both should be perfect. A new baby for the New Year, my dear!'

It was eleven thirty on the morning of New Year's Eve. The Christmas Baby had become imperceptibly a gift for the New Year without troubling the faithful. But there had been few visitors since Christmas Day, when a heavy snow had begun, and had continued to fall.

Time passed. Her vision blurred, Cath raised her head, and saw Miss Lentloe standing over her, holding a bloodstained rag. 'Pray with me, child. Pray for guidance and strength to bear the pain that has to be.' Cath's hand moved down over her body, and rested on her stomach. The baby had stopped moving. 'He shall be called Emmanuel. Think of that name, and imagine his sweet face. Imagine the fingers, nails, hands, eyes. Oh, my dear, imagine his eyes in that sweet face, smiling at you.'

Cath found that she could not imagine her baby smiling. She could not imagine it at all. Even with the baby still, the pain continued. Hours went by, while Miss Lentloe fussed about the room, rearranging the crib already prepared, or sat beside the bed, reading aloud from the Bible, and wiping away the sweat which burst out all over Cath's body.

'Thou hast ravished my heart, my sister, my spouse. Thou hast ravished mine heart with thine eyes. Thou art all fair, my love; there is no spot on thee.'

She was in a fever. At half past three, James left the cottage, and set out through the snow to fetch a woman who was known to use herbs and had sometimes claimed to talk with folk who were dead, but who had more experience in the delivery of children than his aunt. The woman lived in the next parish.

At three minutes past four, Miss Lentloe cut the umbilical cord, loosed it from around the baby's neck, and cleansed the baby with water brought and held in a bowl by Boy William.

'I must hold him high, William, high in the air. He has to be seen by his mother first. That's what we're told.' The snow on the roof had begun to melt. As the droplets fell, they made a rhythmical *chink! chink!* on the window-ledge.

Cath raised herself in the bed, wiped her eyes so that she could see more clearly, and held out her arms for her baby son. A small crumpled ball of purple and blue flesh was placed with great care into her hands. The flesh was cold. Dried blood was under the tiny fingernails. The head lolled forward, and the tongue protruded from the small mouth. Its neck was long, as John's had been, and around it was a black bruise where the cord had strangled it. Her son's eyes were closed. They would never look at her. She could not imagine it smiling.

The *chink! chink!* of the melting snow outside grew louder, quicker, more persistent. The noise filled her head. Miss

Lentloe took the purple lump out of her hand, and began dressing it in the christening gown which must have been a hundred and fifty-eight years old.

'Look at him now. He's such a sweet angel. Why won't you cry for me, little angel? Cry for your mother, you poor little chrisom. Cry for Jesus. Cry for your life, sweet baby. Cry for the One who loves you. Cry for a place in Heaven.'

Miss Lentloe wrapped a blanket around the baby, and descended the stairs. She opened the door of the cottage, and walked out through the snow. She continued walking, talking to the baby as she walked, and not feeling the cold at all.

Stumbling, sometimes falling into deep snow, she walked on for two and a half miles until she reached the edge of the wood. Her intention was to find the hide where she had first seen Cath, but it was too dark, and she could not now remember the path along which she had followed James. At the first clearing she reached, she sat down with her back against a tree, cradling the baby in her arms.

'This is where you might have been born, little one. This would have been your birthplace if I had not found you. No christening robe! No honey for your sweet tooth! Think of that! I looked for you for so long.'

PART FOUR

London

Angel's Pantry

In Shoe Lane, off Fleet Street, close to the Old Bailey, Paternoster Road and Newgate Prison, an establishment for the sale of coffee, tea, chocolate, cordials, and a wide selection of cakes and pastries, to be consumed on the premises, had recently opened. Above its bowed window of mullioned panes, the words 'ANGEL'S PANTRY' had been inscribed in letters of gold and purple.

What distinguished the interior of this small establishment from the many other coffee-houses of London was that it glowed. The small gilt tables and chairs glowed. The drapes of purple and orange velvet glowed. The gilded mirrors, the good china, even the cakes and pastries glowed. The cordials glowed in their glass bottles, green, gold and lavender, potent and comforting. The amber tea, rich chocolate, dark coffee, the whipped cream glowed; even the lemon had its own radiance. On dark afternoons (of which in London there were many), when the gas-jets had been lighted within the shop and screened by shades of amber-coloured glass, calm and comfort was brought to the troubled minds of many persons of the respectable classes, who patronised Angel's Pantry to read the newspapers and make intelligent and informed conversation, while their stomachs gently ingested the comestibles prepared by the sweating Angel below in his cramped and overheated kitchen.

For Angel glowed most of all. He was an Angel in what might be considered, if one judged by temperature alone and leaping flames, a sort of Hell, a broiled white dumpling in a

177

chef's hat, running and skipping about his infernal kingdom, which, though it had the attributes of Hell, was Heaven to Angel. It was what he had always wanted, a step up in the world, a showcase for his creative talent; it had changed his life. He had moved from the greyness, the lack of glow of Warwick, from the smells of brewer's yeast, beeswax and agricultural labourers. He had escaped the darkness of the Good Intent Beer-House. If he was in danger of forgetting that, there was always someone on hand to remind him.

This person was the proprietor of the establishment, who waited on customers in the shop. With her shiny red face, which reflected light, her dress of scarlet satin, and sporting a nose which was the very image of a bluebottle, she was herself the epitome of glow. Rebecca Fleckwindsor was a jewel which had at last found its perfect setting.

Six days a week, Angel's Pantry dispensed refreshment to the respectable classes, and the seventh was a day of rest – though Angel's own efforts were, in fact, redoubled on that day. On such a day, in a small back room, where a group of no more than four persons might be privately entertained, Mrs Fleckwindsor took tea with two friends of long standing.

'In the country, a child who does wrong finds himself shunned. Here in London, a child would very quickly starve if he were to do only that which is right.'

'Do let me press you to a cinnamon circle, Mr Blizard. Mr Bradshaw is quite ahead of you on the sultana slices.'

Bradshaw said, 'Even your great Robert Owen admits that the poor have bad and vicious habits, and that they pass these on to their children. Yet he also blames the schools. But most of those here, who beg, steal and swear, have never received schooling of any sort.'

'Kindness and love have an infinite power with children. Both are difficult to give when one is hungry. Punishment and material reward breed envy, lying and false values.'

'More tea? As a mere woman, I have never understood how one can be trained to overcome temptation. One either jumps in wholeheartedly or backs away from it, only to regret one's timidity.'

'If you were rash enough to walk abroad in the Rookery of St Giles or the Nichol, Rebecca, you would not make so light of others' misery. You would see such sights as would turn your stomach. Infants whose only saleable commodity is their own flesh, meagre as it is! Carnal knowledge rife, even among the smallest children, who perform the act on mounds of human excrement!' Bevil Blizard threw down a cake, and slammed his tea-cup into his saucer, as an expression of his own anger and revulsion, embarrassing himself and his two friends.

A silence followed his outburst, during which the lady wafted both real and imaginary crumbs from the red satin of her dress before she spoke. 'So much excitement all around me, and still Mr Bradshaw has not fulfilled his promise to take me to the theatre.'

'You would be shamed, Rebecca.'

'By a few "women of colour"? My stomach is stronger than that, I think, sir. Do you suppose that a sprinkling of once fine girls did not transact their business at Warwick?' Blizard grunted, but Mrs Fleckwindsor was quick to forestall further political comment. 'And pray do not blame the oppression of the poor for a profession which is as old as time itself.'

'It never boasted so many apprentices as now.'

'I am all spirit, Mr Bradshaw, and the spirit requires food as much as the body; if I am to be kept away from the arts, I shall starve. I ask you to remember that I am also a student of human nature, and am not to be confined by the boundaries set by your chapel upbringing. A play is to be viewed by me within the week, and Angel is to be released from that hell-hole of a kitchen and taken for exercise, or we shall both remove our considerable talents to some other worthy cause.' Mrs Fleckwindsor's dress gave up a quantity of real but hitherto hidden crumbs as she stood to add emphasis to her concern.

The 'worthy cause' was, of course, political, and the probability of her departure remote, since the elevation of the Fleckwindsors from a beer-house in the provinces to a metropolitan coffee-house had been engineered by Bradshaw, whose wife she was given out to be, although she did not allow, or he require, the physical familiarities of the married state. Behind the sugar and spices, the vanilla pods and cinnamon, the best-quality flour (unadulterated with chalk), the currants and sultanas, best butter and cream which crammed the storeroom of Angel's Pantry were pamphlets and unstamped newspapers.

Higgledy-piggledy among the accounts and correspondence of the shop were accounts and correspondence of a different sort.

No, she would not move on, but they needed her as much as she needed them, and all three knew it. She must be humoured. Bradshaw said, 'You shall be humoured, my dear. I shall keep my promise.'

Mrs Fleckwindsor placed a comforting hand on the arm of Mr Blizard. 'Do you still seek your son here?' He looked away from her, accusingly at Bradshaw. 'Mr Bradshaw has told me of your sad news from Gloucestershire. There must be no secrets between partners such as ourselves. If I did not know at all times what is happening, I might by accident betray you. I have been grieved, Mr Blizard, to hear of your son; believe that. My question is from concern.'

'I do not seek my son.'

'If he has, as I have been told, left home to find you, it would be reasonable to seek for him here in London.'

'My son is dead.'

Bradshaw said, 'A boy of eight, Rebecca, could not make his way so far alone.'

The Rookery

'Hallelujah!'

'Keep your hands off!'

The naked man pranced around the room, waving his arms towards Cath, while James stood between them, protecting her. The man staggered and lurched, spitting abuse, stepping on many of the sleeping bodies which huddled together on the floor.

'Leave her be, Spider. She's not that sort.' The man's wife beckoned him back towards the corner they shared. Small children screamed as the man trod on them, and their parents lashed out at him with fists and legs. Cath sank down on the mattress, and turned her face to the wall, covering as much of herself as she could with the inadequate strip of leather provided instead of a blanket. The leather did not harbour bugs, but her clothes (in which she slept) did, as did those of James and Boy William, who shared the same straw-filled pallet, and slept at her feet. All three were covered in bites. So far only Boy William had been able to sleep while the bugs filled their bellies.

'Two-faced Wesleyans!'

'Shush, Spider! Come to sleep.'

James sat on the mattress, watching and waiting for the naked man and the other occupants of the room to settle down into sleep. They were not liked here. They must leave soon. Somehow. They knew the city now, had been here ten days. They had come to London because it was the capital, where fortunes were made. It was to have been a step forwards, not back. Here they were to find work, make a new life together, and forget what had happened. How could they have known that so many other people would have had the same idea?

They had walked for hours along wet pavements under a dome of cloud or fog which hid the sky. The frayed streaks of light from the gas-lamps were almost always green, making those who were healthy look ill, and those who were already ill, near death. The fog exaggerated the noise of rattling carriage-wheels and the cries of the street-sellers. They had started or jumped so many times at one or the other, like rabbits on a battlefield. They had dodged the traffic, and clung to each other, while people with money hid themselves in the passing cabs, with handkerchiefs up to their faces. They had caught glimpses of silks, top-hats and jewels, but nothing blocked out the stench of the sewers. Nothing here was like walking through fields. The parks were not for them. Where they were allowed to walk, it seemed to them that they were always being watched. They had stood outside theatres, looking up, terrified at the size of such places. After the big houses, where the rich people lived and visited, St Giles Rookery, with its vegetable stalls and fish-baskets along the pavements, had seemed like a village, except that the buildings had three or four storeys, and the narrow courts, alleys and passages went on for ever, overcrowded, filthy and dangerous. To live every waking moment with your wits about you is tiring. They were tired. They knew London now, knew the capital well. And only wanted to leave it.

When the naked man had settled again beside his wife, Cath felt the leather cover move as James resumed his place beside Boy William at her feet. He would not sleep, although they had walked all day. The town seldom slept. The night was alive with coughing, sobbing, screaming, music and, on rare occasions, laughter. Mrs Blundell had a laugh which echoed. She was the woman to whom they paid fourpence for their share of this room. It was twelve feet by fourteen; Cath had paced it out. Eight other adults and five children shared it with them. Their fourpence paid for one night's use of this corner and the use of the mattress and leather cover. In the far corner, hidden under a pile of rags behind other sleeping bodies, there was an old man who had been dead two days.

Downstairs in the kitchen, Mrs Blundell was celebrating a windfall, assisted by Tommy, Billy, Mouche, Bark, Harris and Mr Flyte. Half a gallon of gin, two penny whistles and an accordion had been brought in. Herrings were being toasted at the smoking fire. Cath could hear comic songs, the louder scraps of an argument about religion, and Mrs Blundell's echoing laugh, drifting up through the floorboards stained with faeces. The singing, screaming, laughing would go on all night. Only a fight might interrupt it now.

The kitchen was black with soot. Steam rose from three flannel shirts which were hanging by the fire to dry, mixed with the smoke from the men's clay pipes, and did nothing to dilute the more noxious smoke which was periodically blown back down the chimney and spread out around the room in a mushroom-shaped cloud. Mr Flyte laid by his quill, and got up to move the steaming shirts, fearing that they might cause the ink of the thirty-seven begging letters he had recently composed to run. His spirits had not yet entered into the celebration. He blamed the emptiness of his glass for this, and also the wet shirts. In addition, a herring-bone had lodged between his teeth, and would not budge.

Small children ran naked, back and forth up and down the stairs. They splashed their feet in the urine they made, and screamed whenever they slid or were tripped by older children. Their eyes were red and sore from fatigue and smoke, but there was music and food and entertainment to cheer them. Bark and Harris were attempting to perform a negro dance. They grabbed the wet shirts, and swung them above their heads, while Mr Flyte protested, and tried to restrain them.

'I have a living to earn, you barbarians.'

'Suppose your nigger dies on you, what's the best time to bury 'im?'

'I shan't suppose.'

'Ain't autumn the best time for blackberrying?'

> *'Oh, come along, you sandy boys,*
> *Oh, come along wi' me.*
> *Oh, come along, you sandy boys.*
> *Ah'm gonna set you free.'*

The news of Mrs Blundell's windfall, though its nature was unspecified, soon got around the Rookery. The gin was smelt, and strangers arrived at the door without pretext, filling the room almost to bursting, and making further dancing impossible. Folk were pressed to sit on the damp stairs, and the smaller of the naked children were lifted, slapped, and thrown from one stranger to another, resembling underfed cherubs and cupids, as their little white limbs flew through the air from one pair of hands to another. Three older children were despatched to fetch more gin. Mrs Blundell's windfall must have been considerable.

'Are you trying to make out that there is three gods, and not just the one?'

'I'm telling you your God ain't mine, that's all.'

'Well, which is the fellow that's supposed to be keeping an eye on us lot in this hell-hole?'

Mrs Blundell lay back across one of the tables, her rusty black dress up over her knees, her legs swinging in time to the music of the penny whistles. The many hands of strangers stroked her thighs in payment for their tots of gin, and were welcomed. A naked infant, crouched over her head, attempted to plait her hair. The windfall she had received was the result of an imaginative piece of blackmail, and she intended that it should change her life. Tomorrow she would stagger out of this nethersken with its dead bodies, never to return. Every week some old fart died on her, owing rent, and she had to make it up. She would quit the Rookery, and move gracefully towards a peaceful retirement and a steady income for life. Sin was wonderful, the more forbidden the better, the more unlawful the more lucrative. Her nose twitched. Had her new-found status, the gentility which would soon be hers, made her nose more sensitive? Years ago she had rid herself of the sense of smell, yet now she could smell something unpleasant. She turned her head sideways, and squinted, just in time to see the naked Irish cherub vomiting half-digested gin and herring into her hair. No matter! Tomorrow, she would squat below the pump in the court before leaving. She would begin her journey clean. Tonight she had other plans. Tonight she was all for sin.

> 'As I one day was a-hawking my wares,
> I thought I'd invent something novel and rare.
> For as I'm not green, and know what's o-clock,
> So I'll have a go in the pineapple rock.
> Tol de rolay! Tol de ro lie! —'

'So I'll have a go in the pineapple rock.' The echo of Mrs Blundell's laugh drifted upwards.

'Everybody has to live somewhere. We're all put here for a purpose, and reason says we should make the best of it.'

'I do, dearie. I do.' Mrs Blundell's sides began to ache from laughing. Sin was wonderful, and imagination even better. 'Put your hands on my person, Billy, and move them with a little more purpose. Tommy, are you asleep? Give some attention, pray, to your hostess and benefactor. She won't be with you for long.'

Billy put up one hand to catch the hair-oil which was running down his chin, placed it back onto the sideburns which were called 'Newgate Knockers', and curled them around his ears, which stuck out almost at right-angles from his narrow high-cheekboned face. He dried his fingers on the crutch of his tight trousers, and then applied those same fingers to the inside of Mrs Blundell's left thigh. Tommy removed the sickly infant from Mrs Blundell's head, threw it across the room to its mother, and then placed a hand within the bodice of Mrs Blundell's rusty black dress. Tommy and Billy were pickpockets. Mrs Blundell hardly felt their fingers.

'Here, Mouche! Lend me one of your hands, to show these boys how not to be so dainty.' Mouche had once been a stonemason, but was now a maker of counterfeit coins.

Upstairs Cath watched those slits in the window which had not been blocked up against the cold, and would consequently let in the light also when it came. She waited for it. The other transients would leave this room during the daytime, to beg for work, or just beg. For the last three days, she had remained, tried to clean their corner and to sleep while the bugs were resting. In the streets, she had fainted twice. The streets frightened her now. She had gone to the kitchens of nineteen hotels, but the doors were always closed, and there were notices which said, 'NO BEGGING. NO HELP.

NO HAWKERS.' At least in Warwick she had been allowed to show herself, to ask politely and be politely refused, and finally she had been taken on to be Cook's Nose.

The two boys had walked the streets during those three days, not knowing what they were looking for, but looking anyway. They had held onto each other for safety, with James's arm over William's shoulder. Once parted, they might search for a lifetime, and never find each other again. Other boys, well used to the streets, jeered at them, laughing at the way they spoke, at their clothes, at their lack of humour. Small gangs sometimes followed them, taunting them to fight or rob. The London fashion for saying everything backwards confused them. Buying a turnip or a loaf of bread daunted them, when a penny was sometimes a 'yennap' and at other times a 'kennuck', a shilling a 'deaner' and a farthing a 'fadge'.

The day broke slowly. There was enough light to see the mass of bodies lying on the floor, men, women and children, arms, legs and heads tangled together, more bare flesh than Cath had ever seen, all white or grey with dirt. None had caught the sun; there was no sun to catch. Someone had removed, not only the pile of rags, but also the clothes from the body of the dead man. His lifeless eyes stared up at the tiles of the roof. Five tiles were missing, and five thin pillars of cold morning light shone down, cutting through the semi-darkness of the room. He would pay no more rent for his share of it.

There was an old hat stuffed between the slats of the window, and she removed it. It was rotted with damp, and came to pieces in her hands. Clothes lines had been strung in zigzags across the alley outside, forming a cat's cradle, from which hung dirty washing. Below it, barefoot children stood about, few of them summoning up the energy to play. Three Irishmen stood, smoking their short pipes, while their women sat huddled together for warmth in a doorway, and slept. Two prostitutes, who had walked the streets all night, slept leaning against the side of a coster's barrow.

Mrs Blundell was propped up against the pump. Her hair, matted and variously coloured, fell forwards over her face. Her rusty black dress was tangled around her ankles. Her undergarments, in which she had kept the windfall, were ripped into tatters, and what remained of the windfall had been taken from them. The tattered undergarments fluttered in the breeze, and hardly covered her ample body. Mrs Blundell's skin, being London skin, was of the London colour, whity-grey, except for her neck, which was purple and black and glistening with hair-oil. On her chin was a thin trickle of blood, running down from her mouth; it had dried to a dark brown. Sin pays wages in its own coin, and even imaginative black-mail seldom comes to good.

Tommy and Billy would be buying the gin tonight. They knew the city well.

'I'm Joey to those what I like, and a right five shillings worth to those what I don't. This here's Mary, my haybag, so don't you go getting no ideas.' He laughed. 'Scuse the familiars, but we could tell that you three was up from the proverbials, and the city ain't that commonly kind to most country folks.'

Heavy rain was now falling. They had stopped to shelter in a doorway. Joey pushed his haybag, Mary, closer to the door, so that all five young people stood tightly pressed together, with their arms by their sides. If Cath and the two boys had had any money left, they would now have been in danger of losing it to Joey, since the close grouping of the five bodies made it hard to be sure whose hands were where, and whose pockets were whose.

The crush was made worse by the haybag's stoop. Mary had practised this stoop, in an attempt to disguise the fact that she was a good foot and a half taller than Joey. Her practice had made perfect; she now leaned forwards permanently. Her hair, always thin and greasy, was now also wet, and it stuck to the sides of her face among the sores and scabs, some of which were bleeding.

'She works round the back of the Haymarket, don't you, bag?' Mary nodded. 'And does it well, if the alley's dark enough. She don't short-change 'em any. Two deaner a night, she can take, when her sores aren't too wet, or we got the flour on us to dry 'em off a bit.' Mary smiled a shy smile, and lifted a dirty hand up to her face, but Joey slapped the hand down again with a little too much violence. 'That's it, bag! Have 'em dripping all over the gentlemen's faces again.' Mary's expression indicated that she was overcome by remorse for having attempted to scratch her nose. 'She don't talk a mouthful, except if a gent tries to give her short. Then it's all Hell, and "Where's my Joey?", ennit, bag?'

Joey was thirteen, and Mary guessed that she might be coming up to eighteen, but wasn't sure. Joey addressed himself almost exclusively to James, whom he took to be the leader of the group, and ignored the others, though he did refer to Cath several times as 'your haybag there' and twice to Boy William as 'that young toff-tickler'. He could tell they were down, he told James, could easily see that they were on their last. He regretted that the city did not make more use of the prodigious talent flooding every day into its mighty hub. But there they were, and that was life.

He had plans for them all, stratagems by which, if they placed themselves at his disposal and did what he required, he would guarantee them riches. He claimed that it was an act of God which had brought them to this doorway, the work of a father, looking out over his children and guiding their steps. Cath was to work the back alleys behind the Haymarket, charging twice as much for her services as Mary, since Cath had the advantage of being free from sores and scabs, and, as far as his expert eye could judge, not yet having fallen a martyr to 'the glim'. Joey explained in a whisper to James that the glim was venereal disease, but James was no wiser for the explanation, and prayed silently for the rain to stop.

Joey intended that James himself should have the honour of working with him, 'flying the blue pigeon', which was the stealing of lead from roofs. 'You'll have to get used to the terms, you lot. How are you to manage, else?' James would also be hired out by Joey as a 'snakesman', as and when required. A snakesman was a boy used in housebreaking to slide in through the smaller windows, which were often left unlocked, and James was of an ideal build for this task, which would require no special skill, but only a little instruction from Joey, who was experienced in the craft himself, and had also been in prison three times and there consulted with other snakesmen.

As for Boy William, it was clear that Joey regarded him as the jewel amongst them, the one who would bring them real riches; the glint in Joey's eyes grew larger as he turned them towards the little toff-tickler. Dressed out at Joey's own expense, Boy William would be sent out into the more fashionable streets to tease and tickle money out of the toffs. 'Gents and ladies will shower that little 'un with yennaps, deaner, even fasme, if they was moderately drink-taken. I knows what the gentlemen like, believe me. I knows where these type-a toffs lives in their toffkens. I knows when they takes their walks, and where a tasty young snipe should stand to step out and tickle 'em for a good meal. Dozens of good meals. They doesn't like to see too much suffering, you know; they likes their beggars to look healthy and someways attractive. It's no good trying it, if you're all skin and grizzle, but if you've got that hair and those there eyes, and you looks a-cleanish like, why your fortune's near half readymade. A young snipe like this could find his own benefactor. Good hair, good skin. Them bites will go down when we gets a little fresh air on 'em. What's his chest like?'

Since neither Cath nor James could see the point of the question, or know whether it referred to the inward or outward condition of Boy William's chest, neither of which they felt able to describe anyway, they remained silent.

Huddled together as they were, it was not easy for him to do so, but Joey managed to lean forward, and ripped open Boy William's shirt. 'Oh, yes. Oh, very nice! I think we should start him off in a bit of shallow, don't you, bag?'

Mary nodded approvingly at the sight of Boy William's chest. 'Shallow' was a term with which even Boy William was acquainted. It meant begging, half-naked. He shivered at the thought of it, rebuttoned his shirt as best he could, counted three, inhaling deeply, glanced first at Cath and then at James, and dived between Joey and Mary, making as much speed along Tottenham Court Road as his legs would muster.

James followed, pulling Cath after him. Joey pursued for a while, but was hampered by Mary, who had spotted a likely customer.

When all three were safely away, and had stopped to get their breath, Boy William broached a subject which had been on his mind for some time, but which, fearing James's disapproval, he had not dared to mention before, but now, when they had no money, and nowhere to stay, and danger lurked in every doorway (and it was raining), seemed to be the time to mention it. The man who smelled of almonds had mentioned a Mrs Crabtree of 71, Philbeach Gardens, and had instructed Boy William not to forget that name and address. It had been clear that Mrs Crabtree would provide shelter, and might have work for Boy William, and perhaps for Cath and James as well. Although nothing said by the man smelling of almonds could be trusted, what had they to lose by going to Philbeach Gardens, and finding out?

Mrs Crabtree

Perhaps because there was so little light in the streets of the city, and what there was seemed to uglify what it illuminated, within the homes of those who could afford it, light was cherished, mantled in translucent globes or shades of soft and flattering colours, reflected from mirrors and surfaces daily polished, the character of the light itself an expression of the characters of those who cherished it. Angel's Pantry glowed. Everything about Mrs Crabtree twinkled. The front doorstep of her house, which was burnished every day with emery stone, twinkled. The brass poker and firedogs, the cut-glass candelabra, gilt-framed mirrors and bronze equestrian figures, all twinkled.

'So you are the young man who was told to shake my hand?' Boy William had been told that he was to sit tight on that bottom of his before he shook Mrs Crabtree's hand, but, although he was not sure what this part of the instruction signified, he had guessed that it would not be wise to mention it to the servant girl, who had looked at him curiously, and gone off to inform her mistress of his arrival. All three had been allowed in, since it was clear that they would not enter unless they were, and found Mrs Crabtree waiting for them in the drawing-room. She extended a hand for Boy William to approach and shake, and he did. From the moment he had felt the soft thick pile of the carpet tickling the soles of his feet through the holes in his boots, he had known that whatever this lady required of him, he would do, if only in return he were to be allowed to remove his boots and spread his toes into carpet such as this.

'Tea, I think, Veronica, and lots to eat. I'm sure that would be welcomed, don't you?' The maid went for tea, and Mrs Crabtree twinkled at each of her visitors in turn, and received from each a shy nod of the head.

'Come now, all of you, do sit down.' She turned away, allowing them time to take in the seating arrangements and to speculate where their dirty clothes would do least harm. She was a small jolly woman, and seemed to be in her late forties. The colour and texture of her skin and the clearness of her grey eyes were evidence of the good health she enjoyed. Her hair, which shone even more than her skin, had been parted in the middle, and collected into two neat round buns, one covering each ear. Her full dress was black, in contrast to the brightness of the room, and, hanging below the large white puritan collar, was a gentleman's half-hunter watch on a gold chain.

'Feed the body, and watch the soul rejoice.' Everywhere they looked, there was evidence of wealth and comfort. They had stepped from the cold and dirty street into a palace of warmth and colour, the second dazzling their eyes, and the first seeping in through their clothing to make a drowsy pleasure. They were safe now, had found a friend, were to be fed on more than stale bread and turnips. Their fears had been groundless.

Boy William, knowing that, whatever else he did, he must stay awake, had chosen a stool as a seat. It was a cross-frame black and gilt stool, decorated with the carved heads of four leopards, each with a purple tassel hanging from its neck. The legs of the stool resembled a leopard's legs, but there were only four, and they pointed in different directions. Was it one leopard with four heads or four leopards with only one leg each? His fingers toyed with the silk tassels, while his boots moved back and forwards so that the soles of his feet could enjoy the carpet, and a part of his mind tried to decide about the leopard.

Small triangles of bread had been spread with butter, and thin slices of meat or cheese had been placed between them. There were cakes and pastries of different kinds, piled high on a three-tiered cakestand. Most of the paintings on the walls were portraits of children in various unlikely costumes, all smiling and showing a great many teeth. Perhaps they were allowed to walk around barefoot on the carpet and eat food like this every day.

Mrs Crabtree spoke in a low gentle voice which expressed concern, sympathy, reassurance, and above all interest. It enquired whether her three visitors were members of the same family. It asked particularly about Boy William's parents and their whereabouts. It wondered how long the three of them had been in London, and what had happened to them before they arrived. Cath answered all these questions honestly, with some help from James, between mouthfuls of food and gulps of sweet tea, and Mrs Crabtree listened, smiling and nodding, closing her eyes and sighing to indicate her sympathy at the deaths of Cath's baby and Miss Lentloe.

When the tale was done, Mrs Crabtree spoke, and her words seemed to be mixed with the warmth of the fire, adding to their feeling of well-being. They were poor, poor children, set down in a city which was too cruel to the innocent and too kind to the wicked. They had been lucky to escape from the Rookery of St Giles with their lives. It was her wish and her intention to make sure that they never had to go back there.

'Now, as to the charitable work in which I concern myself, I must tell you, my dears, that we are supported by several rich families, who have the kindness to consider that what we do is of singular benefit to mankind. We cannot, of course, accept every young person who applies to us, but those we do accept never look back. That is our boast, my dears. Once inside the bosom of our little family, they never look back. I recall one child, who had been deserted by his mother, being brought to my door in the middle of the night. His only possession was one foul-smelling blanket. We took that child in. We taught him to be clean in mind and in his habits. Now he travels the world as personal servant to a duke.'

A large globe of the world was supported in a circular frame with three legs. The surface of the world had been painted in clear lacquer, and reflected light. It shone. It was singularly unlike the world they had left outside.

'Is it not a sad state of affairs, my dears, when here you are, three young people with no parents or guardians to love and protect you, while so many of my wealthy friends and patrons are kind and generous, but have no children? Happiness has sometimes to be arranged. Very seldom does it drop out of the sky; it has to be worked at. That, in a word, is our work here, and very rewarding work it is.'

Mrs Crabtree's grey eyes twinkled as she glanced round her parlour. Above the fire, on the mantelpiece of pink marble, a small gilt clock ticked quietly. It was supported by two gilt cherubs, and protected from dust by a glass dome. The time was twenty-three minutes past seven.

They had stood in the street outside, and had argued and debated for almost an hour, as afternoon had slipped into evening, and the darkness grew around them. James had noticed one of the curtains move. They were being watched; his suspicions had grown. Nothing which came from the almond-man could be good. He had feared all sorts of things, but mostly there was a fear he could not understand or describe. He had made them swear that they would not be parted. They had taken an oath, all three, to stay together, whatever happened. No harm could come to Boy William if he and Cath were with him.

Now those fears seemed nonsensical. Everything was so reasonable. They were children without parents. He had simply never considered that there might be parents without children, who were willing, even eager, according to Mrs Crabtree, to remedy that state.

'It is simply a matter of making the bettermost of oneself. Never be sullen. Sullenness will not win a friend. Health! That is important too, of course. I walk five miles every day, and expect my pupils to do the same, regardless of age. We traverse Hyde Park. If the ground is not too wet, we do our exercises there, and bring our voices forward; the welkin rings. No one wants a sickly child; that would be unreasonable. Smiling is most important. We smile with our mouths open if we have good straight white teeth, and we learn to smile with our mouths closed should our teeth be less than good. We do not chatter, but speak when we are spoken to. And we never use street terms. Street terms give us away. They let us down. Trousers are trousers, and not "kelks". Bread is bread, and never "scran". And eyes as pretty as yours, Boy William, are not to be referred to as "ogles".' Boy William blushed, as Mrs Crabtree continued to twinkle. She was clearly a lady with a sense of humour; one expects that in a friend. 'Nor are those pieces of old leather with which you are wearing a hole in my carpet to be called "gallies". They are boots, and I believe that your feet would welcome a new pair. A gentleman does not use street terms, and if you place yourself in my hands, a gentleman is what we shall endeavour to make of you. Those of my past students who are now no longer children have found that the grounding in manners and etiquette which they have received at this establishment has enabled them to secure financially rewarding positions in later life. Obedience and the desire to make the best of yourself is all I ask.'

All this was directed to Boy William, who tried to keep his eyes open and to return Mrs Crabtree's friendly gaze, but who felt more comfortable with his eyes lowered, watching the gold half-hunter, which twinkled as she turned it between her fingers. 'We shall overcome your natural shyness,' she said, 'though without pushing you into a pert forwardness, which is far more *mal vu* by genteel people. I believe that we shall easily gain you a position with a rich benefactor, a dear dear friend of mine, a father without a son until this moment.'

There was a moment's silence, save for the quiet tick of the gilt clock, and then James coughed. Mrs Crabtree turned towards him, and smiled.

'Boy William will be preferred, simply by being the youngest. You two will need a little more patience, and I am sure you have it.' She turned to Cath. 'You, dear young lady, shall have a place within a week or two. I have in mind a family which will open their arms to you, and say "Welcome!" You are not afraid of honest work, I am sure, if it be within a considerate and Christian home.' She indicated James. 'Am I right in believing that this young man is intelligent beyond his education?' Cath and Boy William both nodded firmly to indicate that she was correct in her belief. 'I thought as much by his frown. But frowning gives us lines before our time, James. Please smile for me.' James attempted a smile, and Mrs Crabtree appraised it. 'Yes. Much better. Make the bettermost of yourself. You will require a little more thought than the others; we do not wish to waste your talents. Talent is never wasted here.' She rose from her chair, crossing to Boy William, ruffled his hair, then lifted his head to face her, and tickled him under his chin. 'Those eyes will be your fortune, Boy William.'

Mrs Crabtree tugged at a purple tassel hanging by the fireplace, and a servant's bell was heard somewhere within the house. James looked at Cath. There was desperation in his eyes. Cath stood, and explained to Mrs Crabtree, as firmly as she could, that they were not to be separated; they had taken an oath.

'Oh, my dears, how touching and how friendly! I quite understand. Nor shall you be parted, except for the shortest time. But, you see, I have no accommodation for the two of you at present, and we must act quickly. The childless couple I have in mind may find some other young person to reward with their patronage. For William's sake, we must act now; I am about to send a message this very minute. And William can hardly meet them with holes in his boots and quite so much dirt about him.'

She gave Cath a shilling from her purse, and told them both to call at tea-time the following day for news. They were shown out of the room by Veronica, who was a white negress, with thin carrot-coloured hair beneath her lace cap. Veronica's thick lips stretched wide in the smile she had been taught to show off her straight white teeth.

They had been separated. Boy William, left behind, lay in a bath prepared for him by Veronica. The water smelled of almond oil, and the surface of it twinkled.

They had not intended to return to the same nethersken. The shilling from Mrs Crabtree was enough for two nights' lodging as well as food for the next day. Perhaps they should find a better lodging for the night, and pay more.

They were tired, and the effect of Mrs Crabtree's fire and the food she had given them had added to their tiredness. They walked in a daze, holding onto each other for safety, not speaking of what had passed or of their oath, already broken.

Black smoke hung low over the roofs and chimneys, hiding the moon. Every few yards, some man, woman or child would step out of the darkness of a doorway, and stand in their way, or walk backwards in front of them, asking them where they were going, offering them a bed. Hands were held out to them, childish fingers wriggled, offering love, companionship, comfort, sympathy for only a few pennies. The faces offering these commodities stared hard into theirs, coaxing, pleading, threatening. They were green faces, made so by reflected gaslight. Every doorway contained at least one shape, sometimes several, sometimes two shapes coupled into one. In the stillness brought about by the occasional passing of a cab, a single voice would call obscenities across the street to another voice which would reply with even greater profanity.

Their only safety was in movement, purposeful and unhurried. If they ran, they would be chased, and if they stopped, that would be taken as acceptance of whatever was being offered.

As they walked through the Seven Dials, still clutching each other and pacing their strides, the clock of St Giles church struck eleven times. This was their capital city after dark. They had almost reached 'the holy land', the Rookery which they had quitted so eagerly that very morning.

Mrs Blundell's body had been removed from below the pump. Money was now to be handed over to Mr Flyte, who had appointed himself temporary lodging-house keeper. The owner of the tenement, a gentleman farmer residing near St Albans, had not yet been informed of the vacancy caused by Mrs Blundell's demise.

Cath and James sat down in the kitchen awhile to warm themselves, and listened to the talk. Four policemen had entered the Rookery at midday, and had asked questions but been given no answers. They had stood with their shoulders touching for safety, each facing a different point of the compass. In this position, they had been an easy target for the woman who had leaned out of an upstairs window and emptied a bucket of slops over their heads.

The sound of a gentleman's walking-stick tapping against the outside of the door brought the laughter which had followed the story of the four policemen to an abrupt end. Mr Flyte rose from his chair to peer through a crack in the door, then turned back into the room, and indicated with violent waves of his hands that everyone except Mouche and himself should go upstairs.

Cath stood at the window of the room she had left that morning, looking down through the gap in the slats towards the pump and the darkness which surrounded it. The corner in which the three of them had previously slept was now occupied by an Irish family. What little she could see of the men in the court below were only shapes, but the shapes had voices. She listened to the voices, and recognised each in turn.

'Is it wise to speak freely out here?'

'As wise as anywhere.'

'If you are the man who has been recommended to me, you can be trusted with coins.'

'I have an interest in coins, yes. In certain coins. Do you speak of large coins? Heavy?'

'Of the correct weight, we should hope.'

'Am I to take a small coin from you, and return to you a larger one?'

'Much larger, at least in value, and perfect in every respect. It would be delivered here at this hour three nights from now. If it serves, we shall need many more.' This was the voice of a man who had once said to her, 'It grieves me to tell you that he is to be hanged on the hill where the fire was started, three days from now.'

'Where shall these large but perfect coins be used?'

'In the north, by men like yourself, who need them.'

'Like myself?'

'Working men.'

'Politics, is it?'

'Tell me what is not politics.'

'And how will they get there?'

'That is for us to decide.'

'No, sir, I beg to differ. I have been under suspicion before. If it falls again, and falls right, I am the one who will pay the penalty. How will they travel?'

'In a cake.' Angel giggled; his nervousness could be restrained no longer. He wished he had remained at home, in the warm kitchen of Angel's Pantry. '*If you take rid away from Reginald, you're left with the correct letters to form an Angel.*'

Mouche took a great deal more persuading that his counterfeit coins would travel safely from the city and then north, but an agreement was finally reached. A spark flew up from the tobacco loosely packed in his clay pipe, and Cath thought she saw the glint of a small round piece of glass, such as might have been used in a telescope, now held over a roughly drawn map.

'We wasted hours trying to find you in this warren. What is the safest and the quickest way out?' Once Bevil Blizard had used just such a piece of glass in the upper room of the Crown at Otmoor. He had turned it between his fingers, and said, 'But the grass where you were was dry, and the sun very strong.'

Mr Vellacot was a gentleman in his late fifties. He sat on the edge of his seat in Mrs Crabtree's drawing-room, with his back erect, a silk muffler concealing the lower part of his face. His well-tailored clothes were a little old-fashioned, which accentuated the barrel shape of his chest and the narrowness of his waist, and gave him the outline of a pouter pigeon. His eyes, above the muffler, were pale-blue and a little frightened, and what hair he had was turning to silver. When he spoke, which was after a considerable time, Boy William could only just make out what was said. That was partly because of the muffler, and partly because it was Mr Vellacot's habit to speak almost in a whisper.

'What age is he?'

'Eleven years old. I'm sure that is true, in this case.'

'Is he not cold, dressed like that?' It was after midnight, and Boy William had been brought from his bed wearing only his newly acquired nightshirt.

'He's a country boy, are you not, William? They do not feel the cold like city-dwellers.'

'Yes. There's a fog outside.' Mr Vellacot adjusted his muffler. In fact, the whole evening had been free from fog, but he required an excuse for his disguise. 'It is unwholesome for the lungs. Do you experience much fog in the country, William?'

William shook his head. Mrs Crabtree waited for a moment, and then said, 'I think both Mr Vellacot and myself are waiting to hear you speak, William. May I ask you to make some contribution to the conversation? Voices are so important.'

'I don't care for rough talk.' Mr Vellacot's muffler slipped, and required attention.

'Neither do we, eh, William?' William shook his head. 'The boy is a devout Christian like yourself, Mr Vellacot. One would not expect him to swear, use street terms, or ruderies,

199

and I am sure that, indeed, he knows none to use, do you, William?'

William shook his head again. This time the silence which followed was protracted. William decided that the sofa on which the gentleman sat was like a boat without sides, except that it had lions' feet. The gentleman beckoned to him, by crooking and straightening the index finger of his white hand, which was encased, like its fellow, in white gloves. William looked to Mrs Crabtree for instructions, and she twinkled at him, and nodded. He stood, and crossed the carpet slowly to Mr Vellacot.

From the pocket of his old-fashioned coat, Mr Vellacot produced a piece of barley sugar, with a light coating of fluff. He took Boy William's hand in his own, and placed the sweet in the boy's palm.

'What do you say, William?'

'Thank you, sir.' Mrs Crabtree relaxed. Speech had been achieved.

'It's a present.' The nearer one got to him, it seemed, the quieter Mr Vellacot's voice became.

'Yes, sir.'

'The first of many.'

'Thank you, sir.'

'He speaks well. A good boy, I think.' Mr Vellacot turned towards Mrs Crabtree, who was rocking with pleasure. 'I particularly approve the way he doesn't devour the sweet at once. He's saving it, aren't you? Thinking of future pleasure, aren't you?'

'Yes, sir.' Boy William allowed himself an open-mouthed smile. His teeth were white, and reasonably straight. If he were allowed a moment's privacy, he would wipe the barley sugar on his nightshirt.

'And a smile! My goodness! He smiled, madam. That's a very good beginning. He smiled at me, did you see that?' The lines at the edge of Mr Vellacot's eyes moved closer together. Though his own teeth were neither white nor straight, and were in any case concealed by the muffler, he too was smiling. 'Dress him. I'll take him with me.'

Mrs Crabtree laughed her gentle mocking laugh. Her mockery was always friendly, never malicious; no one could take offence. 'That is not possible, I'm afraid, sir. What would my patrons think?'

'There is not to be an auction, is there? I shan't participate, madam. That would be insulting.'

'How can you think of such a thing, Mr Vellacot? But I must insist on a trial period, for your own sake as much as the boy's. Certain matters must be attended to.'

'Procedures?' There was a fatalistic tone in Mr Vellacot's voice, and as he nodded, his muffler slipped.

'Yes, sir, procedures. However I assure you that you have no competitors . . . at present. William, why not shake Mr Vellacot's hand before you return to your bed?'

Mrs Crabtree placed an arm over Boy William's shoulder, and left the room with him. Outside she whispered that Mr Vellacot was not Mr Vellacot, but a duke in disguise.

Veronica was waiting on the landing. Her teeth were very white; he could see them, arranged in a smile, even from the bottom of the stairs. She took him into the bedroom he shared with four other boys, and left him, locking the door.

Separate Ways

'Do tidy Clarinda's hair, and stop Andrew's nose from running.' There were eight children altogether, standing before Mrs Crabtree in her drawing-room. She had placed them in two neat lines, the smallest in the front. In so far as they could, they stood up straight, as instructed, and tried to look proud of themselves.

In Mrs Crabtree's hand was a list, and as she inspected the double line, she would glance at the list, and peer closely at each child, as if stock-taking. This was the list:

Joyce Pimlett. Bolton, Lancashire. Dark-brown hair, green eyes. Age nine.

Eunice Newcomb. Devon. Fair hair, blue eyes. Age eight.

Clarinda Jepson. Nottingham. Black hair, grey-green eyes. Age eleven.

Andrew Salt. Staffordshire. Fair hair, blue eyes. Age seven.

Dunstan Apperley. Gloucestershire. Brown hair, hazel eyes. Age eight.

Nicholas McGuire. Dumfries. Red hair, grey eyes, freckles. Age nine.

Barnaby Semple. Poole. Black hair, blue eyes. Age twelve.

Certain names had been crossed off the list, some ruled out with a blue line, and some with a red. One name was newly added:

William Shiltern. Oxfordshire. Blonde hair, amber eyes. Age eleven.

'Barnaby, will you hand out the hymn sheets?' Boy William became perturbed. His teeth, eyes, hair, the tone of his voice and his avoidance of street terms had all passed muster, but was he expected to read? He noticed that Nicholas, the little red-haired Scottish boy who had been placed in front of him, seemed to have difficulty in telling which way up his hymn sheet should be held, and felt reassured. Mrs Crabtree helped Nicholas. 'Now, children, you will all listen to Barnaby, who has a most beautiful singing voice, and try to follow the words on the page. In that way, you may pick out one or two, and remember what they look like.' She gave a nod, and Barnaby began to sing the twenty-third psalm.

> *'The Lord's my Shepherd. I'll not want.*
> *He makes me down to lie.*
> *In pastures green He leadeth me,*
> *The quiet waters by.*
> *My soul He doth restore again,*
> *And me to walk doth make*
> *Within the paths of righteousness,*
> *E'n for His own name's sake.*
>
> *Goodness and mercy all my –'*

'Thank you, Barnaby. One verse will do this morning. Very melodious, dear! What that means, children, is that God will look after you. He will provide. But I have decided to give Him a little help.' Mrs Crabtree now referred to another sheet of paper, on which she had made some notes. 'Uncle Quilter is collecting you at nine, Nicholas. Will you be clean and tidy for him by then?'

Nicholas nodded. Boy William decided that cinnamon was the colour of Nicholas's freckles. He had been given cinnamon toast on two occasions by Miss Lentloe, and remembered the colour with pleasure. Perhaps there would be cinnamon toast here.

'And what will be your topic of conversation, Nicholas, should he wish you to amuse him?'

Nicholas' facial expression indicated that he found thinking of answers to questions of this sort painful. 'The weather, miss.'

'No, Nicholas. You did the weather on Thursday last. May I suggest that you remember all you possibly can about your visit to the seaside. Express the pleasure it gave you, and indicate your desire to go there again. Yes, dear, I know it was cold, and that lobster doesn't agree with you, but try to remember how much pleasure Uncle Quilter got. Try also to draw his attention to your jacket, which has given of its best. And above all, please try to remember that this is Uncle Quilter, and not Uncle Corcoran. That was last month, and quite a different gentleman.'

Mrs Crabtree smiled her full, open-mouthed smile at Nicholas, who, knowing his cue, practised his own smile back at her. 'Good boy! Now, Joyce, when Uncle Simon arrives at eleven, you are to be unwell with a headache. I wish to speak to him about your allowance, which has become insufficient for your needs. If we should reach a satisfactory agreement, I shall expect your headache to pass away quite quickly.'

Joyce, holding out her dress, gave a full curtsey, and practised her smile. 'Very nice, dear, but keep the lips together. Dunstan! Head up, child! Pay attention! A gentleman by the name of Hensbridge is arriving to meet you at four. We shall have tea in here, and you will wear your suit, and will refrain from scratching yourself, or wiping your nose on anything but your handkerchief. Mr Hensbridge is a farmer, and you are from Gloucestershire; you should have much in common. I shall, in any case, consult my little library, and you will have learned the principal agricultural products of that county by early afternoon, so that you will be able to tell Mr Hensbridge. You may also borrow those wooden animals of Andrew's to bring down with you and impress. This, Dunstan, is to be your last chance to impress and be preferred. If Mr Hensbridge finds you to be as tiresome and as unco-operative a little boy as I do, you will be taken by cab at nightfall to a distant part of the city, and left there, wearing the clothes in which you arrived here. And as for preparation for your new life, should Mr Hensbridge reject you, you will eat neither breakfast nor luncheon. You know, children, do you not, that once I have decided, I never change my mind?' The children nodded seriously. They knew. Mrs Crabtree twinkled at Dunstan. 'So, hold up your head, child. Practise your smile, and let us see what tea-time may bring.'

Eight-year-old Dunstan Apperley wiped his eyes with a

clean handkerchief, lifted his head slowly, and showed Mrs Crabtree his straight white teeth.

'If Dunstan fails again, Mr Hensbridge may also wish to meet you, Andrew, in which case you will draw his attention to the stuffed badger in the library. Eunice Newcomb, have you stopped crying now? Good girl! Veronica did not intend to hurt your head, but you really must learn not to get plum preserve matted into your beautiful hair; it is a woman's crowning glory. Lady Sturton wishes us to take luncheon with her today. Can I trust you not to fall asleep?'

Eunice curtseyed and smiled, and Mrs Crabtree took this for an affirmative answer. 'The rest of you will remain upstairs until Veronica is free to take you for your walk. Barnaby, I am relying on you to help with the younger children until Lord Francomb arrives for you at eight this evening. It may be as well for you to sleep for a while this afternoon, so as not to tire too quickly. I am delighted at the way you and he are progressing, but don't drink too much port wine again, will you? And please remind him about your singing lessons. That poor teacher cannot live on promises. Clarinda, stay behind. I wish to discuss Mr Hartley Cooper's recent behaviour towards you.'

Mrs Crabtree stepped back in order to address her audience in general. 'Very well! And what are we going to do with this lovely day the Lord has given us?'

All the children, including Dunstan but excluding Boy William who did not know the answer, spoke in unison. 'Make the bettermost of ourselves.'

'Quite right! Off you go! You too, William! Off to breakfast! I think we may rest assured that Mr Vellacot will return very soon. Eat slowly, chew every mouthful thirty times, and remember where it comes from. Spare a thought for the poor souls in the Marylebone Workhouse, with logs tied to their legs, and no snuff to bring them comfort.'

The 'procedures' concerning Boy William's adoption by Mr Vellacot were proceeding. The only point which had not yet been agreed was the amount of settlement to be paid to Mrs Crabtree. The good lady explained that if, for any reason, the arrangement should prove unsatisfactory, and Boy William were to be returned to her, his chances of finding a second adoptive parent would be considerably hampered. She was asking two hundred pounds, and Mr Vellacot was reluctant to pay more than half that amount.

As directed, Cath and James returned to Mrs Crabtree's house later that day. On the first occasion they called, Veronica explained that Boy William was out, shopping for clothes. On the second, he was visiting a prospective benefactor, and on the third, he had been taken to a museum.

On the following day, they returned, and this time were received by Mrs Crabtree, who apologised energetically. She explained that William was such a great success that his appointments book was full almost to overflowing. Cath asked if she might see him. Mrs Crabtree twinkled, as she pulled the purple tassel by the fireplace.

Boy William came into the drawing-room, and was hardly recognised by his friends. He wore a complete set of new clothes. His shiny new boots no longer allowed the soles of his feet to be tickled by the carpet. His hair had been cut, and his skin was cleaner than either Cath or James could ever remember having seen it. Such attention had been paid to his fingernails that, without the dark line at the end of each, it was hard even for Boy William to believe that they, and the fingers from which they grew, were his, so he hid one hand within the other, and both behind his back. Cath and James assumed that this new posture was one of those prescribed by Mrs Crabtree as a step towards gentility.

More tea and cakes were brought. Another shilling was given 'to tide them over'. Cath watched Boy William clumsily handling his cup and saucer, and trying to eat a cake without extending his fingers, until finally she placed her own cup in its saucer, took a deep breath, and asked him in a clear strong voice if he was happy with the new arrangements, or wished to be taken away.

Boy William looked first at Mrs Crabtree, then at James, and, finally turning to Cath, replied that he was all right, but wished to know where they were staying, in case he failed to impress and be preferred. James assured him that they would visit every day, and wait in the street if he were otherwise engaged.

'My dears, what trouble you take, and how touching it is

that you should care so for one another. But I don't believe that
William is the sort of boy to forget his friends. Furthermore he
has already made the deepest impression on a rich and titled
person, and I am confident he will be preferred.'

The next day, they were admitted at once, and found another
woman with Mrs Crabtree in the drawing-room. She was
introduced as Mrs Harris, the proprietor of an Agency for
supplying gentlefolk with domestic servants.

'My good friend, Mrs Harris, has offered to assist you to a
situation, Cath, is that not kind? James may stay here for a few
days if he wishes to sleep in William's bed, and will submit to
having a bath first. Our young gentleman of prospects has been
taken to Brighton for a few days by that titled gentleman of
whom I spoke. I am sure he will be spoiled to pieces.'

The Agency was situated in Bishop's Road, Paddington. In
the cab, Mrs Harris removed her hat, unbuttoned her dress,
loosened several undergarments, and scratched herself. It
seemed to Cath that a woman who had to do with gentlefolk
ought not to suffer from the bites of bugs, but she bore herself
in patience.

'We are a very small affair, my dear. If you get too large, you
can't keep your standards high, and standards are what our
gentlefolks likes. Having managed to get this high with the
standards, I intends for to keep them up. Churches and
charities give us clothes. They all know us for our standards.'
The accents of Mrs Harris were not as refined as those of Mrs
Crabtree, nor, however high she kept her standards, was her
diction as elevated.

Above the door at which the cab stopped was the name of
the Agency, with the words, 'High standards are our principle
consern' written underneath, but Mrs Harris steered Cath to
another door, smaller and less impressive, around the corner.

'I'm to sleep in here with you, and show you what's required.
Put you up to one or two tricks like, to play on the gentlemen.
And the first rule is to do nothing until they pays.'

The speaker was a young man in a gentleman's ruffled shirt
(which did not quite fit him) and very tight trousers. He locked
the door by which he had just entered, and put the key away in

a pocket of those trousers. Then he advanced towards her, with one hand held out in greeting.

'I'm Henry. Howjer do? I'm eighteen, I've been at it three years, so I knows what's what. I tells the girls that straight off first thing, 'cos some of them thinks I'm a bit young.' Bemused, Cath shook the offered hand. 'It's not bad work, as work goes, but it do make you sleepy. I'm a sleeper myself, more than anything. Sometimes I sleep when I'm awake. I don't feel the pain when I'm asleep, you see.'

He was already sitting on the side of the bed, removing his boots. It was a nightmare, yet another mistake. She had climbed three flights of stairs behind Mrs Harris, and at any point she could have run away. But the woman had said, 'Later I shall find you a white pinafore and a stuff dress, but in the meantime you'll have to try on what we've got, while I burn those dirty clothes, which are lousy, I shouldn't wonder.' Once in the room, she had been handed a bright red dress of thin shiny material, and told to change. She had asked for under-garments, and the woman had laughed, saying, 'You ain't going to church, dear.' She had asked for water to wash, and the woman had shrugged her shoulders, and pointed to a bowl containing grey-green water with dust floating on top. Then the woman had left the room, locking it behind her. Cath had been alone for hours. Until now.

Henry had taken off his boots, and was squeezing himself, inch by inch, out of the tight trousers. 'They splits so easy if you gets reckless with them.' She was staring at him. He noticed, and patted her knee. 'It's like a family here. You'll like it, once you're in.'

The trousers were round his ankles. He rested for a moment to regain his breath, and rubbed a hand over the lower half of his stomach. 'Couldn't half do with a good sleep right now. My guts giving me hell, something awful. Sharp pain here.' He lifted his shirt, and pointed to his appendix. 'You ever had it?'

Cath shook her head, then left the bed to look out of the window. She was not foolish, and could guess well enough what tricks Henry had come to teach her, but they did not seem to have much to do with desire. Meanwhile he continued with his undressing. 'I looks after all the girls here, and another twenty in Lombard Street. There's not many as wants knocking about, but the one or two which has a taste for it, they wants a lot of it, so that plays me up. It's mostly their fathers to blame. They've been given what-for at home, and when they gets here, they feels neglected.' He was now lying on the bed, completely naked, still holding his stomach where the pain was.

What would happen to James? What was happening to Boy William in Brighton? Clearly Mrs Crabtree was a faithless woman, tricking them all for her own unfathomable purposes. 'Come over here, girl. I'm not a wild beast, neither is you a virgin, is you? After I've shown you what-for, we can have a bit of a sleep, see, before Harris comes banging the door down.'

Cath crossed to the bed, and sat beside him. She removed his hand from his stomach, and replaced it with her own, moving the fingers gently over the spot where he had said the pain was.

'That's very good, girl. Very nice and friendly, that is; you do it very well.' His head relaxed, and his eyes closed, and she gently rubbed and soothed away the pain. The Newgate Knockers which covered most of the sides of his face glistened with oil, as Tommy's and Billy's had done on the night they killed Mrs Blundell. But Henry was a sleeper, and within five minutes, he was snoring to prove it.

'Where did you find her?'
'Crabtree's.'
'Bit old for the Children's Farm, ain't she?'
Cath was standing by the fire with a pan, trying to heat some water with which to wash.

'Hey, you! Do those poor little mites still lose their virginity every week to their wicked uncles?' The woman asking the question rolled about with laughter. 'That Crabtree should be on the stage.'

The kitchen was cluttered with women of various shapes and sizes, all lounging with their limbs sprawled akimbo, their hair loose or tangled. The smell of cheap perfume, of female body odour and of exhaled gin fumes quite masked any scent of cooking there might have been. Apart from Harris, only two women were fully dressed. One of these was Milly, a dumpy woman in her late twenties, who wore six layers of clothing, topped by a man's greatcoat, so as to be adequately muffled against the cold. The other wore the uniform of a parlour-maid, just in case any gentleperson should be misguided enough as to ring the Agency's bell. No domestic servant was ever supplied from these premises, but deposits for their supply were sometimes taken, and excuses then given until the would-be employers grew tired, and sought help elsewhere.

The heat in the room was already oppressive, but a drunken girl of twelve elbowed Cath away from the fire in order to put more coal on. The girl was shivering. 'We has to keep warm. The nights is cold enough. Wait till you've stood half-naked in a doorway all night.' The girl leaned over the fire, staring into it, and speaking to Cath from the corner of her mouth. 'It's not the sin of it that worries me. Daren't think of that much. It's what else I might have missed.' The rims of her eyes were red. 'It's a brutal sort of life, this. If you sees a chance, take it.'

It was clear to Cath that asking for her own clothes back would be of no use. That would alarm Harris, and Henry would be summoned to do his job more thoroughly. If she were to be sent out onto the streets, she might escape.

To her surprise, she was issued with two flimsy petticoats 'for decency's sake', a straw hat ornamented with white feathers, blue ribbons and red paper flowers, a pair of gloves, a bag in which to keep money (when she received some), a pair of shoes two sizes too large, and a hank of false hair in the form of ringlets, the nearest shade to the colour of her own hair as could be found.

After a meal of bread, dripping and sweet tea, to give her the energy to last the night, and wearing the red dress and its accessories, Cath left the Agency in Bishop's Road, Paddington, followed at a less than discreet distance by Milly, half-walking, half-running on her dumpy legs, and shouting for all the world to hear, 'Where are you off to? Don't walk so fast. How can they sees you proper if you moves like a coach and four? Saunter and smile. Make the bettermost of yourself. You looks as if a swarm of bees is after you.'

With a supreme effort of will, and a turn of speed usually reserved only for extreme emergencies, Milly caught up with Cath, and held onto the skirt of her dress while instructions were given.

'Never go into the Inns of Court. Jump out of the cab, or throw yourself into the river first, but do not go into the

Temple. It's unspeakable what happens to those young men when they gets a good class of woman in there. Now Harris says you've got a bit of breeding, and you're new, so this is what we do. Burlington Arcade is best in the afternoon. These are the shops as knows Harris and has rooms in the back for her girls – Glovers, name of Fredericks; Bonnet-makers, name Daphne of Paris; Perfumers, Petite Amour. Now, Jermyn Street is ladies' shoes, and he's called Vincent. Milliner in Bond Street is that old sow from Southampton, Madame Rouchelle. The Strand is easy, right up to Haymarket; every cigar-divan, coffee-shop and chop-house knows us. If a gent wants to go to a proper Accommodation House because he's scared of being seen, you'll have to leave him, and come back to me for an address, but don't let him out of your sight, or others'll have him. Got all that?'

Cath nodded, as Milly paused for breath. 'Here! Slow down. You're going to have to learn to take life easy, or I'll not last the week. We has an arrangement, see? I takes half of what we don't give up to Harris. We could do well, you having a freshish look about you and no scabs that notice. Hiding the money ain't no problem, because I has this friend what I passes it on to, as saves it for us. Harris'll search us both down to our skins and more besides when we takes the clothes back. And don't you think you can run off neither, and keep it all for yourself, because I just keeps after you until I sees a policeman, and then I gets him to take you in charge for stealing Harris's clothes. He has to take you in if I complains, and then Harris sends down a body who's respectable-looking to press the charge, or release you on bail to her good conduct. She's paid Crabtree two and a half guineas for you, so she expects a profit. Them clothes has been up and down the Strand more times than the Greenwich Ferry.'

From Paddington to Piccadilly, once down Bond Street, twice up Jermyn Street, and four times along the Burlington Arcade is a considerable distance to walk, particularly as Cath did it, very fast with Milly holding on tight to her shadow. And still she had not thought of a way to escape.

'I used to come here with my dear, dear mother.' Mr Vellacot's gloved hand held tightly to Boy William's, as they walked along the front at Brighton, watching the sea cascade against the rocks and roll back again. Both man and boy wore heavy overcoats and were muffled against the wind, which made their eyes sting, and blurred their vision.

'We'd bring rugs and food, and sit for hours. She never wished me to grow old, you know. I was most loved when I was your age.' Alternate words were taken by the wind as they left Mr Vellacot's mouth, and thrown inland, away from Boy William's ears. 'Has Mrs Crabtree revealed to you my real name?' William shook his head. The only words he had heard were 'Crabtree', 'real' and 'name'. 'It is of little consequence. You have a good firm hand, William. That is a matter of importance. Never be limp. Mother was always telling me that. "Don't be so limp, Charles, or you'll never do. Firmness is next to manliness. You're too good for the church, and too limp for a soldier." That was her great disappointment.'

A driving rain was now added to the discomfort of the wind, and they took shelter in the coach which had been discreetly following them. Boy William had watched carefully, and had not noticed any sign of a limp in his benefactor's walk. Now, as they sat opposite each other in the stationary coach, Mr Vellacot removed the muffler, and his face was revealed fully to William for the first time. William did not wish to seem to be staring. He glanced at the face, then looked down, then up again, maintaining a perfect politeness, but taking in a little more of the face each time he looked at it, before turning finally to gaze at the rain through the window. It seemed to Boy William that, now he had seen the face of his benefactor, he would not be surprised if the gentleman did sometimes experience difficulty in walking, for Mr Vellacot seemed to him to be very old.

There were cold roast chicken, cold baked potatoes, cold plum pudding and cold brandy sauce. William declined the cold hard-boiled eggs.

A silence followed. Mr Vellacot also looked out of the window, but on his own side of the coach, and said, 'Have you truly never had an uncle before, William?'

William guessed correctly that Mr Vellacot was not referring to such people as Uncle Tom or Uncle Elias, his mother's brothers, and replied, 'No, sir.'

'And this is the first time, then, that you have ever set eyes on the sea?'

'Yes, sir.' The silence was renewed. William remembered Mrs Crabtree's advice that he should help his benefactor a little in the making of conversation, and added, 'It's big, isn't it, sir? The sea.'

'Too big to swim across.'

Boy William laughed out loud at this remark. The waves he had seen had been fifteen feet high at least. Mr Vellacot looked back at William at the sound of the boy's laughter, then smiled himself, and hid his yellow and not straight teeth behind a chicken leg.

'Have you ever been swimming, William?'

'Yes, sir. In the River Cherwell.'

'We must wait until summer for that. Don't eat the skin of your potatoes; there's plenty of food. Have some more chicken.' Boy William, who particularly liked the skin of baked potatoes, moved what was left to the side of his plate, and accepted the chicken.

'And what will you be when you grow up?'

'Don't know, sir.'

Mr Vellacot tittered at a private joke of his own. 'Well, you won't be a duke, will you?'

'No, sir.'

'And you won't be limp?' Boy William shook his head. 'So you might just as well be a soldier.' Mr Vellacot paused, chicken leg in his mouth, and looked at the boy. 'We must have a uniform made for you, mustn't we?'

'He's a rather elderly boy, isn't he? I doubt, madam, whether he is the kind of boy my client is looking for.'

'Then I cannot help your client, sir.'

The elderly boy under discussion between Mrs Crabtree and a fat gentleman, who was sweating so powerfully that her boat-like sofa might soon require bailing, was James. Newly bathed and wearing a clean nightshirt, James had been interviewed by the fat gentleman in Mrs Crabtree's drawing-room. The interview was for the post of foot-boy. James had been sent out of the room while his suitability for the post was discussed.

'I was informed that you were a most obliging person, with all kinds of children at your disposal.'

'The children are in my charge, sir. I do not "dispose" of them. And my accommodation is limited.'

'Then it surprises me, madam, that you clutter it up with such a lubberly boy. No, my client is seeking a boy of eight or nine, with fair hair like silk and blue eyes.' Mrs Crabtree's expression was polite, but noncommittal. 'I don't want a mouse, though, madam. I require a boy with spirit.'

'Your client requires?'

'Quite so. My client. A most particular gentleman.'

'Then I cannot oblige him, and must bid you good day.' Mrs Crabtree rose to her feet.

'On the other hand . . .'

'Yes?'

'If my client were to take this elderly, serious – one might almost say miserable – boy off your hands, would you save for him the next boy you receive who fits the description I have given you?'

'I cannot promise that. Such a child would go to the most suitable home which shows an interest.'

'Then there is no argument, since my client's interest out-weighs all others, and he will match any bid you receive. Within reason, of course. I take it that you don't require much for this elderly boy?'

'Who would go with you as a foot-boy under training?'

'Madam, you are a lady to whom one can speak frankly, and I shall do so. I may confide in you; I think I may; I shall.' Mrs Crabtree may have inclined her head a little to indicate that the fat gentleman might confide. 'My client requires practice in the art of chastisement – in the parental way. His own foot-boy is no older than that elderly young man. He has no need to train another.'

'Then he will find this boy unsuitable, no doubt?'

'And should return him to you?'

Mrs Crabtree twinkled, and shook her head.

Dunstan Apperley

The coach which pulled away from Mrs Crabtree's door contained, not only James and the fat gentleman, but also Dunstan Apperley, who had been fetched from the room under the stairs into which he had been placed as soon as it had become clear that Mr Hensbridge had neither been impressed by him, nor preferred him. Struggling and kicking, Dunstan had been held down by Barnaby and Veronica, while the clothes lent to him by Mrs Crabtree were plucked off, and replaced by those in which he had arrived at Philbeach Gardens.

James had seen none of this. He wondered why the small boy who sat close beside him and opposite the fat gentleman had been reluctant to get into the coach, since surely he must want a position in the household of a gentleman so clearly rich. His own situation was also a puzzlement. He had been provided neither with new clothes nor his own clothes back, but had been bundled into the coach as he was, wearing only a nightshirt. If appearances were as important to Mrs Crabtree as she claimed, it seemed odd that she should send James out to be trained as a foot-boy so very ill-equipped.

The fat gentleman, however, seemed unperturbed by their appearance, and leaned back smiling in his seat, as he watched the small boy whimper and weep more tears onto the surface of a face already scarlet and sore. James wished that he had a handkerchief with which to wipe the small boy's nose.

The coach left the King's Road by Eaton Square, passed

Buckingham Palace, and continued down the Mall towards Trafalgar Square.

'A foot-boy, eh?'

'Yes, sir.'

'Obedience, then, eh?'

'Yes, sir.'

'Everything the master says without question.'

'Yes, sir.'

'Or punishment, eh?'

'I trust your client is a Christian like myself, sir.'

'No, sir. He is not. Nor is there a client. I am he. Your lord and master, rolled into one.' The fat gentleman chuckled, patting his ample stomach. Then he stretched both his arms up and out, and began to bellow like an actor playing tragedy. 'And my wrath is devastating!'

The chuckle became a laugh, and the laugh became uncontrollable. The fat gentleman rolled from side to side, and held his chest. Then one wheel of the coach dipped into a pot-hole, throwing its three occupants about the padded interior, and leaving the fat gentleman with a badly bitten tongue.

'What an elderly, sober and joyless boy you are!' His voice was muffled by the white silk scarf he was applying to his tongue.

Both sides of the Strand were crowded. People stood about under gas-lamps or in lighted doorways. Most of these people, James saw, were women, beautiful women at this distance, wearing dark silk or satin pelisses over their low-cut gowns. Enormous wide-brimmed hats adorned their heads, each hat trimmed with ribbons, flowers and plumes of vivid colours. The cheeks of many of the women were vivid too, bright red or pink, with smiling open mouths. Row upon row of shiny ringlets seemed to drip from beneath the hats, falling over the foreheads of the women, and bouncing beside the crimson cheeks; there was far too much hair for it all to be the women's own. Jewels sparkled at their bosoms, mosaic and shell cameo brooches, gold chains with coral charms.

The effect of the hats, the wide leg-of-mutton sleeves, tight narrow waists and full skirts was that the women seemed to become a sea of gaudy pirouetting bows, turning this way and that, moving on tiny feet but going nowhere, smiling, bobbing and glittering, as they lifted their skirts a little to each and every gentleman in the hope of finding a partner.

No one moved very fast. It would have been difficult for the men to do so, since they appeared to walk on their toes while leaning backwards. They held their stiff, high, padded shoulders, their corseted waists and their round barrel-chests erect, while the women bobbed at them. To James, the people in the Strand were like cocks and hens in a farmyard.

Only occasionally did he see women whose costume flouted the uniformity of their kind. Once it was a fat woman, dressed in a man's greatcoat, moving at a speed which seemed to be too fast for her, as she followed a young girl in a red dress and a cheap hat of rice straw. This girl did not linger in doorways or bob at gentlemen, but seemed to be walking as fast as she could without actually running, sometimes so fast that her shoes, which were too large for her, were left behind.

Along Fleet Street there was less to catch the eye. It was eight o'clock. James lowered his shoulders, and tried to settle them back against the seat. Mrs Crabtree had promised to inform Cath and Boy William of his new address, and to send a message to tell him where they were staying. Together they had been unsuccessful; they had been hungry, cold and unhappy. Perhaps, temporarily apart, they might save enough money to leave London and return home.

The sobbing small boy beside him looked out of the window of the coach at streets which were getting darker, streets with fewer gas-lamps, fewer shops, wine-vaults, eating-houses, assembly halls or concert rooms. They had reached a whole row of unlit houses, then a stretch of derelict ground, piled high with refuse, which had been painstakingly picked over. There was a mound of sewage, or was it a house which had collapsed? The coach had turned east towards Shoreditch.

The eyes of the fat gentleman were closed. The small boy dug his fingernails into James's elbow for attention, and whispered that he needed help, since it was the fat gentleman's intention to throw him out of the coach.

The Shoreditch Road gave way to the Hackney Road, and they passed Nichol Square. The coach pulled to the side, by Birdcage Walk, and came to a stop. The footman could be heard dismounting from his box, and then appeared almost at once at the window nearest the small boy. He flung the door wide, lunged the upper part of his body into the coach, grabbed the small boy by his hair, and began dragging him towards the door. The boy clung to James's right arm, and screamed. Without opening his eyes, the fat gentleman spoke to the footman in what was almost a whisper. 'Do make haste, Swan, or we shall have every rat in the Nichol dismantling our conveyance.'

The heavily-built footman wrenched back the small boy's fingers until they had loosened their grip on James's arm. Then he folded the boy's kicking body within his own arms, lifted it from the coach, took three paces down Birdcage Walk, and flung it to the ground. Then he returned to close the door, adjust his powdered hair, and instructed the coachman to move off.

The fat gentleman opened his eyes, and a faint smile crossed his lips. James got to his feet, opened the door of the moving coach, swung out on it, slid from it to the ground, and rolled over and over in the dirt of the road, partly because he could not help it, and partly so as to hide himself from the footman. But what he heard in the darkness was not the sound of the footman returning to look for him, but the sound of the door being closed and the laughter of the fat gentleman as the coach went on its way.

The small boy was lying where he had been flung. Three of his fingers had been broken, and his ankle was twisted. In his good hand, he was clutching the fat gentleman's white silk scarf. James took it from him, and used it to wipe the boy's face and nose.

'I have to find my father. I think he's in London, but I don't know what his name is now.'

His mother had been ill for a long time, and pined for her husband. She had been unable to tell Dunstan where his father was, or when he would visit them again; usually he had visited at night, and for short periods only. Dunstan had left his home, and walked to Cheltenham. There he had been befriended by the driver of a stagecoach, who had carried him to London, free, on the box. He had delivered the boy to Mrs Crabtree, and received two guineas for him. He had been a kindly man, and had given Dunstan four halfpence of his own, to keep, which the boy still had, so they would not be penniless.

Supporting the boy's weight, James helped him to his feet. He had no plan, no idea of what they should do next, except that they should make their way back towards the centre of the city. They must stay close to the main highway, but not on it, or his nightshirt would attract too much attention. In the city, they might sell the silk scarf. That was as much as he could think of now.

As the boys began moving forwards, they became aware of the sound of other footsteps besides their own, which moved when they moved, and stopped when they stopped. Yet behind them they could see nothing but where they had just come from, and beyond that, blackness. In front, there was the rest of Birdcage Walk, and on either side a honeycomb of narrow passageways and alleys, partially obstructed by refuse and sewage, and all containing doorways and archways in which anything might hide and wait.

James stood still, holding Dunstan close to him, and waited for the other footsteps to move first, waited for a sound which might indicate where they were coming from. But there was only silence. The silence continued for a long time. Dunstan began to tremble. Then, after what seemed like an eternity, the sound came. They heard it.

It was not a footstep. It was a single breathy voice, uttering a single word. It was the mournful pathetic cry of a mother calling to her lost children. 'Boys!' The word was stretched out, lingering against the damp walls of passages, echoing in every side-alley. 'Boys . . . boys . . . boys!' But it was not a woman's voice, not a mother's cry, but a cruel imitation. It told James that he and the small boy were creatures of a game. Their role was to be hunted, while the cry of 'Boys! . . . boys! . . .' went on all around them, the length of the hunt.

'You ain't doing no good, girl. And do you know why you ain't? Because you won't stand still when I tells yer. If I've picked them shoes up once, I done it a billion times.'

Cath was, in fact, standing still. She was gazing at a poster which advertised the Battle of Waterloo, 'A four-hour Reconstruction with Every Small Detail Intact. Military Equestrian

Fetes, Surpassing all Previous Spectacles. And to include Clowns, Elephants, Lions, Wild Animals and Talking Dogs.' She had stopped to read the poster as a means of hiding her face from male passers-by, and had become engrossed in it. As she worked her way through the names of the participants in print of various sizes, she stopped and stared at one item in particular, with a mixture of disbelief and hope. 'See a Huge Cart-Horse and its Diminutive Rider Lifted into the Air by One Man. Frederick the Fearless and Ernest the Able, Strong Man and Dwarf.'

'Here, miss! That gent over there wants a talk with yer.' A boy crossing-sweeper pointed towards an old gentleman with a silver moustache, then did five back-flips to regain his position at the side of the crossing. Milly, finding that she was becoming over-excited at the prospect of a client for her charge, bustled into a doorway, to hide herself behind two large women whose cheeks had been coloured to resemble tomatoes.

Cath adjusted her over-large shoes, and went to ask the boy crossing-sweeper where the theatre advertised in the poster was to be found.

'Don't you know nothing?' Cath shook her head. 'And what about my consideration?' The boy held out his hand. Cath explained that she had no money. The boy indicated the old gentleman. 'Get him to take you to the battle, and you sees me here tomorrow with sixpence, or I'll blacken your character.' Cath looked around, hesitating, and the boy sighed deeply. 'You girls are good for one thing, and that has to be done for yer.'

He took Cath's arm, and led her over to the old gentleman, from whom he accepted a large tip for his trouble, then demonstrated his agility. 'There you goes, sir! Very kind! At sunrise we sweeps, but at night we tumbles.'

The old gentleman with the silver moustache was so drunk, and his speech so lacking in consonants, that Cath was unable to understand anything he said. His two younger male companions spoke in much the same way, swallowing their words amid so much laughter and shaking up and down of shoulders that they were equally incomprehensible, but their female companions, who introduced themselves to Cath as Rose and

Lily, understood everything. At first they were dismissive of Cath's desire to see the Battle of Waterloo, having already seen it seven times themselves in various company, but when it became clear that the old gent with the silver moustache would not stagger a foot further without Cath, both ladies expressed an overwhelming desire to be reminded of that great national victory.

Milly followed the group, walking at a distance, until Cath instructed Rose to hail a cab, and then Milly began once again to run. As Cath waved to Milly from the cab, she wondered whether Milly had told the truth about not having any money, which had caused them to go the whole day without even a warm drink. If it were so, then even if Milly could, by keeping up with the cab, find her way to Astley's Theatre, she would still be unable to get in, since even the cheapest seats cost a shilling.

The sickly-sweet scent of gas induced in Cath's stomach a sense of lightness; it was, after all, empty. She was also rendered temporarily blind by the thousands of flickering pinpoints of light which made up the many candelabra, wherever she looked. Under such circumstances, it might be rash to drink champagne, but she was drinking it all the same. The old gentleman had indicated his insistence that she should by a series of the noises which passed for speech with him, and Rose and Lily had indicated theirs by pinching her arms. So she was drinking.

There were so many mirrors that it was impossible for her to hide her face. During the day, whenever she had been unable to hide her face from gentlemen, she had contorted it, her tongue pushed out over her top lip, her bottom lip stretched wide, her eyes unnaturally wide like a gorgon. Now this gorgon-face, she discovered, had become habitual, and several times she caught herself staring, loose-jawed, grotesque, malign, at some innocent gentleman and his bemused companion, and these gorgon-faces were reflected from one mirror to another. And there was another face, Milly's, also caught in the mirrors of the theatre foyer, a worried, angry, apprehensive face, peering from behind one mock-Roman column or other as Milly attempted to conceal the unsuitability of her attire for an evening at the Battle of Waterloo.

Ernest must be found before the champagne, the dancing lights, the smell of gas, and the tiredness which was now overtaking her all in concert made searching impossible. If her legs were to give way, if she fainted now, who knew where she might wake up? Rose refilled Cath's glass, and winked. Rose knew.

Talking dogs sat on upturned buckets, and barked. Fire-crackers exploded to represent rifle-fire, and there was a boom of cannon from somewhere off-stage right. Horses raced round in a circle, then all together sank to the ground in mock death, before being resurrected to exit, stage left. The Bearded Lady made a surprise entrance as Marshal Blücher, crossing from stage right to left, as if looking for the battle. Would Blücher arrive in time? It would be a damned close-run thing. Two elephants paraded from left to right. A camel crossed the other way. The elephants returned, stood on their hind legs, and trumpeted. Back came the Bearded Lady. Marshal Blücher appeared to have lost his way. The battle which raged off-stage grew nearer. Soon it would be with them. Meanwhile a man dressed as John Bull provided a running commentary, with, as had been promised, 'every small detail intact'. Yes, he had news of Blücher, who had arrived in the nick of time – the Bearded Lady ran triumphantly across the stage, waving at the audience as she went. A bear wearing the helmet of a Prussian soldier danced sideways as lightly as a little girl, and a little girl cartwheeled heavily after it, then did the splits, jumping thereafter into the arms of Ernest the Able, whereat the two of them rolled round the stage in a perfect circle several times, while the largest carthorse Cath had ever seen was led on from stage right by Frederick the Fearless, and stationed stage centre for Ernest to mount.

The mounting itself took a considerable time. Every comic possibility was explored, and some were repeated, while the Battle of Waterloo moved nearer and nearer, and many thousands of lives were lost. As the sounds of the gunfire, the sturdy defiance of the English, the despairing charge of the French, the groans of the wounded, the screams of the dying, the huzzahs of our jolly fellows giving three-times-three for their general and the malevolent curses of the vile Bonaparte, all reached a crescendo, Ernest finally achieved his seat on the carthorse, and promptly slid off again, to cheers from the audience. A dwarf was making Napoleon wait.

Angel Fleckwindsor rose from his seat, and moved forwards in his box, his white hands beating together in applause. Cath saw him, then quickly realised that he was not alone, for, protruding bravely round the velvet side-curtain of that same box, there was a nose. She knew that nose. It was the very image of a bluebottle.

'Will you take command of Mother's army? She was always Lord Essex, considering the Roundheads to be less limp.'

Boy William and Mr Vellacot were standing in a room at the very top of the house. Set out within the room were a multitude of miniature soldiers, some mounted and some on foot, gun-carriages, tents, walled castles and all the appurtenances of war. There were trees, and strips of blue cloth to represent rivers, and ingenious arrangements of sand within green canvas to represent hills. The Battle of Edgehill was in progress.

'I shall be Prince Rupert. He was very dashing, you know, but inclined to be rash.' Portraits of Mr Vellacot's ancestors, wearing military uniforms, lined the walls and looked down at the proceedings. None had been trained by Mrs Crabtree; none showed even the merest glimmer of teeth.

'This is Digby, Astley, Willoughby and Aston. Over there is Radway, and this is the hill they call Sunrising. Below it are the three villages of Tysoe.' Mr Vellacot consulted a small notebook. 'When we postponed hostilities because of mother's illness, the sun was at four o'clock, and the king was viewing the battle through his telescope. What I have written here is that, from where the king stands, any Roundhead on Sunrising would catch the sun on his helmet, and the whole hill would appear to be on fire.' He closed the book. 'Mother would not approve. She always insisted that her side won, though we know that the battle was indecisive. Twelve hundred were said to have died. There were no surgeons, and the following day saw a fierce autumn frost. Do say it would interest you to do battle with me.'

Boy William positioned a cannon to point at Mr Vellacot's Cavaliers.

'I have decided to meet Mrs Crabtree's terms for your

223

settlement, William. If you decide that you will be comfortable here, I see no reason why you should not stay, do you?' Mr Vellacot held Prince Rupert in front of his mouth, as he smiled and waited for a reply. Boy William examined the painted blood on the neck of a Roundhead, and placed him face-downward on the side of Sunrising Hill. He would not be rushed.

Running and stumbling, half-dragging, half-carrying the smaller boy, he darted through the honeycomb of passages. The sound of sticks being tapped rhythmically against bricks. Against iron. Against a glass bottle. Livets of green wood being scraped along walls. He knew that sound well, knew the sound of footsteps following, many more than before, ten or twelve pairs of feet, all multiplied by their own echoes, and mixed with the scraping of wood and the banging of a stick upon a can. James ran.

The sound stopped when he stopped. All noise stopped then, and there was silence, until the voice began, always the same singsong taunting, threatening. 'Be good boys now . . . Come away home.'

Then he would be in movement again, pulling and heaving the injured boy with him, trying desperately to find a way out of the hunt. At every corner he expected to see a face . . . grinning . . . smiling . . . feel a stick come down across his shoulders or pierce him in the stomach. But he felt nothing – nothing but the boy's weight, and the stitch in his side. He saw nothing, only more corners, more archways, leaning walls already half collapsed, more and more passages. And he heard nothing but the livets scraping, the sticks tapping out their rhythmic message.

Suddenly to the right there was an area of open ground. More refuse. Piles of cinders. Hills on which weeds had sprouted, bindweed, fern and bramble. Behind them the honeycomb of noise, and in front, open ground. No cover, but for the tall dung-heaps and hollow patches of ground, where one could fall through a thin shell of earth, and sink thirty feet into a ready-made grave. He knew, had been told in the nethersken, of many being buried alive in such places.

At the edge of the open ground, he placed the small boy on

the grass, and took the fat gentleman's white silk scarf, which he held in the air above his head as he watched a line of nine bodies in silhouette emerge from the honeycomb of passages. All carried sticks. All moved forwards in step.

James wrapped the scarf around a stone for weight, then stood and hurled it towards the line of silhouettes. The tallest body collected it up, unwrapped it from the stone, and wrapped it round his own neck. Then the line began moving forwards again, and the taunting singsong voice began again. 'Please be good boys, now . . . Come away home.'

He dragged Dunstan to his feet again, and began running towards some derelict buildings close to a church. He was surprised that the line of bodies stopped moving, allowing him the start, perhaps pleased that the game was to be extended. The drumming of stick upon can continued, but remained where it was; it did not follow them. Their way to the Shoreditch Road was blocked, but they reached the buildings, and passed through the back yard of one of them, climbed over a high wall, and landed safely in the churchyard.

The drumming was slow, and remained distant. Exhausted they crawled just inside the entrance to a small tomb, and rested there, huddling together for warmth, and listening for any sound of danger. The drumming grew slower and no closer. Time passed, and no one came. They stretched out as best they could, and waited for strength to return.

They conversed fitfully and in whispers. James asked about Boy William and where he had been taken, but Dunstan knew nothing more than that the benefactor's name was not Vellacot, and that he was thought to be titled and very rich. He thanked James for helping him, and asked if they might stay together until he had found his father, but seemed to have no idea where his father might be, or even what work his father did, except that it was dangerous and secret.

James agreed; he also had people to find. They would return to the Rookery, join up again with Cath, put word around that Dunstan Apperley was looking for his father, then set about finding Boy William. They must also get what honest work they could, and leave London as soon as possible. If they failed to find Dunstan's father, they would travel with him to his home, since his father was bound to return there sooner or later. That was their plan. To have formulated it pleased them both, and gave James strength to contemplate the long walk ahead supporting the crippled boy.

Rested, they crawled out from the tomb, blinking and rubbing their eyes to adjust them to the moonlight. Then they noticed that they could no longer hear the tin drum. There was no sound at all. The silence was complete, as it had been before. The small boy started to shiver again, clinging to James, but refusing to be lifted to his feet. Shrinking back against the ground, shivering with fright, Dunstan began to hiccup, and could not stop. The hiccups became louder and more urgent, breaking the silence.

'I can't lift you up like that. You'll have to help me.' James had not noticed the line of silhouettes stepping out of the darkness. He saw a pair of large, stained and blistered feet standing close to his own, then looked up towards light trousers and saw the ash livet being twisted between large hands. Then the broad shoulders, blocking out the moon. He heard the singsong voice he now knew well, saying, 'We saw the coach. We knows you've money.'

Sobs were now mixed with the small boy's hiccups as he cowered at James's feet.

'No. Only the scarf. We were thrown out of the coach. We've nothing.'

'He was pulled off. You jumped. You must have got something off there, or you wouldn't have jumped.' The large youth waited, then said, 'He was pulled off, so he can go.'

The small boy ceased sobbing, and held his breath to stop the hiccups and maintain the silence as James helped him to his feet. If he had moved away slowly on his injured feet, he might have been safe. But, once on his feet, he tried to dart past the large youth. The four halfpence clinked together in the lining of his jacket. The large youth flicked out the livet, striking him on the back of the head.

Dunstan's knees collapsed under the weight of his body, and he lay in the mud of the graveyard, perfectly still. The line of silhouettes moved forward to rip the clothes from his body, and tear at the lining of the jacket for the coins.

James was ignored. Once the small boy had fallen, and it was seen that he would not get up again, the job of stripping the body occupied the youths completely, until each had either a coin, a piece of clothing or a torn rag in his hand. Then fear of discovery sent them scattering in different directions.

James felt the small white chest for a heartbeat. Finding none, he dragged the naked boy back into the tomb, and covered him with dead leaves. Outside the tomb, he knelt in the mud and prayed that Jesus should receive the soul of eight-year-old Dunstan Apperley. Then he stood, and walked on towards the centre of the city.

Confrontations

Those taking refreshment in the front room of Angel's Pantry included Ernest the Able, Frederick the Fearless, the Bearded Lady, Milly and a policeman who should have been patrolling Fleet Street. They took their ease there as guests, not customers.

Mr Bradshaw and Bevil Blizard were away in Bedford, attending a political meeting, and would not return until the following day. Mrs Fleckwindsor, having discharged her primary duties as a hostess, and assisted in pushing back the delicate tables and gilt chairs so as to enable Milly and others to attempt handstands, had taken Cath into the adjacent room. She listened carefully to Cath's story, and when it was finished, filled both their glasses with a generous quantity of port wine.

'I never imagined that I should miss the greyness of Warwick, my dear, but human nature in London is far too complicated for a mere student like myself. Certainly the two boys must be found, and then we must decide what next to do.'

'I think James will return to the Rookery, to Mrs Blundell's. He will expect to find me there.'

'The late Mrs Blundell's lodging-house?' Cath looked at her. For a mere student, Mrs Fleckwindsor seemed to be uncommonly well informed. 'The gentlemen had some dealings there. They may have mentioned her name.'

'I saw them. I heard them talking to a man named Mouche about some coins which were to be taken north, hidden in cakes. Angel sounded frightened.'

'My dear, he was beside himself. I'm sure he lost a stone in weight that evening.' Mrs Fleckwindsor peered through the crack in the door, satisfied herself that the policeman was fully occupied in attempting the performance of a back-flip, assisted by Ernest, closed the door carefully, and lowered her voice. 'Since you already have that dangerous knowledge, your possession of it has given me a wonderful idea. Even if domestic service were to be your future, surely you would be happier performing it somewhere other than in London? I have in mind somewhere where the people would be more appreciative of your natural qualities, would cherish you, and protect you from loneliness.'

'I am not alone. I have two friends. That is more than many have. We have sworn not to be separated. But it is true that we should like to leave London. Together.'

'Mr Bradshaw and Mr Blizard shall speak to their friends. Is it true, my dear, that you can read and write?' Cath nodded. 'Self-improvement is most fashionable these days amongst the working people of the north. Teaching women to read may suit you better than housework.'

Relaxed by the port wine, Cath explained that she was reluctant to meet Bevil Blizard again. She described the stoning of the prisoners at St Giles Fair, and her conviction that he was behind it.

'But the prisoners escaped, did they not? You yourself escaped.'

'Some did.' Cath remembered the blind man lying in the cart, trampled by the escaping prisoners. She went on to speak of Bevil's unexplained knowledge of what had happened at the fire on the hill they called Sunrising, of how he had played with the magnifying glass from a telescope, and remarked that the sun had been very strong that day.

'Correct me if I am wrong, my dear, but surely, if one is to make fire by directing the sun's ray through a strong glass, then the glass must be close to the fuel? To have started a fire which began so close to you, Mr Blizard must have been close also, and you would have seen him. I think the wine and your imagination may be beginning to tease you a little. I cannot claim sainthood for either of the two gentlemen, and certainly they have, on occasions, broken the law in the cause of freedom, but that must be done or how else can our laws be changed?'

Singing and dancing had begun in the next room. The Bearded Lady tapped out the rhythm of a jig with a knife on a plate, while Milly and the policeman spun round and round, and Frederick jumped up and down carrying Ernest in his arms.

'But even the laws we have protect us a little. The bawd you call Harris has no claim against you under the law's provisions as they stand, for if she could prove any consideration, it would be an immoral one, and bad in law.' Mrs Fleckwindsor drained the contents of her glass. 'My time spent on those hard public benches in the courts was not entirely wasted.'

'What will happen to Milly?'

Mr Fleckwindsor got to her feet a little unsteadily, and opened the door to the front room, where Milly, sitting astride the Bearded Lady's shoulders, was attempting to dislodge Angel from the shoulders of Frederick the Fearless. 'I think we have to face the fact, my dear, that she may do herself an injury.'

He walked one minute, ran the next, his bare feet splashing through pools of water. He could not decide between the two. Walking was too slow; running might attract attention. Rain drummed on the top of his head like large pebbles, and ran down his forehead, getting into his eyes. He was blinking, shaking his head from side to side to see where he was going, with the nightshirt clinging, wet and heavy, around his thighs, slowing him down and tiring him.

None of the street names was familiar to him. William Street; New Inn Yard; Holywell Lane; Old Nichol Street. He knew the names of only the larger streets in the centre of the city. He repeated aloud the name of the street which led to the Rookery of St Giles, afraid that he might forget it. 'Oxford Street.' He feared that he might be travelling in circles, or moving away from the centre of the city, away from his friends.

He had never thought before of the coincidence that the first Londoners he had ever met were in the Fair of St Giles in Oxford, and that then, when he came to London, he should lodge in the Rookery of St Giles off Oxford Street. That would help him to remember the name. 'Oxford Street.'

He had run from the main street of Bishopsgate into Threadneedle Street because he had seen a policeman, and had become lost from then on. There was no one from whom to ask the way, no one he dared ask. Shadows appeared briefly from the shelter of doorways, but the owners of those shadows did not show themselves. He was only a pair of bare feet, flapping through water, a drenched nightshirt with no pockets to contain anything of interest. The shadows remained within doorways. They were waiting for the rain to stop.

He leaned against a wall, and tried to choose between six streets. He lifted the front of the nightshirt, and squeezed out water. If he could find the River Thames, he would follow it to get closer to the Strand. He had glimpsed the river from the windows of the carriage; it had been on his right.

He watched the flow of the water in the gutter. What could not get into the now flooding sewer would surely run towards the river. He followed. He ran down a street called Walbrook, which later became Dowgate Hill, with the rushing gutter-water covering his ankles until he smelled the river, saw in the moonlight the tops of sailboats moored against the quay, felt the extra coldness of a wind from the sea. James turned his back on the wind, to follow the river inland towards South-wark Bridge.

By Puddle Dock he stopped under a gas-lamp to squeeze more water from his nightshirt, and catch his breath. Bent double and gasping for air, he noticed that his left foot was bleeding. He had broken a toenail; it was hanging half-off. He had not noticed the stinging pain until now, as he watched the pink diluted blood mixing with the rainwater around his feet.

He lifted his right hand to brush away something cold and wet from his lips, and felt fingers which were not his own tighten with a sudden jerk over his mouth, while a large muscular arm slid around his waist, pulling him backwards.

He was secured, like a fish in a net, and like a fish he wriggled and kicked to be free. But the arm lifted him off the ground, and the hard calloused hand gripped his mouth and jaw, keeping his head facing forwards with such strength that any sudden movement from him might break his own neck.

231

Imprisoned in this way, he travelled backwards some fifty or sixty yards, until the rain and the dark sky disappeared, and above his head was even darker canvas. A small dog was growling, a low threatening purring hiss of a growl. He could not see the dog, dared not move his head to look down, but felt a warmth close to his injured foot. It was hot breath, panting breath, then a dampness again, but this time a warm soft dampness.

'Still now, or Agatha will take your leg!' The dog was licking the blood from his bleeding toe, and speaking to its owner between licks, purring, whining and grunting, explaining to its mistress that it liked the taste. For it was a woman, although her voice was deep and coarse, who had caught James and brought him home. She lowered herself onto an upturned barrel, and sat with him perched on her lap, still tightly gripped.

'Make a squeal, and she'll go for your throat. She's a ratter, aren't yer, gal?' Still he could not see the dog, but the tone of its conversation changed in answer to the woman's question, and he imagined its lips curling back to reveal teeth specially sharpened for ratting.

His own mouth was uncovered, and a small lamp was lit. The arm around his waist had been exchanged for a hand gripping his left wrist and holding it against his right shoulder-blade. He saw that the canvas roof was part of an old sail, many times patched and repaired, secured at one end to the side of a building, while the other was held to the ground by large stones. Rain dripped in where the sail had been repaired, but most of it ran down the outside, or trickled down the bricks of the wall and soaked into two sacks filled with straw. In this retreat were pieces of coal, a pile of splintered timber, rivets and washers from barges, a tangle of frayed rope, pickings from the river-bed or from the barges themselves.

He could see the dog now. She returned his gaze, licking her lips, and complaining that the meal had been inadequate. The bleeding had stopped. He did not try to look at the woman. She was behind him, and he was afraid to move. She had forced him to stand while she had lighted the lamp, using only her free hand, and he had remained standing. The woman had lighted a

232

pipe for herself at the same time, and resumed her seat on the barrel. He waited.

Mixed with the smell of tobacco smoke, there were the smells of raw onion, fish, sweat and the woman's baleful breath. He heard the wheezing rattle of an unhealthy chest.

'Now, here's a gentleman friend for you, Agatha. Here's a nice young man come to see you. Did I not tell you I'd find us some company?' The woman's free hand was placed on James's hip-bone, and moved the hip so that he was obliged to turn and face her. The dog's voice warned him that any other movement of his feet would constitute a threat.

'Rain puts Agatha in low spirits, and since we're out of the liquid sort, I feels it with her.' She smiled, open-mouthed, showing a full set of rotten teeth. Her face was the colour of bullocks' liver. 'Got any money?' James shook his head. She continued to smile, while her large hands patted the outside of his nightshirt, the fingers feeling for coins sewn into an inside pocket. Enormous pendular breasts hung down over roll upon roll of fat, each roll wrapped in rags of a different colour, all sewn or knotted together. But the arms were muscular, and very strong.

' 'Tis a gentleman's nightshirt. Am I right?' James nodded. 'Then what's a gentleman doing without a coin at least?'

'I'm not a gentleman.'

'Then 'tis someone else's shirt you're wearing?'

'My clothes were taken.'

'What rogues people be!' The woman shook her head and tut-tutted. 'Been in the river?' James shook his head. 'Not come off a boat?' He repeated the action. 'Then why you running through the night in all weather, when there's shelter all about?'

'I have to find a friend.'

'What did I tell you, Agatha? Always someone worse off than us. We has friends, young muddies like yourself, what picks the river clean. They calls to see Agatha. Brings her presents. Seems you come empty-handed.'

'I'm sorry.'

'So's we, ain't we, gal? 'Tis an offence to pick along this part of the water without asking leave and bringing a gift for Agatha. Bitta coal. Stretcha timber. Lump of iron. Heel of fat.

Something or nothing, 'tis the thought that counts. Suppose we give her that shirt?'

'I've nothing else to wear.'

'Cold out. You're getting too close to a man to go tripping through the West End, all skin and bone and everything on show. Ain't life a problem, though?' She waited, watching his eyes, her head on one side. 'Best be the shirt, then, eh?'

'I wasn't picking the river.'

'That's what you says now. My guess is you been mudlarking in the rain, and got something nice and precious hidden to collect when it fairs up. Where you come from?'

'Oxford.'

'Knows it well. Not much to find on the river they got there. That's how come you don't know about Agatha and her liking for presents. Ignorance never stands up in a court of law, though, do he? Rules is rules; she has to have her liking. That shirt'll get us a tidy drop of gin. Saucer of that makes her sleep like a real human. Don't it?' This last question was directed at the dog, which barked an affirmative reply. 'Seems you been outvoted. Good thing you had a shirt, at least. Lord knows what Agatha could have asked for else. She be a crafty bitch from Bristol, and knows how to get her own way.'

There was the sound of rain hitting the canvas roof and a low-spirited growling from the dog. The woman waited for James to remove his nightshirt.

'Have you got something else I could wear?'

'We ain't no gents' outfitters, are we, Agatha? What there is, is what you see.'

'Couldn't you sell some coal? Or those?' James nodded towards the rivets and washers.

'Them's capital. Our savings, hers and mine. We never touches capital. Bad economy, that. No, the shirt will do for us. We've set our hearts on it.' The woman gave a playful tug at the shirt. James looked round the shack, desperately searching for something else he could wear.

'Agatha gets awful spiteful if young men keeps her waiting.'

'You can't leave me with nothing. Some old rags would do, anything so as I can get to St Giles.'

'That's a terrible bad place. Who'd want to go there? They'd have the shirt off your back, soon as look at you.' She was grinning now. 'Landlord of the Bear has a boy your build. Should get enough gin for the three of us. Warm you up, that will.'

'The sacks. I'll wear those.' The woman shook her head slowly. 'Then I won't give the shirt.'

'Agatha has her way of taking what ain't given generous like. Only trouble is, she takes it a bit at a time, and don't know when to stop.' The dog growled in agreement.

'Then she'd better start, cos I ain't going naked for no dog.'

The woman bent down, and lifted the dog up in one arm, holding her close to James's face. What he had imagined proved to be true. Though her nose was almost touching his face, so that she was too close for him to focus on, he could nevertheless tell that Agatha's teeth were large and had been filed to sharp points. The woman lowered her a little, so that her muzzle was level with James's throat, and released his wrist. 'Agatha is waiting for her present, boy.'

James looked down at the dog's head, then at the woman, then back at the dog.

'Tell him to hurry his undressing, gal, or we'll miss getting our gin.' She jerked the dog forwards, causing her to snap excitedly at James's neck.

'Let me turn round.'

Still carrying the dog, the woman moved behind him, so as to block the way out. James went behind the barrel, faced the wall, then lifted the nightshirt up and over his head. Without looking round, he held it behind him for the woman to take.

'Ain't that a nice present, Agatha? Just what you've always wanted.' James heard the woman whisper something to Agatha. He turned his head to look, but the woman had already gone, and only the dog remained, crouching at the entrance to the shack, and grumbling to herself.

He turned on the spot to face the dog. The straw-filled sacks were to his left. As he stretched out a leg to try to draw one closer to him, Agatha jumped to her feet, and let out a threatening growl that was more like a roar.

Slowly, and without moving his body, he rested his hands on the barrel in front of him. He tilted the barrel slightly, and felt the bottom with his toes, to discover whether it was open or closed. It was open.

James rubbed his injured toe against the rim of the barrel to make it bleed again. He lifted the barrel first one inch, then two, then a little more. The dog moved forwards, and complained. James wriggled his bleeding toe, and the growl of complaint became a whine of interest. The barrel was heavy. He was now holding it about a foot and a half off the ground, and Agatha had stopped moving forwards, and was looking round for her mistress. James moved his foot from side to side, and regained the dog's interest. She came closer to him, pawing the ground and sniffing the air as she came, until she reached the other side of the barrel, where she stopped again, looking up at him. Agatha's head turned. She was about to move sideways, about to go round the barrel, but James thrust his bleeding toe out sharply, touching her nose, then brought the barrel down as the dog jumped forwards.

A moment's fear, as the instep of his foot was caught under the rim of the barrel, and had to be quickly rescued. Then he was free. He ripped open the end of the nearest sack, using a rivet and a piece of sharp coal, pulled out the straw, and made a hole for his head at the other end. He tied a length of frayed rope around his waist. Though not strictly necessary, it gave his costume a more natural appearance. The sacking was wet and cold, but the important parts of him were covered, and he was able to limp from the canvas shack out into the rain. Behind him as he went, the sounds of Agatha's scratching and barking, as she went round and round the inside of her new kennel, grew more distant.

'Your coachman is a dwarf, is he not?' Tea had been served. Mrs Crabtree stood at her window, admiring her visitor's equipage.

'And my footman a giant, yes. Isn't it amusing?' Mrs Fleckwindsor used one large hand to spin the globe of the world and the other to bite into what she considered to be an indifferent maid-of-honour. 'So you understand why the boys I seek must be the prettiest you have. Appearances are so important, don't you think?'

Costumes had been hired, borrowed or stolen for the day. The coachman, Ernest the Able, was dressed as Alexander the Great, with helmet and plume. Frederick the Fearless stood behind as King Alfred, wearing mock crown, thonged boots and a sheepskin cloak. The brougham was the most expensive they had been able to obtain, and its coachwork had been brought to a state of high polish. The hastily printed (but immaculate) visiting card on deckled paper bore the words, 'The Hon. Rebecca Fleckwindsor, Combined Charities for the Relief of Destitute and Orphaned Infants'.

'You must meet many orphans in the course of your charitable work. Would none of those do?'

'Heavens No! They are all so ugly. Destitution and the lack of loving parents combine to render them morose; it marks the features. But the young person I met while visiting my aunt, Lady Cheverley in Brighton, the young person from your own establishment, was quite another matter. A most attractive boy. My aunt has known the boy's benefactor for some years, and says she has never seen the gentleman so happy.'

'He introduced the boy to your aunt?'

'They met on the Esplanade.'

'That boy is very special. I have no one else like him. Have you tried a Domestic Agency?'

'My dear, they cheat one so. They promise the world, but the servant you would settle for never arrives. First it's the mumps, then the measles, a death in the family. A situation, one would think, is their last consideration. I have my own suspicions of these agencies. I have made my husband promise an investigation which will result, I am sure, in the closure of the majority of them.'

Mrs Crabtree noted that information seemed to emerge sideways from her visitor, and none of it was comforting. There was an aunt who lived in Brighton and was acquainted with Mr Vellacot, and a husband, it seemed, who, though his profession was not specified, had the power either to conduct investigations or cause them to be conducted.

Mrs Fleckwindsor was reading from a list. 'I need an honest hard-working girl of about twelve, and two boys of eleven. The boys must match in height and colour, for they will be dressed as twins, and brought out to wait, as pages, at special functions. Their training will be extensive; I demand the highest standards for my staff. Their future careers will be assured.'

'I have no one who fits your descriptions.'

'And you are my last hope! However, since I hear that you give refuge only to the most attractive and gifted of children, I shall see what you have, and make do if I can.'

'That is not possible.'

'They are all sick? Pray do not let that concern you. I have suffered every illness known to man, and sent them all packing. I am built like a horse.' Mrs Fleckwindsor pointed to the ceiling, and appeared to be ready to ascend to it. 'Your sick room is upstairs?'

'No one is sick. They are not available.'

'But surely the children you keep here are orphans, are they not, or they would be with their own parents?'

'They are orphans.'

'Then how can you say that they are not available, when their availability is clearly at your own discretion? I am offering to take three off your hands. I am offering homes and employment to three orphans.'

'You are very kind, but I have no one suitable.'

'Surely I am to judge of their suitability, since I am the lady into whose establishment they are to be received?'

Mrs Crabtree did not reply. She was watching a second coach draw up behind the first. On this the more conventionally attired coachman was the Bearded Lady, whose beard was nobly displayed over a greatcoat of bottle-green. Angel was costumed as a constable, and Bevil Blizard as a senior police officer, while Mr Bradshaw appeared as himself. James, wearing clothes found for him by Ernest, his face obscured under the brim of a large hat, stood at the rear as a foot-boy.

Mrs Fleckwindsor glanced at the gilt clock on the mantel. The coach was three minutes early. 'I am insulted, madam, by your refusal. As one who has, for many years, been engaged in charitable work on behalf of poor children, and as the wife of a Justice of the Peace, I am not accustomed to being considered unsuitable either as a protectress or employer of orphans.'

'I did not say you were unsuitable. I said that children of the sort you require are not here.'

'And I offered, madam, to alter my requirements.'

Outside in the street, Constable Angel had left his post at the rear of the coach beside James, and was adjusting his tight costume preparatory to opening the door of the coach for his superiors. James remained where he was.

'Do you accept money for these children, madam?' The question caused Mrs Crabtree to turn sharply from the window.

'Certainly not.'

'Then how can you afford to keep them here?'

'I have patrons. They donate gifts.'

'Am I to believe that, if I had offered a gift of sufficient magnitude, the orphans I require would already have been packed into my coach, and driven away?'

'You may believe what you wish, madam. Allegations have always to be proved.' Mrs Crabtree drew back the curtain for a better view of the policeman outside. This was a movement Mrs Fleckwindsor had expected to have to perform herself, for it was the gentlemen's cue to approach the house. 'Your husband has arrived. He is waiting outside.'

'No, my dear. I wait for him. Inside.' The doorbell sounded, and already the gentlemen were pushing past Veronica in the hall.

'Then you did not come here to find servants or to rescue orphans.'

'Oh, but I did. And I shall have them, every one.'

The children had been brought from upstairs, and now stood in a line by the window. Veronica continued to tidy their hair and straighten their clothing. Mrs Crabtree had always emphasised that there were no situations in which appearances were not important.

'I wish to know the whereabouts of a boy named William Shiltern, and a gentleman known to you under the name of Mr Vellacot.'

'This lady has an aunt who knows the gentleman. She can tell you.'

'It may go better for you, madam, if you cooperate. Withholding knowledge of the whereabouts of a witness is very serious.' No reply. 'What is the real name of Mr Vellacot?'

'He never gave it.'

'But you know it. You have entered into an agreement with

239

him. I do not believe that you would enter into a binding financial agreement with someone whom you knew to be using a false name. Come now! The game is up. Why protect him?'

Mrs Crabtree gave a warning glance towards Veronica, and said, 'I do not play games, sir. I find homes for orphaned children; that is all. There is no harm in that.'

'The children you keep here are not orphans. They have been stolen.'

'Not by me. They present themselves as orphans.'

'Untrue, madam. William Shiltern spoke to you of his parents. We have a witness to that, a girl sold by you to a brothel-keeper.'

'You have a witness of bad character, then, it seems. The children stay of their own free will, and are grateful for what I can do for them. Many of them gain advancement. Their expectations before they arrive here are negligible, and through my good offices they are enabled to meet persons of wealth and breeding.' She nodded at Barnaby Semple, who began quietly to sing the twenty-third psalm. 'Clothes are found for them. Lessons are given. Any talents they may possess are nourished.' The singing grew louder; it was Barnaby's talent, and had been nourished. 'We live as a family here. My children are cared for as well as any.' Her voice had grown louder to match the singing, which was now very loud. 'I care too much sometimes. It breaks my heart when they impress their benefactors, are preferred, and leave me. I weep sometimes to see them go through that door for the last time.'

'Bitch! Murderess! Stop!' It was Bevil Blizard who slapped Barnaby across the face to stop the noise. His voice shook as he tried to control the intensity of his emotion. 'And do you not buy these children, madam, whom you advance in such a way? Did you not give two guineas to a coachman for one such, brought from Gloucestershire to this establishment? You! –' He addressed himself to the whimpering Barnaby. 'Did you know Dunstan Apperley?' Holding his face, Barnaby nodded. Other children nodded. 'Will you tell me, madam, that *you* did not know Dunstan Apperley?'

There was no reply. The fire in Mrs Crabtree's hearth, long unattended, had gone out. Its twinkling flames were no longer reflected from the polished furniture, and the room was cold and had the dullness of the February weather outside.

Bevil said, 'We have a witness, who was with the boy when he was thrown from a coach in the Nichol by one of your caring benefactors. He was lamed by the fall, and shortly afterwards murdered by a gang of youths. I would like the name of that benefactor, madam; I would like it now. I would like the name of the man who threw my son out of a coach in the roughest part of London, after the boy had been starved and mistreated here by you. His name, please!'

'I do not know his name.'

'Mr Vellacot's name.'

'Or that, either.'

'You, then! Tell me!' Bevil grabbed Veronica by the wrist. She shook her head. Pulling her with him, he pushed past the others into the hall, and opened the cupboard under the stairs.

'You locked my son in there without food. Had he been stronger, he might have survived.' He pushed her into the cupboard, and closed the door. 'We shall be taking everyone away soon. This house will be locked up. In a day or two I shall return for you. If I remember.'

Mrs Crabtree and the children were packed into the two coaches, and both coaches driven noisily off. The children would be cared for temporarily by a friend of the Bearded Lady, who would assist those who had homes to return to them. As for Mrs Crabtree, since it was unlikely that she was technically guilty of any crime (whereas Bradshaw and Blizard had impersonated the police), a rough justice had been decided upon – the justice of Dunstan Appleby. She would be driven to the Nichol, and pushed out of the coach in all her twinkling finery. She was likely to be stripped, perhaps beaten, perhaps murdered, as Dunstan had been murdered. It was possible that she would survive any or all of these fates. That was in the hands of God.

The coaches had gone. The doors of the house had been banged and noisily locked. Silence. After ten minutes, Veronica began to scream. Bevil, who had been waiting outside the door, returned.

'Please! Please don't leave me. I gets scared of the dark. I only knows what I am told. I'll tell you that. Please!'

He opened the door of the cupboard, to find her shaking with fear.

'That's what you did to my son.'

'No, sir; it was her. He knew she was going to let him out. Send him away. He was brave, sir. Told me he was looking for you.'

'And the man?'

'She knows, sir; must do. I heard him say he'd come back if she had the right boy for him. He beats his boys, sir.'

'And Mr Vellacot?'

'His coachman brought the money, and took the agreement. I never knew the address.'

'But you know his real name. Did the coachman not tell you?'

'Only because it was a joke. He make up a name out of the same letters, sir, as his real one.'

'Vellacot?'

'Tollcave. But careful, sir; he is a lord. I only knows what I'm told.'

'And if I were to take you with me to find him?'

'Me, sir? I wouldn't dare, sir. But if I dare, I'd start with Finchley.'

It was a large house in its own grounds. The sound of Boy William's voice issuing military commands led James along a wooded drive, and the gentlemen followed. Standing to attention on a neat lawn behind trees, was an elderly gentleman who wore the bright red tunic of a soldier, and held a toy musket. Boy William, wearing a similar uniform but with higher badges of rank and far too many medals, marched backwards and forwards, inspecting his one-man army.

Mr Blizard was still dressed as a policeman, and, since it had been considered unwise to send Constable Angel with him, Mr Bradshaw had become his subordinate. Mr Vellacot dropped the toy musket at his feet, and his body became extremely limp.

'I was given to understand that William is an orphan.'

'If you had asked the boy himself, my lord, he could have told you that his parents are still alive.'

'Why should I upset him by enquiring after parents I thought to be dead? Are you to take him from me?'

'I'm afraid so, my lord.'

'And if he wished to stay?' James was examining the medals on Boy William's tunic. 'He would lose a considerable fortune by leaving. His parents might decide that they would rather . . .' His voice trailed away. He was watching James and Boy William laughing together, as James displayed his injured foot, and described the escape from Agatha. 'He has been happy here, I think. Why else should he agree to stay with me, knowing his own parents to be alive?'

'He had quarrelled with them. And he had fallen into Mrs Crabtree's power, my lord. His choice was not between yourself and his parents, but between yourself and her.'

'I must see the parents. Talk with them.'

'They live in Oxfordshire.'

'Near the River Cherwell?'

'Then you did know of them?'

Mr Vellacot lifted his head, and stared at Bevil Blizard for a long time before he spoke. 'I ask you to remember that you are speaking to a gentleman, sir. Is it the disposition of your class to be suspicious of mine?'

'Perhaps, my lord. Or perhaps it is because I myself have lost a son recently.'

'I would not knowingly steal another's child. I am sorry for you. Your grief must be unbearable. William said only that he had swum in that river.'

It was agreed that, since Mr Vellacot had no legal right to Boy William's company, William must go with the officers. However, nothing stood in the way of the noble lord's approaching William's parents himself, and acquiring that right. William was consulted, and told Mr Vellacot where his parents might be found.

'Will you write to me, William, while you are away?'

William looked to James for guidance.

'I will help him write to you, sir.'

'Then I shall visit your parents, William, and afterwards, if that will please you, I shall come and find you.' William did not commit himself either way. 'You must take some of your clothes. And you will need money.'

Bevil Blizard indicated that his party would wait on the lawn, and Boy William followed Lord Tollcave into the house.

The elderly gentleman had become, during the course of the afternoon, an old man.

'One day we must complete the Battle of Edgehill, William.'

'Yes, sir. I would like that.'

The old man and the young boy shook hands, and the old man's hand waved limply as the group walked away from him down the drive.

To the North

At six o'clock on the morning of March 1st, 1831, a covered
cart moved away from Angel's Pantry in Shoe Lane, heading
towards north London and the suburbs. The occupants of the
cart were singing very loudly, a song about freedom and the
joys of travelling light. The driver was a giant of a man,
wrapped in many layers of coats, capes and mufflers against
the cold. Within the cart itself were Cath, James, Boy William,
Ernest and the Bearded Lady, who were not, in fact, travelling
particularly light, since the cart was laden with all manner of
costumes and equipment needed by show-people to entertain
in the towns and villages of the north of England.

Adding to this weight, and carefully packed in separate
boxes, were thirty-seven Commemorative Cakes, to be delivered to various Working Men's Unions and Friendly Societies
in such towns as Bolton, Saddleworth, Middleton, Rochdale,
Oldham, Bury, Todmorden and Kendal. These cakes were iced
and variously decorated. Some bore the words 'Cleanliness',
'Sobriety', 'Order', 'Peace', 'Reform'; one very daringly (it was
bound for Widnes) the two words 'Universal Suffrage', but the
boldness of the demand had been a little diminished with a
pattern of hearts, flowers, and doves with olive branches.
Some were decorated with flags. Angel had gone to considerable pains to make the white hands on the pitch-black flag of
the Lees and Saddleworth Union look as if they were joined.
Words were easy, but the fingers of the two hands had kept
running into each other, or had been too delicate, like the
hands of women (none of the Unions or Friendly Societies were

at that time demanding votes for women). Many times he had scraped off icing which had become grey as a result of his attempts to portray exactly the firm and manly clasp of union and friendship.

Twelve of the cakes were to be eaten on August 16th, in commemoration of the Peterloo Massacre in 1819. The other twenty-five, all of which bore on their tops a cameo portrait of Robert Owen in white icing on a chocolate base with the words 'Our Social Father' contained in a pink scroll, were to be consumed in celebration of Owen's sixtieth birthday on May 14th. Baked within each of the cakes were fifty counterfeit golden sovereigns, the work of Mouche.

Mrs Fleckwindsor had asked Ernest how the Battle of Waterloo would proceed at Astley's without himself and his friends. He had replied, 'Vere is werry many dwarfs, strong men and bearded ladies in London, all vaiting to get into the Battle, a werry successful show. It vould not surprise Ernest if hostilities vos still in progress ven he return.'

Cath did not expect that she or the boys ever would return. They would assist in the delivery of the cakes, and she would deliver letters of introduction to people in every town they were to visit. They would choose one of the towns as a place to start a new life. It was true that she could read and write, though not at any advanced level, and perhaps it was also true, as had been suggested, that she could teach others to do so.

In her own village there had been a Dame School of the meanest kind, run by an old woman for pennies. The woman had been as much child-minder as pedagogue, and had done little more than beat the catechism and a few biblical texts into her pupils. Yet Cath had learned from her, had wanted to learn, and had done so in spite of her. Would she become such a woman in her turn, growing old without realising it, scorned by those who knew better, and feared by the children?

No, she would not. Mr Blizard had spoken to her of two very different women, Hannah More and Sarah Trimmer, who had served working people by teaching them to read and write. Bevil had said, 'Any man who can write his own name clearly will stand up and fight for his rights with more energy.' He had told her of Robert Owen's belief in the full development of the potential of all human beings, even women. To teach, one must know how to do, and wish to share that knowledge; she needed no other qualification. She was a blank sheet of paper, on which only the best of ideas should be written out. She had the character of a good person; this was the only essential. She could teach simply by example.

Well, she did not feel like a blank sheet of paper. Too much had happened, which could not be rubbed out. But Bevil's words had filled her head, and had inspired her with a desire to attempt what he suggested. 'The young are our future. You must be part of it.' It was to be a new life. James would help her, and Boy William would do what he could. They must move forwards, and never look back.

At one time she had suspected Bevil of having himself started the fire on the hill they called Sunrising, of having started it deliberately, and allowing the blame to fall on John. She had said so to Mrs Fleckwindsor, who had mocked her out of the belief with common sense. But Bevil himself told her that he had, indeed, been on the hill, though several days before the fire. He had stopped to talk with the men who were cutting the hay, and had later discovered a hole in his pocket, and the loss of his telescope glass. The long grass had lain in the field and dried to tinder, until that afternoon when she and John had lain side by side in the heat of the afternoon, and talked of their future. *Only the sound of yellowhammers rising suddenly from the stubble had stopped their laughter.* 'We shall never be certain,' Bevil said, 'whether it was my glass or your match which started the fire.'

It was less than a year ago, and now seemed an eternity. Many details she had once believed to have been burned into her brain had now been forgotten. She must forget them all. That was the past; it was dead, her lover and her child both dead and in the past. She, James and William were alive. Somewhere in the north they would make a new home.

They stopped at a toll-gate on the outskirts of the city. Ahead of them the countryside stretched itself out, ready to be viewed. Boy William stopped singing, took Cath's hand in his, and said, 'What will happen to us now, do you think?'

'We'll be alright now. If we stay together.' James nodded in agreement.

'Course we will, Boy. Ain't you learned anything?'

She was almost seventeen. She was still young. It would soon be summer.